DRAGON FORM

Blood of the Ancients Book 13

DAN MICHAELSON

D.K. HOLMBERG

ASH
PUBLISHING

Copyright © 2023 by ASH Publishing

Cover art by Damonza.com

All rights reserved.

No part of this book may be reproduced in any form or by any electronic or mechanical means, including information storage and retrieval systems, without written permission from the author, except for the use of brief quotations in a book review.

Chapter One

AROWEND

Arowend struggled to hold his form.

That wasn't uncommon, though it did surprise him, given the amount of essence he now had control over. Arowend thought he knew everything about the essence, but after leaving the tower, he realized this wasn't the case, and the unity was more intricate than he'd originally thought.

He closed his eyes, balling his hands into tight fists as he concentrated. His physical form manifested once again. Opening his eyes, he held his physical form into place as parts of himself began solidifying.

There was something about how his body solidified, which left him feeling like things were now easier and harder than before. He now had greater control over the essence, yet he didn't know the extent of what he could do with it. Sometimes, he felt the manifestation stretching away from him, even as he attempted to make sense of it while holding on to it.

Arowend looked around.

The cavern was dark, with a faint glow emanating from the walls, reflecting the hidden energy buried within. He suspected the glow was tied to the unity, though not the part he connected to.

Shifting his focus back to his form, he tried locking it into place once again, preparing for whatever might come. Yet, nothing came.

Rob had not returned, and as time passed, Arowend wasn't convinced that he would. After defeating the heralds, Rob isolated himself from everyone. And with Rob gone, Arowend knew he needed to continue on.

He strode forward, walking deeper into the cavern.

The shadow of a man appeared at the end of the cavern, and at the sight of him, Arowend held onto his essence. The man, who was bound to a chair, looked up as he approached.

"Somebody else has come to taunt me?"

Arowend's skin tingled as he felt the Eternal's power emanating. Luckily, Rob's essence connection still entrapped him.

"The other one has been visiting?"

This was news to Arowend. He thought Rob had imprisoned the Eternal and left him alone in isolation, so he was quite surprised to learn Rob had visited.

"I'm not here to taunt," he explained, "I'm here for answers."

He flowed forward as opposed to walking. Arowend needed the upper hand in this conversation, and since flowing intimidated most, he hoped it would do the same for the Eternal. But the Eternal looked unimpressed.

As he manifested in front of the Eternal, he found his solidity taking hold once more. He paused, crossing his arms over his chest and focusing on the power of the unity that he felt all around him.

"Quite the trick."

"No trick," Arowend shrugged.

The Eternal turned, tilting his head slightly as he studied Arowend. His eyes blazed with essence, though they faded rapidly.

"A memory," the Eternal said, laughing, "That's what you are. Yet, you have decided that they are more than that."

Arowend trembled with anger as he stared down at the Eternal.

Even though the man was imprisoned, he had the upper hand because deep down, Arowend knew it was right.

Lately, he'd been feeling out of place because he wasn't entirely sure about what he was and what he could do. He felt useless, something he hadn't felt in a long time. And even though a small part of him knew it wasn't true, the others certainly supported him. Ever since the tower had given him access to the unity, he felt like he was something more than before.

Arowend wanted to think that it mattered, he wanted to believe that it meant that he had access to the kind of power that he had always tried to draw, the kind of power that he'd been chasing before he'd nearly been destroyed, but all it took were a few words from somebody like the Eternal to make him question everything.

He shook his head.

'I have to stop doubting myself," he thought.

He may no longer be the Netheral, and he may no longer possess the essence he had before, but he was still Arowend.

He turned to the Eternal, who was sitting on the chair with a smug look on his face.

He wanted the man's name, but he knew he wouldn't get it through threats and force, and he needed to progress further to use the dragon mind connection to steal it.

'Even if I could use it," he thought, *"It isn't what I want to do. I don't want to be that person anymore."*

Arowend knew this was the only path to becoming the person he once was. And if he could achieve this, he would no longer fear the Netheral that was still a part of him.

But the Netheral was still part of him. As much as he tried to ignore that, and as much as he tried to pretend that it was otherwise, the Netheral still was buried inside of him, a part of him that he had become.

"You did come to taunt me," the Eternal accused, "Much like I suspected. The other one does that as well. He saunters in and boasts about all these things he has accomplished as if his slight success will ever make a difference for what is to come."

Arowend flickered, his form shimmering for a moment until he solidified it again. There was no point in hiding what he was. The Eternal saw right through it.

"And what is to come?"

The Eternal looked up at him as his lips slowly curled into a sneer.

"I think you'll have to wait and see," he replied, "That's far more intriguing, isn't it?"

Arowend lowered himself until he was at eye-level with the Eternal. He stared into the man's eyes, looking past the gleam of malice. There was something else within its depths, and it spoke volumes.

"I think you want me to know."

The Eternal tipped his head to the side and frowned.

"Why should I want that? It'll be far more intriguing when you get to experience it yourself. No surprises, as it were."

"And you still think that the others like you are coming to save you?"

The Eternal laughed.

Oh, they'll come. And whatever talent you might have acquired here will be needed. You will be begging, but once I'm freed, I will ensure you do more than beg."

The malice in his words was familiar to Arowend, as it was the same malice that Arowend once had and used when he had been the Netheral. He hated that he recognized it, but it was better to recognize it and know how it felt than to ignore who and what he had been.

"Do your heralds look anything like this?"

Rather than connecting to the dragon mind connection, which could be dangerous, Arowend drew upon the essence he felt around him. There was unity trapped within the walls, and given his newfound connection to it, Arowend pulled on that power. He closed his eyes and tipped back his head as it flowed out of the walls and into him.

Keeping his eyes shut, he formed a series of images

and willed it out of him. Opening his eyes, he focused on the moving pictures playing before the Eternal. He was careful only to show the heralds and hide any images of Rob's people.

He showed the heralds falling.

The Eternal watched the pictures with a bored expression, and when the essence disappeared, the man looked up at him and shook his head.

"Did you think this show of essence would impress me? Just because you've seen other heralds doesn't mean you can defeat them all."

"I haven't shown you how we defeated them," Arowend said.

He held his form for a moment, but then he released it. His form swirled, forming a cloud of essence that drew power from the unity that filled the room. Arowend drew upon this power and pushed it outward, aiming it at the Eternal.

"Do you think you could handle a memory sweeping through you?"

The Eternal nodded, looking unbothered.

"I can."

"Do you think you could hold your essence when a memory of the unity sweeps through you?"

The eternal paused, and for the first time, Arowend saw him hesitate.

Seeing the Eternal worried would typically be a reason to celebrate, but Arowend kept his expression neutral as he felt the Eternal's gaze sweeping across his face as he sized him up.

"Unity?" the Eternal smirked, shaking his head in disbelief. "You think that you've found something unique and powerful. What you will find is that —"

"What is going on here?"

Arowend spun around.

Rob was striding towards them, his face hidden in the shadows of the cavern. He was dressed all in black. Essence radiated from his muscular build, but Arowend sensed something different. It no longer felt nearly as profound as it had before. He sensed… uncertainty.

Rob glanced over at Arowend, and the dragon mind link between them flared.

"Are you tormenting him?"

Arowend shook his head.

"I'm trying to get him to talk," Arowend explained. "I wasn't sure how often you were coming here, so I figured it made sense for someone else to approach him. We need to know more about this other entity."

Rob stood before the Eternal, his essence radiating outward and looping steadily around him until it constricted downward. The eternal's eyes bulged as his face contorted in pain, but no sound escaped his lips.

Arowend stepped forward. He was taken aback by Rob's anger and the strength of the force he was using. It seemed almost inhumane to inflict this pain, but then he wondered if Rob was aiming his pent-up rage at the Eternal responsible for one aspect of it.

"He hasn't been willing to talk," Rob said, still speaking through the dragon mind link and twirling his fingers as he tightened the constraints, "But maybe it's good that you came because you may have to do to him what you did to the others."

Rob took a step closer to the Eternal and spoke aloud.

"That is no longer working, and I've decided it's time to return your essence to the rest."

Arowend didn't like Rob's threat because even though it was very similar to what he'd been threatening to do to the Eternal, he now felt as though he was being forced to take action, and didn't want to target the Eternal. But if Rob commanded it, what other choice did he have?

Do I fight?

It all came down to what he was, and there wasn't a simple answer. Was he just a memory? And if that was all he was, then maybe he had no choice but to answer and do what Rob wanted.

But, what if he was more…

How can I not be more?

Rob saw him as a memory, and most of the others did as well, except Tessatha.

Not only Tessatha. Serena sees me differently, as well.

He felt it in her essence, especially when they'd been inside the tower, fighting alongside each other, trying to help find their way free. Serena was more like Tessatha.

And I am more like Rob.

Which was probably why Rob thought that Arowend would be willing to do what Rob said. They were similar to the point where Arowend had taken on Rob's form when he had first started to manifest. He didn't know what he looked like and hadn't remembered who he was then, so he used a familiar aspect, and it had been Rob, for better or worse.

"I'm not so sure I like that idea," Arowend said.

"We have to get answers from him," Rob said aloud, though, through the dragon mind connection, he focused on Arowend. "I'm not going to force you to do anything you don't want, but he doesn't need his power here. If he were to escape, think of what he might do."

"I also think about what we might lose if we strip it away." When Rob turned, Arowend just shrugged at him. "I don't know what kind of power he possesses, but I do know that he has some connection to essence, and essence grants additional abilities the longer you connect to it."

"And?"

"There must be things that we can learn," Arowend said.

Rob fell silent before finally nodding. When he turned his attention back to the Eternal, he squeezed his own essence, tightening it around the Eternal's neck in a way that left Arowend wondering if he was doing it for show or if this was something that Rob enjoyed doing. He never would've thought Rob was one for torture, but…some things and experiences can change a person.

Given all that the Eternal had done, it wasn't surprising that Rob wanted vengeance. He remained silent as he watched it play out.

"I think we should let the essence claim you again," Rob said, looking to the Eternal. "Maybe then you'll decide to talk. And if not, perhaps we'll bring the others in here and line them up before you. Wouldn't see what happens to them if you don't talk to be fun?"

The Eternal smirked, but the humor didn't reach his eyes this time. Unlike Arowend, Rob was dangerous, and the Eternal knew it.

"I like your claim of gathering the others."

Rob circled the Eternal, playing with the tightness of the essence around the man's neck.

"Oh, it's no claim. And I do have the others. I'm questioning them, as well."

"Then you will see how much they know."

"I will," Rob said, pausing before the Eternal. "But perhaps it'll be better if you suffer along with them."

With that, he compressed his essence.

The Eternal gasped as he struggled to loosen his hands from the essence binding his wrists.

Arowend was aware of how Rob did it and the heaviness that he constricted down upon the Eternal, but he was hesitant to say anything.

"He's *our enemy," he reminded himself silently.*

This was somebody who came to their realm, wanting to destroy them.

Why did Arowend have a hard time with that?

But, of course, he knew that answer. It was because something similar had been done to him. He had been destroyed and shattered because others had seen him as a danger. Others thought he was seeking information he shouldn't have, and others had decided that they would instead strip away his essence than allow him to prove himself.

Arowend didn't expect the Eternal to prove himself, but the similarities made him uncomfortable.

When the Eternal collapsed, he looked at Rob.

"Have the others talked?"

"Not the way I hoped they would," Rob said. "They either know something and don't want to talk about it, or none of them really know, but they are trying to pretend that they do."

"And if it's the latter?"

"Then I'm not sure how we'll find what we need to know."

He sensed Rob's irritation, but more than that, he sensed his uncertainty.

And it was one that Arowend understood. They had to find the strength and power to defeat this other entity, but how could they handle it if they didn't know what it was? How could they prepare for it if they didn't know what they were dealing with?

"I could look with you."

"I would like that," Rob said, "I have something I need to do first, though."

"Then I will do something myself."

He tried to hide the sadness in his voice but was slightly disappointed, although he knew he shouldn't be. This was Rob, after all, and Rob had his own purposes and needs, but sometimes it felt like Rob was keeping him out of things.

So many were keeping him out of things.

With a quick disruption of his form, he's stretched upward, streaking through the temple overhead and up into the sky above the land. He hovered briefly, looking down in a nebulous form, until an idea came to him. It was something that he should've done before, someone, that he should've gone to before, but now was the time.

The only question Arowend had was how Nelah would react to his presence.

Chapter Two

SERENA

Serena looked up at the tower.

Her memory of the last time that she'd been here was still quite prominent in her mind. Although it was mere days ago, it felt like an eternity. Those days had been tormenting, and she'd wondered if she was going to escape the tower or whether it was going to hold her indefinitely.

Her skin prickled as she remembered the ways that the tower tried to trap them, as it tried to keep them all inside. The tower would test them; if they failed, they'd remain imprisoned within its walls.

Serena still wasn't entirely sure she had succeeded, even though she now had access to the unity essence. Sometimes, she wondered if the tower recognized they were needed elsewhere and simply released them.

It was strange for her to think of the tower as having some sort of conscious thought, but that had been her impression when she was inside, especially because the tower welcomed her and then tried to counter everything they had done.

As she looked up at the tower, the energy flowing from it pulsated like a living being, and she was bound to that energy in a way that she hadn't been before.

But that wasn't even entirely true, either. She was bound to the palace, and the palace itself had also started to take on some of the unity. It was holding onto that unity energy as though it was trapping the energy within its walls, and Serena wasn't sure if it was harming things, changing things, or simply what needed to happen. She didn't get the time to study it as much as she wanted to.

And since they'd stopped the heralds, Tessatha wasn't around her. She had been trying to work with Arowend to make sense of the progression that the three of them had undergone. Serena would've liked to have them around, partly because she appreciated their company and felt a growing affinity for Tessatha.

But Arowend was…

Arowend.

He wasn't the Netheral any longer. She saw his devotion to Tessatha and his willingness to help and fight beside them. So, she couldn't take her anger out on Arowend the way that she had before.

And it had been anger.

How was that any different than what he had done?

"You've been standing there a long time," a voice said behind her.

Serena spun around and saw her father holding his notebook clutched against his chest and a leather satchel hanging off his shoulder. His deep blue eyes glimmered against the midday sun.

He walked toward her, his gray cloak fluttering with the light wind.

"I've been trying to decide what I'm going to do here," she said.

Keeping her gaze on her father, she felt the awareness he had inside and wondered if this was because of the unity essence, as she'd never felt this before.

It felt strange.

"You went into the tower once. Do you intend to go again?"

She shrugged.

"Well, the tower is something beyond what I ever imagined it could be," Serena said, "and I do think that the tower is somehow alive, so maybe I need to."

Her father pulled his notebook out and glanced down, flipping through the pages. Once he stopped, he held out the book, and she leaned in. He'd drawn an image of the tower. There was a hole in the middle, and she and Tessatha were entering it.

Her father sighed.

"I had to draw this. I thought that if this were the last time I would see you, I wanted to remember it."

She looked up from the drawing.

"You didn't try to come after us?"

She tried to hide the disappointment in her voice because she wasn't completely disappointed. Her father was still a dragon soul. And he still had far to reach, partly because he wasn't excited about gaining a different connection, and deep down, he felt that he didn't really deserve it.

In some ways, he wasn't all that dissimilar from Rob. Rob was happy to gain power and chase progression, but he had done it for a specific reason. He chose to gain power, not for himself, but to protect others. It was a refreshing change for Serena.

Maybe because he's like Father.

She hadn't even considered that before, but it did make sense.

"I doubt that I would've been able to get into the tower in the first place," her father explained, "And I quickly saw that I didn't need to. *He* came after you."

She pictured Arowend rushing into the tower after them.

"You don't fear him?"

Her father frowned, stroking his cheek as he thought about it.

"I should, but at the same time, I'm not sure it would do much good for me to fear him. *He* has done nothing to harm me. And when he has found himself again, it seems as if he has begun to help."

"I think he has," Serena said.

Her father held her gazing, studying her expression.

"Do you fear him?"

"Not any longer," she answered honestly.

When he was the Netheral and was more powerful than her, she indeed feared him. She saw how the Netheral used his power to corrupt and attack, but since then, she began mastering her essence, and now she was at the same level as Arowend.

Or seemingly so. She couldn't transmute forms, which she believed would only happen if she elevated to dragon form. And right now, she wasn't sure if that was possible.

Then again, I saw what he could do with those heralds.

That had to be significant. He had stripped power away from the heralds. What would happen if he tried to do the same thing to her? To Tessatha? To Rob?

But he wouldn't, and after everything that happened to him, she wondered if he still could.

"Do you hate him?" her father asked.

"I feel like I should."

"Because forgiveness is hard," he said, looking down.

"Do *you* hate him?"

"He's not the one I have a hard time forgiving," he said, finally looking up at her. "It's strange, isn't it? He caused significant suffering and took things from me — including you — for a long time. But I also feel like I gained something. In a way, perhaps a measure of insight I wouldn't have gained otherwise. So as much as I suffered because of him, I feel as if I must also be thankful for what I learned. Perhaps that's a mistake, but it's how I feel."

"But you have a harder time with my mother."

"I do."

"Why?"

"There are many reasons," he explained, looking past her and at the tower with a dazed expression, "and I'm not even sure I can define some of them. I simply accepted them then, as that was all I knew. It wasn't until I was taken away from it and was given an opportunity to see the world differently and feel essence in a different way that I started to understand. The Netheral was broken and had lost some part of himself, so anything he had done to me was... well, not necessarily understandable, but forgivable. But your mother, the things she did and how she used essence. She knew what she was doing. She had always known. She knows a lot more than we can imagine, and that knowledge troubles me."

Serena replayed her father's words in her head.

Deep down, she knew this should trouble her too, but her mother was trapped within the palace.

She never forgave her mother because her mother didn't deserve forgiveness. But she wondered if it was wrong to forgive Arowend and not her mother.

"I think we both need to find a way to let go," Serena said.

"Perhaps we do," he agreed, glancing back at her before nodding toward the tower. "What have you learned?"

"I think these towers are some final essence endpoint," She shrugged. "We have this one, and Rob has helped one of the realms create another similar one, but beyond that, I'm not entirely sure about it."

"He has done more than just help them create one, hasn't he?"

Serena nodded slowly and felt him through the conduit she shared with Rob. She had always felt him since he had formed that conduit, and she appreciated the connection and the power, but ever since the battle with the heralds and what Rob had done, she recognized that he had something greater than before. While she had taken on the unity and came to appreciate the realm's power in a way she hadn't before, Rob was now linked to a second unity.

She could feel it, even if he denied that he was connected to her in the same way as he was connected to this realm. And it might be no different than how he had linked the various realms, adding fire, storm, earth, life, thorn, and water to him.

What would Rob become if he could do the same with these unity essences?

And what if he became something greater than he was now?

It could become so great that he wouldn't remain in their realm.

She tried not to think about that and hated the idea that Rob might eventually get to the point where he couldn't stay, but if he continued to progress, wasn't that possible?

"You know that he has," she said softly.

"I didn't say it to upset you," her father said.

She smiled tightly. "You didn't upset me. It's all of this. It's me. It's this essence. It's what we're doing. And it's the uncertainty that I have."

"What have I always told you about uncertainty?"

She looked over at him, arching a brow. When he said something like that, it always brought her back to how her father treated her when she was younger. He worked with her to understand the essence and helped her try to make sense of that power. She had learned to question. It was something that her mother had never really appreciated, but then again, Serena had always been more like her father with the way that she questioned the world. She might have her mother's essence — and now, more than her mother's essence — but she had always been more like her father.

"You taught me to ask questions and to keep searching for answers."

He nodded with pride.

"Exactly. So, what are you going to do now?"

Serena looked up at the tower. "I suppose we have to go back in."

"We?"

Serena shrugged. "Well, maybe just me. But either way, I have to go in, find the answers I'm looking for, and see if the tower might provide me with more information."

And the more she thought about it, the more she knew that this was the only way to get more answers. The tower had been sentient, she believed. It seemed aware, from how it created different doorways and how it had answered her when she spoke. Arowend had said something similar, as well. There had to be answers inside, answers that they could find, and all she had to do was dig deep enough that she could uncover them.

"Do you want to come?"

"I'm not sure it would be safe for me."

"You might learn something," she said. "For all we know, you might even progress. Isn't that what you taught me, Father? Understand the world so that we can understand our place in it?"

He regarded her for a long moment. "I don't like this side of you, Daughter."

"Which side is that?"

"The side that knows enough to throw my comments back at me." He snorted, and then he looked up at the tower again. "I suppose I could go in with you. That is if the tower permits it. It may not, after all."

"You're right. It may not."

But then again, she thought it would. She wasn't sure why she believed it, only that it did seem as if there was some part of the tower that was waiting on them, some part that was simply anticipating their arrival, and if she were to get up to it, she hoped that they could get the information that she wanted.

And she wanted to know.

She took her father's hand, and they strode forward. He tucked his notebook against his chest, shifting his satchel over his shoulder. Serena was tempted to take to the air, but her father couldn't travel like that, so she decided against it. Instead, she made her way across the rocky ground, feeling the unity radiating from the tower. It was a pushing and pulling of power, of the essence, that flowed in and out of the tower itself. She still couldn't determine whether the tower was a mere construct or an actual entity, but perhaps with the amount of power it displayed, it didn't even matter.

As they neared, she noticed a doorway had formed. It was closed, but a series of symbols worked into the stone. She stopped and stared at them. She didn't recall seeing these markings before, and she didn't recognize the writing. She looked over to her father, who had hurriedly pulled out his notebook, changed pages, and begun to draw the markings. Serena used a different technique, borrowing from Tessatha's lesson on creating essence memories, and she sealed those down inside herself and shared them with the librarian, hoping that he could work on the answers while she was inside.

"Are you ready?" Serena asked.

Her father looked over at her. "We still haven't decided if the tower will accept us in."

Serena looked at it, and though she didn't know, she could feel the unity essence within the tower. It seemed to be linked to some part of her, so she felt the energy flowing and pulsating all around her. She didn't have a good handle on that energy, only that she could detect some part of it in a way she had not when she'd been here before.

She approached, and unsurprisingly, the door pulled upward, creating a darkened opening.

"See?"

Her father breathed out heavily. "I do see. And I am a little concerned."

"No need to be concerned. This shouldn't be unsafe. We should be fine."

He watched her. "Didn't you say you were trapped inside here the last time?"

"Did *I* say that?"

"I believe you said you were trapped, had essence constructs attacking you, and had to find different strategies to escape. That you barely managed to escape."

"But we *did* escape," Serena said. "And we came out stronger."

"I've never cared for being stronger," he said. His voice was soft. "That is what your mother and I disagreed on."

"I didn't know."

"I don't mind having progressed, as it has given me a greater understanding of things than before, but I didn't need to. And I don't know that I need to keep trying to."

Serena looked behind her. "Then you can stay behind," she said. "I don't want to push you into anything that you don't want. I'm just looking for information. Answers. I feel like there must be some inside of this tower."

"And what if the tower traps you again?"

Serena couldn't explain to her father why she thought that was not likely. She felt a connection to the tower and the unity essence she hadn't had before. The answers were inside. If only she were willing and able to go inside and claim. There had been artifacts that were there that she and Tessatha had uncovered, and if she had a chance to study them, she had to believe that they could find more than what they had before.

But it was more than that. It was the connection that she needed.

How could she explain that to her father?

There was something to the tower itself, some aspect of that power, that she felt she needed to understand... and speak to.

It was sentient, which meant that there were answers. But until she entered the tower, she wasn't sure she could get those answers.

"We aren't going to be trapped," she finally said.

He held her gaze for a moment. "I'm not letting you go by yourself. So, I'm coming with you."

She squeezed his hand, and together they walked forward into the tower.

Serena panicked when the door closed behind her, and her father was ripped away from her. The same thing happened to her and Tessatha, the separation that the tower forced upon them, but her panic eased rapidly. Despite not having her father with her, she could feel him. It was almost as if the tower gave her an awareness. Not only that, but it was almost as if the tower tried to reassure her.

"Do not harm him," Serena said, unsure if it would make any difference.

"I will not."

"Good. Now. I have questions."

Chapter Three

ROB

Rob stood over the Eternal.

He lay motionless, which left Rob questioning if he was trying to mask something from him, though he wasn't entirely sure if he was. He'd use a considerable amount of the essence to bear down upon the Eternal, thinking that this would restrict him and give him an opportunity to torment him, if only a little.

Is that what I want to do?

He had seen Arowend's expression, the concern in his eyes, and the horror that flashed across his face every time Rob did something horrible.

Rob had never acted like this before, and judging by Arowend's response, he wondered if he was being too forceful. He kept telling himself that the Eternal deserved it, but maybe he needed a different approach because he needed answers. The other heralds were no help, which left the Eternal. And in his desperation to get those answers, perhaps his questioning method was too vigorous.

Am I changing?

That thought lingered within him, a question he didn't have the answer to. He didn't want to become like the Netheral, but the worry on Arowend's face made it clear that he thought Rob was.

It was difficult for him to react differently, though. He had seen his people and his realm tormented by that power, and Rob was worried that they wouldn't survive what was coming.

He had helped others progress but couldn't be sure it was enough.

He took a deep breath and made his way out of this chamber, pausing inside the temple. It was a small building with bookshelves filled with ancient tomes. The manifestation of the librarian continued working through them, barely looking over at Rob as he appeared. He had rarely paid much attention to Rob, which wasn't surprising, as he was more attuned to Serena. Bonded to her and tied to her link within the palace.

"Have you found anything?" Rob asked the librarian.

The thin essence manifestation turned to him, holding a book. He held physical form quite well, much better than many others. There were not many essence manifestations that could maintain that physicality. He was dressed in a manner unlike anybody would in the current time, which wasn't terribly surprising given that he was last alive several hundred years ago. He wore embroidered silk flowing from him and a thin, wire-framed spectacles that fell to the bridge of his nose.

"I've been searching for answers, but it seems as though they're difficult to uncover. These volumes are older than many of the others we've uncovered so far, but they still don't provide me with what I am looking for." He glanced over to the bookshelf before turning his attention back to Rob. "I will keep looking, of course."

"And Serena?" Rob asked the librarian.

"She has taken a different approach. She seeks a different sort of understanding."

Rob closed his eyes for a moment and focused. When he did, he felt the conduit between him and Serena begin to form, and through that conduit, he was aware of her. He could tell where she was, even though he wasn't entirely sure what she was doing. Then…

Then he felt it. There was a sense of unity all around her. It was potent and radiating through her. He had a strong suspicion about what she was doing and wondered if it was safe for her to do so, but he wouldn't say anything to Serena. If she chose to risk herself, it was her choice, not his.

He opened his eyes and looked at the librarian.

"Can you ensure that she's safe?" Rob asked.

"There is very little I can do to ensure anything with that one," he said.

"But you can tell me if something happens."

"And what am I supposed to tell you, master?"

At this point, Rob simply didn't know if there was anything that the librarian could share, anything that would make a difference other than to reveal that Serena was in trouble. And given his connection to her through the conduit, he would know. There wouldn't be any way for her to mask that from him.

"I would like you to help her as much as possible."

"Of course," the librarian said.

Then he turned back to his book, leaving Rob alone.

It amused Rob to a certain extent. The librarian was different from what Rob would've expected, and he continued to change as time passed. As they continued progressing with the power in the realm, he was exposed to aspects of unity that he hadn't been to before. That unity seemed more profound now than it had been, to the point where Rob felt it through him. Had Serena not been connected to the unity, he wondered if she could use the librarian the way she had before. She needed to progress for her to maintain that connection.

He stepped outside the temple.

He could feel Arowend off near the northern realm, and for a moment, Rob wondered what Arowend was doing before deciding that it wasn't for him to be concerned about. He had to let go. He was aware of that power and that Arowend was doing something, but whatever it was that Arowend had elected to do was not at all for him to be concerned about.

And so, he ignored it, taking to the air.

He felt the presence around him, that of his realm, and the power that existed all around him. He took it in before heading off to the north, streaking over the water, reaching the boundary between his realm and this other entity. He tested it, making sure that the boundary itself was secure.

As he focused on the essence below him, he noticed

the Oro and his kind were still active in the water. He had barely spoken to Oro since he found the unity. Perhaps it was time that changed. Either way, he needed to keep working with them, trying to help forge a connection so that they could become greater than they were.

He drifted onward. The boundary between his realm and Alyssa's was destroyed. It was a smooth transition, as if Rob could simply move between them without any weakness forming as there once had been. That shifting was fortuitous, as he thought he would need to use what he could feel and what he could find beyond to understand better the dangers that existed. So far, he had not explored anything beyond Alyssa's realm, but he knew he needed to do so as time passed. He hoped he would find answers from the heralds to help him know more about what he had to do, but they were silent.

Frustratingly so.

Either they didn't know or were too afraid to share it.

And if they didn't know something, how had this other entity kept its presence quiet?

Not necessarily quiet, but they had not seen it enough to know whether there was anything they could do with it. That was what Rob still had to figure out.

As he neared Alyssa's realm, he felt the essence. It wasn't as potent as his own realm but grew more potent over time. He could feel it building as if it were cycling through and finding a way to restore what had been stolen. Rob had to hope that over time the essence would continue to grow and that they would find the power they had stolen from them before and give them an opportunity to become something more.

But so far, it had not been easy.

He slowed for a moment, and as he did, he felt something bubbling up against him. He focused on the sense of Alyssa, and he called to her. It took a moment to feel her coming toward him, but when she did, she hurtled on a streak of energy. But there was no cloud, no realm, not how there had been when he first encountered Alyssa.

She also looked different. She no longer held onto a cloud of essence that reflected her domain. Now she traveled the same way that he traveled. She had a red jacket and dark blue pants, and there was a tracing of different colored essence around her. She hovered in front of him. "Is there another attack?"

"No," Rob said, hating that this was the initial assumption when he arrived somewhere.

Was that how he was perceived?

Or was it going to be more like the way that the Netheral — Arowend — had started to look at him, watching him with worry in his eyes as he thought about whether Rob would do anything dangerous and whether he would take some sort of approach that would attack others.

"What do you need?"

"I just wanted to see how things were going."

She frowned and turned away from him, looking down at her realm. Rob could feel the connection she formed with her essence, as a part of him was linked to it in a way that allowed him to know what she was doing, even though he couldn't feel anything more. In some way, it reminded him of his connection to the other essences of his realm before he had awoken and learned how to utilize them. He could feel it in this case, but he wasn't sure he could draw upon it. And even if he could, he was still determining if it would be safe to do so. They needed the energy to restore and recover to become something more, but that would take time.

"We've been trying to make sense of everything that happened here," she began, "and this tower isn't making it easy. I can feel the energy from it — the unity, I suppose you would call it — and although it seems to be building, it's doing more than that. It's spreading power outward. It is sort of cycling that power, and it's nothing like we've ever seen before."

"We have the same thing in my realm," Rob added, nodding at her. "If you'd like to, you can study it, see what it means, and if there's anything you can learn from it."

"I have enough here. I need to understand," she said.

"Such as helping your people progress?"

Her brow furrowed, and she pressed her lips together in a tight frown. "I'm not sure what's going to take for anybody else to progress. It was hard enough for me to do so, and it was because I could feel the way the power flowed and could push it outward. But now there's no other power to help anyone else progress. It seems as if this is the only opportunity." She looked up at him. "You didn't tell me I would be the only one."

"You don't have to be the only one," he said.

He told her what happened to Serena, Tessatha, and Arowend inside the tower.

"With enough time, you could help your people, but they need to find a way into the tower, and from there, the tower will decide how much testing it would put them through and if they will progress. I'm unsure what's involved, as I didn't experience it myself, but I know what Serena encountered and how she was tested."

Rob hoped it was something similar and that the people of her realm could progress by doing what Serena did. But uncertainty meant danger, and Rob couldn't guarantee that no harm would come to those that entered the tower. So far, Rob had survived progression, but he believed that there was a chance he wouldn't survive in the future and that there were others who couldn't survive it.

"We have so few," she lamented. "And some are afraid to risk what they have already gained."

She looked up at him, searching for any reassurance that it wouldn't be dangerous, but there wasn't anything he could say to reassure her. The only thing he knew was that others survived it.

"I wish I could help you more," Rob said.

"More?" She started to laugh, edging closer to him. The closer she got, the more he felt the power within her radiating. It was the essence, unity essence. He felt it flowing around her. "You've done more than we could've ever managed. Our people have returned to their land with hope for the future. That is so much more than we could have ever thought was possible."

She beamed at him, but Rob could only return a grim smile.

"And yet, I don't think it's over," he confessed. "I'm going to find my way past your realm and see if there's any other way to link additional places. I believe that's the only way we'll be able to overpower what is to come."

She paused for a moment, watching him.

"Is that necessary?"

"Is what necessary?"

"Well, whatever it is you intend to do. Is it necessary? I get that you're trying to figure out what needs to happen, and you think there is this other entity out there that we need to stop, but does it have to be you?"

Rob pointed to the darkness beyond them.

"You've felt that power. You've seen the danger of the sub heralds and heralds, and you —"

"And I now have a way of defending myself and my people. Do we have to go chasing after it? I'd love it if we didn't always look for danger and give ourselves a chance to recover. Wouldn't our people need that?"

It was something that he'd heard before, but at the same time, and though he wished he could do what she said, he knew that he needed to find the danger before it found them.

Most people didn't understand this, or maybe they did, and they simply chose to look away, thinking that if they needed to, they would take action. And until then, they'd work on progress.

Rob knew he needed to find whatever was out there and stop it. And only when he succeeded could he find peace.

"I can leave you to your people," he said.

"Rob…"

He raised his hand.

"I know what I'm doing," he said, floating in the air

and feeling the energy around him. "I realize I might be the only one who feels it's necessary because if we don't chase the entity, we will be targeted again. Giving this other entity time to recuperate and prepare for us gives it a greater chance of destroying us. By moving forward and going on the offensive, at least to a certain extent, we're giving ourselves a chance. And that's all we need, a chance."

Alyssa looked down.

"And I want to give my people a chance, as well," she replied, finally. "They've struggled and known nothing but running for so long that they deserve an opportunity to have things slow down, even if for a little while. I'm not saying that we're not going to help you, but I am saying that you need to give us an opportunity to try to make sense of what we can do and what we can be. And if you do that, we should be able to find a way, and maybe answers, that we couldn't find before."

Rob floated toward her tower as she followed closely behind.

It was taller than before, but it was small and slender compared to the one in his realm. There was a sense of unity within it; as she suggested, it was pulsing, and the power within it was growing, but this also meant that it could still take time to become what it indeed could be.

"And did we have that time?"

That was the question that plagued him, as it was one that he didn't have an answer to, and deep down, he knew he needed the answer to understand whether they would be capable of stopping what was coming.

More than that, he believed he would have to find

other towers. And that would be the key to helping link power and creating a barricade that this other entity could not pass.

Rob also thought linking the towers, gaining that unity, and combining it inside himself and others might be key to the next step in the progression.

And then…

The progression might stop this other entity.

Always progression.

When he finally tore his gaze away from the tower, he saw Alyssa drifting to the north as she headed deeper into her realm. Rob felt her energy and wondered if she hoped he would heed her advice.

But he had to explore.

That was what he needed to do, if only so that he could find more power and be ready for additional dangers and what else they might encounter.

Rob would be ready to take the next step, even if others were not.

Chapter Four

SERENA

SERENA SEARCHED THE INSIDE OF THE TOWER. THE essence she felt was potent, and the unity seemed to radiate around her, giving off something that reminded her of the palace, only tenfold stronger. Maybe even more than that. Everything about it was massive and intense, giving off a wave of power she could scarcely track. She wanted to make sense of it, partly because she felt as if there was some part of it that she was meant to claim.

The tower had spoken to her, and although it hadn't said much, it was time for Serena to get answers. She could feel her father and was aware of what he was facing, so she wasn't worried about him.

She knew her father well. She didn't know what he would encounter, but she hoped he would be allowed to progress if he wanted. She saw the amusement in his mind as he worked through a puzzle, so she was confident he could get through this.

She tried not to let that satisfaction fill her, but she couldn't hide it. She was pleased by the fact that her father wanted more. He initially hesitated, and she sensed his hesitation. She knew there was a part of him that wasn't sure what he wanted for himself, but here... here he was finding himself, allowing himself to become something more and giving himself a chance. And that was all that Serena wanted for him.

"What is your purpose?" Serena asked, turning her attention back to the library.

She guessed that this was the ground floor. There was a massive open foyer with the walls curling away and no other adornment inside. A staircase at the back of the room led upward, giving her more access to the tower than she had before.

There were no decorations. No sculptures. No paintings. No carpet. No artifacts. There was nothing but the stone. Nothing but unity.

But she didn't need much more. She could feel the energy and something glowing around her, to the point where it seemed as if it were radiating out of the walls and pressing inward, almost as if it were pulsing and pressing through her. She smiled at that, feeling the energy as though some part of it was meant for her.

The tower didn't answer.

"You obviously have some sort of a purpose," she continued, spinning herself slowly as she gazed at the walls. "And I'm hoping we can work together to accomplish whatever you're trying."

The essence continued pulsing within the room, but other than that, she was met with silence.

"Can you answer?"

As the essence continued radiating, she wondered if this were the only way the tower would communicate.

"My purpose is unity," the tower said.

The voice filled the room, clear and strong. She looked around, waiting, but nothing else happened.

"And that is all?"

"That is all that I can describe," the tower answered.

Serena smiled, amused.

She wondered if that was all the tower could share with her. If so, it meant that the tower didn't have as much awareness as she thought, even though it was much stronger than Serena could comprehend.

And yet, she felt something more from the tower even before she entered. She saw how the tower commanded the essence, creating constructs as it tried to test them.

"Are you here to test us?"

Serena focused on her thoughts, trying to create a series of images that she would normally use to help communicate with the dragon mind, and sent that outward, hoping that she could link to the tower as she attempted to do so.

"There is some testing," the tower answered.

"Who wants you to test us?"

Could there be something greater? If so, then Serena needed to ask the right questions to get her desired answers. If there was some other entity out there that wanted them to be tested, then she could find the answer and learn just what was. But…

She wasn't sure.

"Essence wants you to be tested," the tower said.

Serena paused and looked at the walls of the tower, confused.

"The *Essence*?"

"Essence wants you to be tested," the tower repeated.

The unity pulse got stronger as it flowed through Serena. She felt linked and noticed that there was something about the tower that was seemingly trying to guide her toward the stairs. So, she followed it.

As she walked up the stairs, she opened the connection she shared with Rob and realized that he was beyond the borders of his traditional realm.

Was he visiting with this other woman?

She knew he wanted to connect and understand the power, mostly because he had wanted to make sense of the different unity he had uncovered, so she wasn't surprised that he would do that, but she was accustomed to him sharing something with her when he did. The fact that he was silent left her feeling like he was keeping things from her.

She had to stop thinking like that. Rob wasn't hiding anything from her.

Rob was... Rob.

He was likely trying to figure out these towers as he was trying to find a way to progress. That's what he was always after, after all.

And yet, sometimes, she wanted him to slow down, to give him an opportunity to try to understand just what it meant for him to progress so that he could understand each step in the process. But this was Rob, and he never took that time because Rob wasn't sure that he needed to. And so far, he was right. He'd managed to draw upon power and had done things that others could not. But it also meant that he was in far more danger than others.

She continued up the stairs, and she shifted her focus to Tessatha.

Lately, she'd been working with Arowend as they tried to make sense of their power and better understand the unity. Because of this, they were always distant, and Serena found herself missing Tessatha and their connection.

She stopped and gasped as she felt Tessatha's connection.

She was curious to know if the tower would try to restrict it as it did before. Thankfully, that sense of Tessatha lingered in her mind, returning to her rapidly. Serena probed, reaching for it, and then told Tessatha what she was doing.

"I'm heading up the stairs inside of the tower. If you can join me, I would appreciate it. Bring Arowend."

"Arowend is not with me," Tessatha said.

"Where is he?"

Tessatha sighed.

"Arowend is finding himself."

This surprised her, and perhaps this was the reason that Arowend turned to Tessatha only. Everything she knew about Arowend was difficult, as she wasn't sure what to make of him. She'd been struggling with him to the point where perhaps her father's advice was good, as he was not the same entity that had targeted them harmed them, and tried to attack them. He was not the Netheral.

At least, he was not *entirely* the Netheral. She

suspected that a part of Netheral remained deep within, even though the rest of him was Arowend. She needed to understand better what Arowend was going to do, what he could do, and whether there was anything that Arowend might need from them.

She had to find forgiveness, much like her father had suggested.

"Find me," Serena said.

She returned her attention to the stairwell. It was wide and smooth. The stone itself radiated the unity, which thudded beneath her boots. She wrapped herself in the power of unity. She didn't know if the unity would be upset if she were trying to get away with drawing upon more power than she should, but at this point, it didn't really matter. She reached the landing, which contained a long, narrow hallway with doors lining either side.

"What is it that you want me to find here?" Serena asked.

"You must understand the essence," the tower said.

Serena shook her head, looking at the line of doors before her.

"You know, it would be easy enough for you to share with me what I need to know," she countered. "We're connected, and essence can speak to essence."

Her words were met with silence.

Serena decided to check on her father. She found him in another room; he was not alone this time. Another essence manifestation was present, though Serena wasn't sure who it was. She felt her father's concern, and a part of her wanted to go to him, thinking that maybe he needed her, but she felt reassurance from the tower as if it wanted to remind Serena that she didn't need to go to him.

"I can tell that you're speaking to me somehow, but I would like a more direct conversation. I want to know your purpose. I want to know our purpose. And we need to know more about what it will take for us to stop this other entity."

Silence.

That wasn't surprising; the tower had been very selective about what it said to her. She started down the hallway when she felt a presence arrive. It was strange, but it seemed as if the tower gave her that awareness and wanted her to know something or someone was there. She focused on it and realized that it was Tessatha coming in through the same door that Serena did.

She waited, sending a dragon mind connection to Tessatha, letting her know where she was and how to reach her. It didn't take long before Tessatha came running up the stairs, radiating the power of the unity as if she were to shield herself within it. She was also linked to the tower itself, doing something similar to what Serena had done, but her connection was a little different, and the power that she was holding onto was different, in a way that left Serena thinking that perhaps Tessatha was more concerned about returning to the tower than Serena had been. When she saw Serena, she skipped the last two steps and stopped before her. Tessatha wore a dark gray cloak with a matching jacket and pants. Serena didn't recognize the style, as it didn't fit with anything from any of the current realms, which left her thinking that either Tessatha had it made in her old style or maybe it was nothing more than a manifestation.

"You came," Serena said.

"I wanted to help," Tessatha replied with a warm smile. "Especially here, where we don't know what you might encounter."

"The tower is keeping things from me," Serena explained, looking up and trying to focus on the tower's energy. "But it seems like it's not sure why."

"And you've been asking it?"

Serena nodded.

"I've been asking, but there might be something else that I could try." She focused on the librarian and manifested him next to her.

She hadn't done that in quite a while and certainly never tried to do that inside the tower the first time she was here. The librarian shimmered for a moment before he took control of the manifestation and stood across from her, drawing upon the unity from the tower itself.

Something about him felt different than before, almost as if he were more solid and perhaps better connected than he had been.

"The master did ask me to keep an eye out for you," he said.

Serena frowned at him.

Rob asked the librarian.

That surprised her, even though Rob had his own way of doing things and perhaps thought that was his way of ensuring she was as safe as possible.

"There is something here," Serena said. "Can you feel it?"

"I can feel a presence," he said, looking around, sweeping his gaze until he turned to the ceiling overhead. "And I'm not entirely sure what it is, only that the presence is calling to some part of me. It feels like it's connected to me."

"I think you're feeling the tower," Serena said. She looked over to Tessatha, who frowned but said nothing.

"Why should I feel the tower?"

"Well, given the newfound connection that the palace has to the unity and how that is tied to what's happening here, I think you're changing."

"Progressing," the librarian said with a whisper.

Serena hadn't considered that before. *Was that what was happening?* What would that mean if the librarian and the essence manifestations were progressing?

The soldiers are likely progressing, as well.

She had known that, at least partially, and understood that there was a power that was changing and that she had felt some part of it shifting within these manifestations, but she had not considered the possibility that they might be progressing in the same way that she, Tessatha, and…

Arowend had progressed, as well, hadn't he?

"The tower said something about essence guiding us," Serena said, looking at Tessatha. "The essence is the key, but I'm not entirely sure what it means, nor do I know what it is about the essence we're supposed to uncover. What I do know is that something is changing. And if the unity is spreading, and Rob does what he intends to do, linking other towers and blending it even more, what do you think that will mean for our essence?"

Tessatha shook her head. "I'm not sure that it matters," she said.

"It matters," Serena countered. "It has to matter. There needs to be something to what we are doing, some purpose to it, that we can make sense of."

A small part of her worried that there might not be any purpose behind what they were doing or the connections they were making, leaving her uncertain about the significance of their endeavors. She strode down the hall and stopped before one of the larger doors. Most of the doors along the hall were small, narrow, seemingly made of stone, and not marked with ancient writing. The one at the end of the hall was much larger and set into the wall with the runic markers that appeared to describe the power within it. The ancient writing was illegible to Serena as she had not learned it, but the librarian approached, holding out his hand and tracing it with his finger. The unity essence flowed from him and into the writing, which caused a faint flash. The door slowly opened. It reminded her of the first time they were in the tower.

"How did you know to do that?"

The librarian shrugged, stepping aside, and gesturing for Serena to enter.

"The essence told me."

Serena looked at him for a moment and tried to feel the power inside them, wondering if perhaps there was something more that she was supposed to feel, something more that she could identify from him, something that would help her know what kind of power he had. If it was only essence, then perhaps he was progressing. But maybe he was linked in a way that she needed to understand better. It may help her gain insight into what the tower, the palace, and the essence that helped manifest this librarian had given her.

She stepped into the room.

It was tall, with a towering ceiling high overhead. A series of symbols were written all around her, reminding her of the markings on the door and the kind of power she had seen before. Tessatha stopped behind her, sucking in a sharp breath.

"What is it?"

"I've never seen writing like this before," she said. "This is old. Ancient. Older than anything that we've ever encountered in this realm."

"What are you trying to show us?" Serena asked, looking up at the ceiling before her gaze skimmed to the writing on the walls. It seemed as if the tower wanted them to find something here, but Serena wasn't sure what that was, nor did she know if there was any way for her to understand it. However, she was convinced that the tower did want them to find something.

"You must understand the essence," the tower said to her.

"That's what this is?" Serena asked, looking around. "This is your way of helping me understand the essence because if that's the case, I need to understand the markings here better. I can't read them."

"You must understand the essence."

Frustration started to build within Serena, but then something else changed. She felt a connection between the tower and her form. Within that connection came the kind of knowledge she had shared with the librarian. It was knowledge of these markings, and as Serena looked at them, she realized that she *could* read them.

And her breath caught.

They spoke of power. An ancient power. Something old, older than her, older than the dragon queen, and older than the individual realms. They spoke of the unity, but then they spoke of something else—a hunger, a desire, and a danger that was trying to draw upon this power.

Something ancient.

And for the first time, Serena understood what they were facing.

Chapter Five

ROB

Rob looked off into the distance. He half expected to find something out there but, so far, had not. He was looking for evidence of the heralds, perhaps subheralds, but found nothing. He didn't even know if there were any more heralds around or if he and the others had already defeated them, leaving this other entity weakened to the point where there was no longer any danger for them to worry about.

He hoped that was the case, but he wasn't sure.

He struggled to move forward with the towers and unity essence because even though he knew they had to be bonded, he didn't know how to make that happen. In his mind, accomplishing that goal would be similar to how he linked the different realms in his land. And when it came to mastering the realms, he at least had an idea of the different kinds of power that had been there and how they were linked together. But in this case, with this other unity, he didn't know how to track that kind of power.

And even if he found it, it meant leaving his own realm, finding another place, and risking himself. Could he do that?

Rob feared what would happen if he tried to leave this space and push himself beyond the boundary of what he felt comfortable doing. He worried that he might not be strong enough or have enough power. And he worried that whatever entity was out there had progressed to the point where it was beyond anything they'd ever encountered.

This is why he pushed so hard. He needed answers. It was the only way he'd know if they were in real danger.

Maybe I am pushing too hard.

He wondered about what would happen if he pushed too hard. What would it mean? He didn't want to push beyond what was possible or cause grave danger to those who stood with him. More than that, he also didn't want to become something he wasn't. He didn't want to change so much that he was not the person he'd always been.

But hadn't I changed already?

That thought stuck with Rob every time he thought about progression. He had changed dramatically over the months since he began pursuing this power, trying to understand what it was and how he had it. And during this time, he became something more. But he feared what this change meant for him.

Deep down, he thought this change was for the best.

It allowed him to do so much by finding a way to link

the world in ways that it hadn't before, and Rob felt that everything he did, needed to be done.

But everyone who had power likely felt the same thing.

He wished he had an opportunity to talk to Arowend about what he'd done and how he felt when he was the Netheral, but Rob didn't want to push him. He needed Arowend, that connection, and to know what Arowend might know and what he could do so that they could continue.

Rob drifted along the boundary.

Even now, he felt that power beyond him and the strange presence of energy, so much so that he didn't dare go beyond what he had already pressed, fearing that he might find something beyond that boundary that was too dangerous. Rob didn't want any additional problems and wanted to be careful with everything he encountered. He needed to ensure he'd fully mastered the power within his realm before linking with other realms, like Alyssa's.

He drifted.

Off beyond the boundary, Rob had never explored. He saw the sweeping expanse of the water from the ocean that drifted outward. He felt the essence change, something different from the water surrounding his realm.

Rob had fought the creatures that were within that essence, and he'd survived everything that had been there. But still, he didn't know if there was any way for him to understand that essence and maybe find a way to link to it so that he could fully master the connection around this realm.

Alyssa found a way to connect to it, allowing her to create unity. Rob wondered if she was linked to water or only to the kind of water around his realm.

Rob still had so many questions that he needed answers to, and so much of that he felt was tied to the past. He hoped that he could save the future by answering these questions of the past. Right now, there was too much going on and too much that he still didn't understand. All of it left him feeling like he needed to keep digging, trying to find the answers, but he wasn't sure how hard he had to push because everything he had found so far had been beyond him.

A strange pressure pushed against the boundary.

Rob made his way toward it, feeling that pressure, and focused.

There hadn't been any sort of pressure against his boundary for quite some time. Ever since the heralds came, in fact. To the point, Rob had started to feel as if that pressure was not going to recur, giving them an opportunity to find a way to continue to progress, to push more and more of his people to find a way to become more than they had been before. Rob hoped that they could gain the necessary power that they needed so they could counter this other entity. He'd been encouraging as many of them as possible to find a way to link to the different kinds of essences. Serena understood how to find the unity, and over time, Rob had hoped that the others would enter the tower and be tested in a way that would allow them to gain that essence, as well. That was going to be the key, he suspected.

Eventually, the unity would be the predominant essence, and then…

Then he had to think that the people who came after him, who had not yet touched essence for the first time, would be bonded to the unity from the beginning. They wouldn't need to go into the tower to gain that connection.

It was only him, the people that already had an essence, that needed to do something like that for them to find the real power, the connection that they shared so that they could become something more.

He focused on the boundary, and even as he did, he still didn't feel anything more than what he had already uncovered. He pressed his way along it, probing and hoping that he might find something here, but even as he worked his way along the wall, he still didn't feel what was out there. Was it invisible in some way? Rob would've thought that would be impossible, but the reality was that he didn't really know the true extent of the essence, nor did he know what was possible with it, as this other entity was wholly more powerful than him, and probably progressed well beyond what Rob was. And because of that, he knew he had to be careful with the kind of power that was out there. He had to ensure that he could protect himself.

So far, his boundary held, but for how much longer?

Eventually, this other entity would show itself. And there was a part of Rob that wanted that and felt as if they *needed* that.

But he wasn't ready for it.

That was why Serena asked Rob for patience, and he knew she was right.

He did need to have a measure of patience, as he did need to try to find a way to wait and see what they might uncover, which would hopefully give them the answers they sought about the way to progress. But it was difficult for him to do that. Rob recognized that the essence was growing. His essence was growing. And more than that, he felt as if there was something to the different types of unity essence that he needed to link together for him to master what was there fully. That unity essence was going to be the key, but Rob didn't know what it was going to entail. If he could find more towers and more unity, then maybe he could link that together and find a way to overpower this other entity.

Perhaps this was the way to succeed without putting his people in danger.

This was his hope. He wanted to find a way to save his people without putting them into battle, as so many of them had battled enough not only with his other entity but before, back when the Netheral was the Netheral. And even before that, he suspected. His people have been fighting for far too long. Rob wanted to find a measure of peace. He wanted to find a way to bring that to them so that they didn't have to battle, and they didn't have to prove themselves, just so that they could gain essence. Shouldn't they be given the essence just because they deserve it?

This thought plagued him.

When he was younger, back when he was still in the

valley, essence had been so restricted. So rare. And Rob had felt as if he were so different. He tried to push those thoughts aside, but they stayed with him more than they probably should. He was now something more. The boy who had no essence, who never had a dragon forging, was now one of the most powerful in his realm.

Not one of the most powerful. He probably *was* the most powerful. He was linked to Alyssa's realm, and because of that, Rob had gained something more that others could not even fathom. He was thankful for this, but even as he focused on it, he sensed that there was something else he needed to understand better.

That strange pressure on the boundary began to build again, and Rob headed toward it, focusing on what he could feel, and then…

Then he recognized that there was something more. He saw shapes on the other side of the boundary. At first, Rob couldn't tell what they were, but he could *feel* something.

As he approached it, Rob started to move carefully, sliding forward, and he began to build on his own essence, drawing upon what he had from his realm and borrowing from Alyssa's realm. The link that he shared between those two essences and the unities that he shared between those gave him the opportunity to draw upon more than he would've otherwise.

Rob had never fully drawn on Alyssa's realm, but now that he was here, he wasn't sure that it was something he should hold back from.

A cluster of shapes burst through the boundary.

Rob was ready.

He had seen shapes like this before. They were subheralds. They looked monstrous. Birdlike, with massive, leathery wings and strange twisted arms and legs with a beak attached to an almost humanoid head. The essence radiated from them was unlike what he felt from the heralds, almost twisted as if it would shred his own essence.

And before he had mastered unity, it had actually done that. It had drawn upon his essence and managed to overwhelm him to the point where Rob had started questioning whether he had enough strength to overpower this strange subherald.

He twisted, creating a lance of unity essence, and he sent it streaking toward the nearest of the subheralds. When he blasted the first of them, it tried to wrap its wings around the bolt of the essence, but Rob had enough control over the unity that he angled it forward and bent it between the wings, striking the subherald in the chest. The creature fell.

The other four started to surround him.

Rob let them.

The last time that the subherald surrounded him, they had attempted to trap him and hold him, using some sort of essence that could overwhelm him. But now he wasn't quite as afraid of that. He was still connected to his realm and had his power, so he didn't worry about what would happen if they gathered around him. They had power, that was certain, and even as they surrounded him, he could feel that power starting to constrict, as if it were trying to squeeze down upon him, but Rob had enough strength to push outward and counter what they were doing.

Then he began to focus on each of them. He created four distinct bursts of the essence, the unity striking out, and he shot it toward each of them, crashing into their chest, and as one, they fell into the water below him.

Rob thought that the essence below him would take care of it, but he hadn't counted on the fact that during the fight, he had drifted beyond the boundary of his own realm and beyond the boundary of Alyssa's realm.

Something surged from the water.

It was unexpected. The power that came up from the water was a different kind of essence, something that Rob had never experienced before. He braced himself, shielding himself with the unity essence, then pushed downward with it. He sent a cascading burst of energy downward, and as soon as it struck, he felt it slithering past whatever was down there, the essence was still trying to grasp at him, and he managed to push it away.

For now.

How long would something like that work?

As Rob pushed back towards his realm, he felt a series of other subherald coming toward him. As he had suspected earlier, they were masked, and now there were a dozen of them, all surrounding him.

Rob turned in place. He swept his gaze around him. The subheralds all had a uniform appearance, almost as if they were constructs of power, which they could absolutely be. Rob didn't know if this other entity had so much strength it was able to create this subherald, but if so, would it be all that different from the soldiers and the librarian that Serena was able to manifest from the palace?

It probably wouldn't be all that different.

He wondered if there might be some way for him to disrupt them without targeting each of them individually. Maybe he could cut them off from essence.

But he didn't have Arowend's connection essence nor the nebulous form that permitted him to try to sweep through them. Rather than waiting, he focused on their power and started to target them the same way he had before. He began to build power and target them, shooting his energy out in bursts that came out of him in a dozen different ways, targeting each of these strange subheralds in the same manner as he had before. As he did, Rob could feel the essence striking, whatever it was that he hit, and the resistance they were trying to use against him. Rob pushed more power from him, trying to counter what they were doing, and as he did, he could not feel anything more. He felt that resistance, but that was it.

Then he felt something else.

It was behind him.

It was vast, powerful, and…

And felt similar to the unity.

But there were different aspects of it. Different contours that he could almost feel.

Was this the other entity? Was this what he was going to have to deal with?

He had to focus on these subheralds first. Deal with them. Take them down. And…

Something came up in the water, and Rob targeted

downward, pushing himself straight up with a burst of unity while also pushing downward with a blade of unity.

He heard a strange, horrifying shriek, and then he shot upward until he got above the subheralds, and above whatever was emerging from the water below. Then he turned his focus back to the subheralds, shot outward with a dozen more blades, and began to twist them until the subheralds were shredded.

As he suspected, the subherald simply dissipated. They were essence constructs, not real. Maybe they were essence memories, no different than Arowend, who was an essence memory.

And if they were, they were powerful essence memories.

He hovered, focusing on the distant sense he detected. It was considerable. Rob was aware of the power and aware of how it pressed on him, but he was also somehow aware of vastness, as if some part of that pressed against him. It was a deep energy that felt as if it were connected to the world in a greater way than Rob had managed.

If he could understand that connection, maybe he wouldn't have to fear anything more.

But how was he supposed to find that connection on his own?

That power began to press through him.

Attempting to slide *into* him.

There was some aspect of it that felt almost alive.

And essence could be alive. Rob had certainly experienced it. He also understood that the kind of power he was feeling was incredibly potent, and he needed to find something within it that he could counter. However, he knew he couldn't do it from a place that was not his realm. What he needed, instead, was to try to find other places, other towers, and other unities.

But Rob wasn't sure how he was going to do that. The other places would be disconnected from him, which meant that he was going to risk himself. He needed some other way to try to travel to those towers, places, and link to them for him to gain power.

But how could he?

How could he counter what he felt out there, and how could he stay alive if there was this much power pressing on him?

He lingered on this side of the boundary for a little while longer until he retreated. It was too potent for him, and Rob didn't want to risk himself, as he could still feel that slithering energy starting to work through him. It wasn't until he got back through the boundary where he had access to the full unity once again, both his and the linked unity, that he could sweep away any additional influence and ensure that nothing else was trying to touch upon him.

Only then did Rob finally relax.

Only Rob couldn't relax. How could he? He had never felt anything quite like that before, and the power that he had experienced out there, the energy that he was aware of, was so much vaster than anything that he had ever experienced, to the point where Rob didn't know if there was going to be anything that he would be able to do to progress to that kind of potency.

He turned away.

He would have to find something. And the answers were not going to be found beyond his borders. Somehow and some way, he was going to need to find them inside of his borders, even if it meant going into the tower to discover its secrets.

Chapter Six

AROWEND

Arowend drifted above ground. He didn't mind staying in this nebulous form, as he enjoyed staying separated, a little more than essence in a cloud that floated. There was a part of him that felt as if he were more himself, like this was the way he was supposed to be, but there was also a part of him that was what he had become. That was the Netheral part of himself, and though Arowend was aware of it, he worried about what would happen if he were to stay in this form for too long. Would he eventually lose awareness of himself?

He did not have an answer to that and wasn't sure there was an answer. Tessatha had been working with him, trying to help him learn more about what it meant for him to be the essence in this form. Not an essence memory. At least, that wasn't what he wanted to call himself, though Rob and some others referred to him that way. He was simply essence. He didn't know what that meant for him, nor did he know whether he could gather that power back together in a way that would help him hold the link inside of him, but increasingly, he felt that he needed to find the key so he could fully understand just what it meant for him to have this power. He could use it when dealing with this other entity they had to face.

I had used it.

And there was that part of him that dreaded what he had done. He had stripped essence off. Was that what he needed to become?

An essence weapon.

He didn't like that, but he wasn't sure that there was anything that he could say about it, anyway. Once it helped the people that he cared about?

But...

He also felt that same bothered sensation, as he couldn't help but question if others viewed the same weapon that had destroyed him in the same way.

So, he floated.

In a cloud form like this, he was aware of the unity in a way that he wasn't when he was down on the ground or even when he was in his physical form. He was aware of how the unity flowed, working its way from what had once been the nexus and then pushing outward, creating a steady energy that turned into something of a cloud. Arowend could feel it was sweeping out into the land and working in a way that made the other essence a part of it, but merely a part. He could feel the other essences and how they existed, but he could also feel the way they pulled apart for him to find something more.

And that was what it came down to. It always came down to finding more.

At least, that was Rob's impression of it.

But hadn't he been the same way?

Even when he was alive, Arowend had attempted to find more. He wanted to bridge the different forms of the essence, something never done before. He remembered the others. It took a long time to get those memories back, but now that he did, he could remember how the others fought him, each of them the head of their own house and leader of their own type of essence. They all feared what would happen if Arowend were to bring those different powers together. They feared essence.

Shouldn't it be feared?

From up here, Arowend didn't think there was anything to be feared when it came to essence. It felt as if it were a part of everything. It felt like life.

Even though he wasn't alive. Not really.

But isn't essence alive?

These questions bothered him in ways he couldn't fully understand, but he kept trying to work through them, wanting to make sense of what he had become and find a way to know more about himself. The essence might be alive, but it didn't mean that Arowend once again lived because he had essence.

But then, he had memories. Didn't that mean that some part of him was still there? Memories were locked in essence. Tessatha taught him that, yet memories were not all he was. The essence reflected something more.

He had to push aside those memories, ignoring his fear about what had happened all that time ago and what had changed for him and what the others had done to him. It wasn't easy, but it was necessary. Forgiveness was necessary.

It was the same thing that he asked of those he had harmed.

And he had harmed plenty.

Arowend drifted before he started to focus on a different kind of power that he felt below him, and then he headed directly toward one specific focus of it. From above, it was an odd sensation. Especially because it had taken him so much time to master the unity, he felt something that was specifically ice and a heavily concentrated form of it at that. He knew he had to be careful with what he was doing and where he was going, as this was somebody that he had harmed more than any other. But he needed to go to them.

He needed to make amends.

If the others were still alive, those who had harmed him, would they make amends with him? Arowend doubted that they would. How could they, as they had caused him so much pain and…

And he had suffered. He had become the Netheral. He had used that rage and anger to become something else.

When he landed amidst a pile of snow mixed with ancient stone debris, he felt the city that had once been here. It was once a vibrant place, long before his time, back when essence flowed from one place to the next. His time had bridged essences, allowing the lands to be connected, but no one had bonded them in the way he wanted. He could feel that essence now, even though there was only a memory of it here. As he strode forward, he formed himself once again, taking on the Arowend form, though, for a moment, he was tempted to take on that of Rob. Maybe he would get a better response if he went in as Rob.

Because he could.

He was similar, wasn't he?

There was a time when they'd been different. But even then, they weren't that dissimilar. Arowend wanted to bring the essences together, and Rob had done it. Arowend had found himself when Rob had done that, and now…

Now he was more than what Rob was, at least in some regards. Rob might be linked to the unity, bridging from one type to another, but Arowend could use essence in a way that Rob could never unless he was willing to leave his body, which Arowend would counsel him against. He wasn't sure it was safe, and no one should make that commitment unless they had to.

"I see you," a voice said from a distance.

Arowend froze.

He could scarcely make out the other entity, but now that he paused, he could *feel* her. Her essence was highly concentrated, radiating ice's power far more than he had expected. She was at least a dragon soul. He didn't feel any of the other essence within it. Now that he had access to unity and the way that he bonded that power, it was possible that he would not even know what she was or what she was doing. That power continued to build from her, spreading outward in a way that left Arowend feeling something considerable from her.

"I came to find you," he said, bowing his head.

Two other arctic cats were behind her. They were actual arctic cats, not physical manifestations of the essence, not how Eleanor was.

The Nelah.

She might not be the Nelah anymore, but she had been when he targeted her. He owed her more than he thought he could provide. More than an explanation. He owed her an apology.

"I came to say sorry."

Eleanor prowled forward.

She flowed, almost as if she were drawing upon the ice as she moved until she was right across from him. A blaze of cold came from her, washing outward until it slammed into him, but there wasn't anything violent in it. There was something almost soothing. It had been quite some time since he felt the ice and its power. He felt as if he were connected to something more, some part of him, that he had wanted to be.

"You do not need to come and apologize," she said, her voice low.

He wondered if she was speaking aloud or through the dragon mind connection. He suspected it was the dragon mind connection, as arctic cats had no way of speaking otherwise.

Behind him, and behind her, there were other arctic cats.

More had come.

Arowend was now surrounded.

He felt the effect of the circle that they formed. They were trying to hold onto power so that they could trap him and hold him here. It might work, or at least, it might've worked back before he was connected to the unity, but now he didn't think it would.

But maybe because he was in their realm, and because they had progressed — all of these arctic cats feeling him as if they were some sort of dragon soul — they might be able to hold onto him. That kind of thing was impressive. Though he was targeted by it, he knew that it was an impressive use of power. It was the kind of thing that he would have wanted to understand before, but even now, he wasn't sure that it made much difference if he tried to understand it, as he still thought he could lose his form and sweep away from them. Either going down, deep beneath the ground, or heading up.

Or I could sweep through them.

That was what he'd done to the heralds, and although he knew he could do it, he didn't want to.

"Do you intend to hold me?"

The Nelah came toward him, moving carefully. She still slithered, moving upon the power that Arowend found amazing. It was the kind of control he would've wanted back when he was still in his physical form. Her control over ice and this power left him marveling at what she could do.

"Are we in any sort of danger?"

"I don't intend to harm you if that's your question. I came to apologize, and I came for answers."

"He deserves no answers," one of the arctic cats behind her growled.

Arowend could feel the power coming off that arctic cat and recognized that it had been bound to him at one point. Back then, he attempted to use that kind of energy and corrupted it.

He bowed his head to that arctic cat. "And I apologize to you. To all of you." He shifted his essence, sending it away from him, trying to connect to all the arctic cats so he could share how he felt and the depths of his regret. He suspected he would have to do this with everybody he harmed. That was the only way he was going to find a way of making amends, but even as he attempted to do so, he felt resistance. He recognized that something was coming off him, and some other aspect of it was trying to press into him. They were opposing him. "I am sorry."

"Enough," the Nelah commanded.

Arowend thought that she was talking to him, but that wasn't it at all. Her essence radiated outward, and it slammed into the arctic cats. When she did, the pressure against him eased.

The fact that he had been able to change forms suddenly changed as well. He was no longer bound the way he had been, which he marveled at, but then again, he also marveled at the fact that these other arctic cats could hold him. He doubted that they would be able to hold him for long, but the fact that they were able to hold him at all was still impressive.

"Come with me," she said, and she slithered off, gliding across the land.

Arowend followed her.

Glancing back, he saw two of the arctic cats following. They were both massive and radiated considerable power, leaving him thinking they were dragon souls or something more. They might have become dragon blood, as Rob hadn't restricted anybody from advancing if they wanted it. He had even encouraged it, something that Arowend found amazing. Rob really was different. As hard as it was for him to acknowledge, there was something about Rob he thought he needed to be more like.

"What is it that you would like to know?"

"I want to know how you tolerate this," he said, deciding to get to the point. "I'm like you, at least because we are both forms of the essence. And I'm struggling with it."

She paused, and then she took a seat, crouching to look up at him. There was an intensity in her eyes. She had manifested her physical form, but she had done so with such an intensity that it seemed as if she were truly connected to it, something Arowend had not yet done.

"Is it difficult for you?"

"At times," he admitted. "And I don't like the fact that it is, but I can't shake that. I feel as if I am out of time and out of place and…" He breathed out. "And I still struggle with what I was."

"Then you are as alive as any," she said with a small smile. "If you didn't struggle with what you were, you could not become what you must be. That is all that we are."

It sounded like a riddle to him, but it also struck him as sage advice. Even though he had existed for hundreds of years, he felt as if Nelah had been alive for longer than him. Maybe what he really needed to do was to visit with the others.

Serena had spoken of the Sultan and the advice that

she had offered, so maybe she would help him, as well. And then there was the one from the earth realm. Gregor was not one that Arowend had much experience with, but perhaps he had some advice for him, too.

"I don't know what I'm supposed to do."

"You serve," she said.

"But what do I serve?"

The Nelah got up and stepped toward him, almost seeming as if she drifted out from her essence form before manifesting directly in front of him. And then he realized what she was doing. She was losing her form before retaking hold of it. It was an impressive use of essence. He wasn't even sure that he would be able to drift back and forth quite as effectively as what he had seen from her. It was amazing.

"You serve essence."

"But what does essence call me to do?"

She leaned toward him, and for a moment, Arowend felt the power that she radiated. It was considerable, and she had a way of using essence that he still didn't fully understand.

"Only you can find the answer to that. You must listen to what it's calling you to do, be open to it, and be ready to respond."

"What if it calls me to harm others?"

That's what Rob suggested he do, and it was something that he didn't want to do, not if he didn't have to. He had done enough of that.

"Would that fit with who you are?"

"It fits with who I was."

"That wasn't the question."

"No," he said. "It wouldn't fit with who I am."

"Then essence won't call you to do that. I don't know what it will call you to do, and I don't know how it will call you, but I do know that eventually, the essence will find a way to ask you what you need to do. And you must be ready. Only you can be. Only you can know what it's asking."

"What is it asking of you?"

"To come here."

Chapter Seven

SERENA

SERENA FELT THE ESSENCE ALL AROUND HER. SHE TRIED to make sense of it, hoping to understand some part of the unity that flowed through the tower. But even as she attempted to do so, she could tell that there was some aspect of it that was different from what she'd felt before.

Distantly, she was aware of her father. Serena appreciated that the tower permitted her that awareness. Her link to the tower felt similar to the dragon's mind connection. She was gifted with the ability to understand what was happening with her father, but she couldn't see the entire picture. When she closed her eyes, she saw what her father was doing, the way he handled the essence, and the challenges he faced.

She saw the challenge he was about to face, and she was worried it would push his boundary, especially since his connection began to change.

Was he progressing?

That was certainly her hope for him. She wanted him

to progress, but he was a dragon soul, so for him to progress to something more, using the unity was going to involve something more than what she had experienced before. Maybe it wasn't even possible for him to do so, or perhaps he could, and the tower would permit it.

She glanced around. Tessatha was standing on the other side of the room, studying the markings on the walls as she tried to make sense of them. Somehow, Serena had gained the knowledge of those markings given to her from the tower.

Serena walked over to her.

"You were saying something about these?" Tessatha asked, and she paused, looking over her shoulder at Serena. Her brow furrowed, and her deep blue eyes glittered as if reflecting some of the unity in the room.

Or perhaps they were simply radiating unity. Tessatha had grown powerful, and she'd begun to demonstrate a significant connection to that essence. Then again, all of them had. Tessatha was just the one who had managed to draw upon that.

"I was saying that the tower gifted me some knowledge, and I'd like to try to make sense of what else is here."

Serena fell silent as she looked at the markings, trying to make sense of them.

"I feel something. I don't know what it is, but I'm increasingly questioning what the tower wants me to learn. Is all of this some sort of a relic?"

"I think we've decided that this was some sort of a construct, but whatever it is, it's powerful enough to be dangerous for us."

Serena focused on the unity that she was feeling and felt as if there was something the tower was trying to give to her, but even as she attempted to do so, she couldn't tell what it was, only that she was aware that it was there.

"What more do you think we can find here?" she asked, looking over to Tessatha.

"Well, I think that if we can piece together the language here," she said, turning her attention to the librarian who'd joined them in the room, and was pausing to take notes by using a mixture of essence and ink as he did, something that Serena found quite different and amusing, "we could track down some of what the tower is trying to tell us. Isn't that what you suggested? That the tower is trying to tell us something?"

That was certainly Serena's impression, but the challenge was that she didn't know what the tower wanted them to know or how they'd learn it other than the writing in there. And the writing didn't seem to provide them with enough information about what was happening, only that something was happening. If Serena had an opportunity to spend the time to study this, she might be able to learn something more and gain the knowledge that the tower was trying to funnel to them.

"It's about power," Serena said. "But I can't find more information than that. All I can tell is that it speaks of power and something that has come here before, and...." She frowned, running her fingers along a particular etching. The writing here was smaller than in the other places, which made it harder for her to study. The tower might've given her the knowledge to read certain aspects of the writing, but it didn't allow her to take it all in at once. If only the tower would give her that. Then again, the tower had continually offered them gifts, not only with their progression but with whatever it was offering her father. She shouldn't complain about it. "I don't know what it's trying to tell us, but there are these connections." She paused as she looked around. "I wonder what we might find if we were to go to the other tower."

"I don't think we can go to that tower," Tessatha surmised, "Not yet. Not unless we had a connection to it, the same way that Rob does."

"Perhaps we could link to the people who occupy that tower," Serena suggested.

Wouldn't that help? If she were to connect to the woman Rob had helped, maybe they would be able to communicate in a way that would help them find answers.

What kind of answers would they uncover? What would there be that they could use?

Nothing.

At least, there was nothing that Serena thought would benefit them, given everything they were dealing with and everything they may still have to deal with.

"Rob seems to think that the key to all of this is how the towers are connected," Serena said. "And from what I can tell here, this speaks of a higher power, but it doesn't tell us how to access it. I think Rob needs that so that he'll know how to stop this other entity."

"We can keep working," Tessatha said.

Serena nodded. "Yes, we can keep working, and I feel like the answers are close by, at least with what the tower wants us to see, but I don't know if we'll find them quickly enough."

"There has been no sign of this attack, so I think we have time," Tessatha said.

Serena wanted to believe that they had the time they thought they did, but at the same time, she also recognized that there had been increasing movement around them, the sense of power that was starting to build, leaving her feeling like something was taking place. If that power continued to work toward them, and this other entity continued to move, how much time did they really have? Rob believed that progression was the key to all things, but Serena had come to know that it wasn't just progression. It was knowledge. And here they had a tower that was trying to give her knowledge, but she didn't feel as if she had the necessary time to work through it so that they could understand what the tower was trying to show them.

Was this what Rob felt?

She knew that he was helpless with some of the struggles they'd been dealing with and the fact that they had to keep fighting without giving him an opportunity to stop, study, and try to use the essence of memories that might provide him with the answers he wanted. And yet still, he had managed to learn what he needed. But it had been harder.

Did they have to do it alone?

She had the librarian, and the manifestation of power that the librarian offered her, so perhaps they didn't. There was a way that they might be able to use that power, something that she had never attempted to do before, but maybe now was the time for her to do it.

She focused on him and on the unity that she felt within herself, the connection that she had to the tower — and it was a connection which she felt more distinctly now than she had before — and began to try to draw upon that energy so that she could create another librarian. In the past, when she manifested other librarians, they had done so in different locations and never in the same one. But this time, she needed knowledge and information, and she felt like anything that she might provide to the librarian, and that he might provide her, would come from this connection and from giving her what she needed so that she could understand the power that existed here.

She created another, and then another, and then paused.

Three librarians. Would that be enough?

Tessatha was watching her with an unreadable expression. She was trying to make sense of the power that Serena was using and how she was manifesting that power.

"I'm going to leave him here to study," Serena said.

"Do you think that is wise?"

"I have a connection to him, and anything that he learns, he funnels back to me."

Tessatha focused on her dragon mind connection. Serena felt that link forming, solidifying in a way that hadn't before, and she focused on Serena. "How long will that be the case?"

"I am connected to the librarian."

"You are, but if — he — is connected to the palace and possibly even to the tower. At what point do you think that connection will no longer be enough?"

Serena never gave that a thought, but maybe she should have. The possibility remains that the librarian may choose to funnel power to help the palace, and maybe the tower, and might even ally itself with the tower rather than with Serena.

But she felt as if she were connected, and that connection was significant. She thought that if she were to be able to use some part of that power, the librarian would help her.

She had to trust.

She linked to each of them. She used something of the conduit that she had shared with Rob, though she didn't open herself quite as much to them the way Rob did with her. She appreciated the openness, and she knew that it was going to be necessary for the two of them to share what they did because the two of them shared more than just the connection. They also occasionally share power. In this case, she needed to share knowledge. She opened herself and pushed out what the tower had offered her, though it seemed that the librarian had already known.

"Help me find whatever is written here and make sense of the tower."

One of the librarians, who was there before, glanced briefly at the others before nodding at her. "We will find what you need, Mistress."

Serena let out a heavy sigh. "I think that's all I can do now."

"You don't want to stay?"

"I was staying mostly because I was concerned about my father," she began, and when she did, she could feel the sense of her father out there, still in the tower, though some part of him had changed. He was safe. She no longer had to worry about the tower harming him, though Serena never really had to worry about that. She knew that the tower was not here to harm, at least not somebody at that level. Maybe a different level?

That was odd. She couldn't help but question if the tower would've harmed them had they not worked the way they had.

"He has progressed, I think."

Tessatha nodded. "The tower will be useful for such things, I think. Perhaps this was the original intention for this construct."

"But who made it?" Serena asked. "That's what I've been wondering. It seems as if whoever made the tower, and whoever had the power to do so, is going to be key to understanding how we can *use* the different towers, and whether they can be linked, to stop whatever is coming."

Tessatha said, "The answers will either be here or elsewhere.". "Which is something that I enjoy. We can continue to study, look, and see if the answers are found around us, and then…." She shrugged. "Then we might find what we've been looking for."

Serena wished it was that easy, but maybe to Tessatha, it was as simple as that. She was a researcher, and she had worked before she had lost time doing similar things. For Serena, however, though she was also a researcher, there was a part of her that was more than that. It had been hard for her to accept that, but she was also a doer. Rob had shown her that about herself. She didn't like to be trapped and isolated. She wanted to be the one to go and fight when it came down to it.

And lately, that had been necessary more than she would've liked.

"What are you going to do?"

"There are additional things I can look into," Tessatha said. "I'm trying to make sense of the tower and the different powers here, and I'm hopeful that we might be able to uncover something more. Once we leave the tower, I intend to return to some of my studies. Maybe what I find will add to what you're doing. And there is something that I'm concerned about that I'm going to look into."

"Is there anything that I can help you with?"

"Not yet," Tessatha said. "I feel like I need to do this myself, and I feel like I'll be better off alone until Arowend joins me, and it may amount to nothing. I don't want to say anything because I don't know that there's anything there, and I certainly don't want to make you concerned."

The fact that Tessatha had something she thought would Serena was surprising. But what might she learn? There were things that Serena needed to do, as well, so she decided to leave.

She looked up, focusing on the tower. "Will you permit me to depart?"

There was no response, but she felt a connection within her, that of the tower, and she followed that connection. Tessatha stayed with her, and the two of them headed back toward where she thought the staircase was going to be, but it was not there. She found an opening forming in the tower and strode toward it. She stepped through into daylight and realized that she was on ground level. Some parts of the tower had changed.

She smiled, though it was mostly to herself. Being in the tower was such an odd experience, to feel the way it was changing, but at the same time, there was something about the tower that she thought she could learn, maybe even master a measure of control over. It would take time, though. But increasingly, it seemed as if the tower wanted her to take that time, as if the tower itself was trying to give her that gift of understanding, but Serena had figured out what it was so that she might be able to master it.

"I can never get over how much it changes each time we're there," Tessatha said.

"I think it wants us to struggle with that," Serena replied. "It's what makes me think that the tower is far more alive and more aware than we were ever aware of before. The more that we see, the more that we do, the more that we experience, the more that I come to question just how much the tower is trying to play with us."

Tessatha looked over, back at the tower, her gaze darkening momentarily. "I don't like the idea of some sentient tower playing with us."

"I don't think it intends to harm us, though."

At least, not now.

But if it did, Serena wasn't sure what they could do to protect themselves if the tower did try to harm them. There was so much power within the tower, so much essence it was drawing through it, drawing off the other places within her realm, that she could feel it bubbling up and wondered if that connection, and the way it formed, was meant to distract.

"It certainly attempted to harm us when we were inside and trying to progress," Tessatha said. "And whether that was only a test or something more, it doesn't matter. It was there, and it was dangerous. What happens if someone else enters the tower it wants to target?"

"Maybe the tower can help defend us, then?"

"Did you think the tower wanted to defend this realm?"

Serena almost answered yes, but then she started to think about it. Was that what was happening?

The tower didn't seem like it intended to try to help the realm, only that it was connected to it. The power that was here, the power that was flowing through it, was so much more than what Serena had ever experienced. Yet, even as she was connected to it, she still didn't know if the tower itself was trying to offer them something, or if it was trying to take something.

This was even more reason for her and the librarian to try to get the answers they needed so that they might better understand what was happening here and to know if there was going to be any way that they might be able to protect themselves from whatever it was that was here. And to protect themselves from whatever it was that was coming.

"I hope that it does," she said.

"We can hope for all we want, but essence doesn't follow such things. Essence chooses its own path."

Serena wanted to argue with that, but that had also been her experience. Essence didn't have any real preference. Or if it did, it was at the instigation of whoever it was drawing on.

She focused, testing for the connection to the tower, and wondered if maybe there was going to be something that she might be able to use, some part of that connection, which might help her know more about what was out there, but she could not feel it.

The only thing that she could feel was unity. The same unity that was changing everything in this realm. And that change, more than anything else, was something that Serena knew was significant and perhaps necessary but also dangerous.

And perhaps it was time that she tried to understand the unity better, so that when she came back to the tower, she might fully understand it as well.

Chapter Eight

ROB

Rob hadn't expected to see anything. He had been drifting, trying to make sense of the essence around him, when he noticed a pale tracing of fiery essence in a familiar location. He was not at all sure why it was so familiar.

He drifted closer to it, thinking that it was tied to Serena or perhaps tied to something of the dragon queen, but as he neared, he found himself slowing, his heart hammering.

It was the essence, incorporate essence.

And there was a reason that he recognized it.

Rob dropped to the ground. He tried to focus, thinking about that essence. He tried pulling it together, but it didn't function as it should even as he attempted to.

"Mother?" Rob spoke softly while trying unsuccessfully to gather the essence of memory to him. He was certain that this was his mother, certain that she was nothing more than a memory now, as he had been chasing word of her for quite some time.

The essence fluttered, turning toward him, a little more than a swirl of the essence—some ice and even a little fire—before it suddenly drifted away. Now, he did not doubt in his mind.

An essence memory. His mother.

He found her.

After all this time that he had others searching, he was the one who found her. Rob stood in place. Distantly, he was aware of where that essence memory drifted. He thought he could gather it up, perhaps even call that memory into himself, but he didn't want to. He was curious about what would happen.

He watched for longer than he probably needed to because, after a while, he knew what he had to do. It was only a short journey to his valley. He landed near the boundary and found the outpost much like it had been before. Rob called out to his father with a pulse of his dragon mind connection.

His father appeared, moments later, emerging from the outpost, half-dressed, eyes wide, as he staggered toward Rob. His face was grizzled, his eyes carrying the same look they had when Rob had been younger, a mirror of his own. He was slightly larger than the last time Rob had seen him and was dressed in a black jacket and pants. Essence filled him in such a way that it hadn't been the last time he'd been here. He had progressed. Rob was thankful for what he had, knowing that it was possible, and hopeful that his father would continue progressing.

"Rob?"

"It's me."

His father yawned, rubbing his eyes.

"What... What are you doing here?"

"Shouldn't I come to visit my father?"

His father swept his gaze around him. "I know that you're busy. I can feel it. Sometimes I can almost hear your voice and the things you tell your friends."

That surprised Rob. He didn't expect his father to have the power to hear him, but he was still thankful for it. It told him that Rob still lived.

"I only came because I found something."

"What did you find?"

"I found her."

Rob said no more because his father needed no further explanation.

"You found her?"

Rob nodded. "She's gone, but not gone." Rob focused on his father, focused on the dragon mind connection that he could now force between the two of them, and gave him the image of what he'd experienced. "She's not fully intact. And I don't know if she can be reformed."

"What are you talking about?"

"Essence memories. Sometimes when people are lost, you can bring them back. At least, in a certain way."

"That is not what we would do."

"Maybe not," Rob said. He had been too excited; maybe that was part of the problem. He understood essence in ways that his father did not, and he understood that losing the essence, becoming nothing more than an essence memory, was not the end. It was just one part of life, such as it was. Eventually, everybody would become an essence, wouldn't they? In Rob's mind, it seemed as if that was something to look forward to.

But maybe not for his father.

"She's gone," he said again.

His father wiped his eyes, and he looked over to Rob. "Why aren't you more bothered by this?"

"I'm sad," Rob said. "Sad because of what we've lost. Sad because she is no longer what she'd been. But she can be something else now. She can still be found."

"And how would you find her?"

"She can be found here," Rob said, tapping his chest. "And here." He tapped his forehead. "She's in your memories and mine. She's all around us."

His father sighed.

"Would you like to stay and visit for a while?"

There was so much that Rob needed to do, but maybe this was the connection he needed to make right now.

"I would like that."

He took a moment to survey everything in his realm, testing whether there was anything that would prove dangerous, but he didn't feel any additional attempts to press through the barrier. Not that he fully expected it, as he'd defeated the subheralds trying to attack, and he thought that he had scared them away—at least for now.

The memory of that other entity pressing toward him came back, though. There was power there, and it was unlike anything Rob had ever experienced. He needed to find a way to uncover more unity and link more power so they could be safe from it.

He reached Alyssa's realm. From above, he was aware of the power blooming within it, the essence that lingered through the tower. Given that he'd been drawing upon that power, he felt as if he were connected to it in a way that he had not been before. Not directly, and not the way that Alyssa had, but he did feel as if some part of him were able to access it. That had to be significant, didn't it? Because of that connection and what he had done, he'd managed to survive during dark times before. It also allowed him to extend his influence beyond what he wouldn't have otherwise been able to do.

Essence.

That was the key. For so long, Rob tried to make sense of his power and how that essence flowed, yet he couldn't fully grasp it. And now, as the essence was working within him, Rob knew there was a connection to him and the realm around him. He also recognized that essence might not be enough.

Maybe it was about knowledge.

He thought that was the key when trying to understand what was needed for him to become a dragon soul. He had used the essence memories around his realm to grasp more than he would've otherwise until he had to stop. There hadn't been the time or the opportunity, as those essence memories had gifted him with certain aspects of what he might need, and it wasn't enough. *He* had not been enough. It wasn't until he had begun to explore and experiment on his own that he found what he needed.

That was what he had to do now, wasn't it?

Certain places around his realm were ancient. Older than old and tied to the world in ways that Rob still didn't fully understand. Now that he was connected to the unity and he had a way of using that power, Rob thought he could and should find a means of linking to that power well enough that he could use it. Those memories and that knowledge were going to be key.

Rob just had to find it.

He paused momentarily, hovering above Alyssa's land, and wondered if he could use some memories here. Essence memories of any realm would be useful even if they were not of his own realm. Rob could use those to try to understand what had happened.

As he focused on the essence below him, he realized that the essence stripped away by this other entity and the heralds that served it had damaged those memories.

Of course, they had. That had been clear to them from the very beginning, as the others like Alyssa made it clear that they had lost so much of who and what they once were because of what the heralds had done to them. They wanted to take that knowledge. At the time, Rob thought that it was because they wanted to help prevent them from finding what they needed to do to progress, but maybe there was another reason for it. Maybe what they had done was to strip away knowledge of what this other entity was and who the heralds served so that they would be able to keep them from succeeding.

Or maybe there was something else that Rob still had to find.

He moved on.

The answers weren't going to come here, and as he paused over Oro's realm, he tested whether there was anything within the essence that he might be able to find. He was unfamiliar with Oro's essence, even though he had it as a part of the unity and was bonded to it. That essence made it so that Rob could link to certain aspects of power, but something else was difficult for Rob to grasp fully. He struggled to test whether there were memories there he might use. The answers might be there, but they eluded him, indicating that he needed to return to his own realm. By the time he arrived, he was ready. He knew that there had to be ancient, distant, and buried essence memories he could draw upon. The key was using his newfound unity essence to master it. But as he attempted to focus on what was there, Rob could feel…

He could feel hints, nothing more.

And maybe that was because of the unity, the way the essence had been blended. Some part of it had been distorted with the unity, so as Rob attempted to focus and probe for those essence memories, he found some part of it changing and some part of him changing.

He was drawn, and for a moment, he hesitated until he realized what it was. He smiled and allowed himself to be pulled forward until he reached the Borderlands and a cluster of trees that pulled him downward.

When he landed, Maggie manifested. Somehow, despite her manifestation, she looked older than before.

Her back was a little more stooped, her hair a pale silver and pulled up into a bun, and her green robes reminded him of the essence that flowed through her. He suspected that he had not been speaking to her nearly as often as he should, and he didn't know how much she had grown, though he had given her the opportunity to continue to connect to the essence and find her own connection to the unity. As far as he knew, she had, but her connection was different because she was different.

"You've been difficult to reach," Maggie said.

"I wasn't trying to be difficult," Rob said. "You are aware of what we've been doing and what we faced. It requires vigilance, and it requires —"

"Do you really think you'll find another way to progress?"

"I think that it's possible," he said. "But I don't know that it's going to be easy."

Maggie laughed and turned to one of the trees, raising her hand. The trees around him were enormous, and as far as he could tell, a similar type of essence radiated around here. There was an energy that was beyond the usual connections that existed. A brief surge of life essence flowed through the tree. It was combined with a bit of unity, though maybe it was only unity, and Rob felt life most of all. That connection was surprising and unique, and it was not at all what he would've expected.

"Has it ever been easy to progress, Rob?"

"Early on," he admitted. "At least, once I reached dragon forged, but after that, it was merely a matter of consuming enough essence. Now it's about something else."

"It's always been about something else," Maggie said. "The challenge is that most know what it is, yet you did not. Still, you found your way, fumbling and stumbling along until you managed to reach for the kind of power that others could only dream of." She turned to him. "And now you seek to join our land with others."

"It's not the first time I've attempted to do that," Rob said.

"It's not, but what you intend to do now is quite a bit different, isn't it?"

He wasn't about to argue with her, as what he intended, and thought was necessarily involved more linkage than what they had already done. Rob still wasn't sure what that was going to entail, and he didn't know if it was even going to be possible for him to do it, but he felt as if he had to try.

"It's different. It's the only way that I think that we're going to be able to be safe from this other entity."

"And what if that's what the other entity wants?" She frowned and turned to another tree, pulling another strand of life essence from within it. "You have been changing things here. I haven't argued, as it feels necessary," she went on, though something in her tone left Rob wondering if she truly felt that way or was merely saying it for his benefit. "Over time, I can feel the essence shifting. I wonder what that means for us, and I wonder what that means for our realm."

"You can still use it," Rob said.

"I can because I've bonded to more. Others… Well, others find this a bit more challenging than they once did. I don't know what that means."

Rob knew there would be difficulties, especially for those who were still on their journey to understanding their essence. Those who had just become dragon forged, or dragon skin, would likely have the hardest time, as the unity had the essence that he was calling through the realms, was a combination of all the different essence, but it also might make it so that they wouldn't be able to reach for their own kind of essence quite as easily as they had otherwise.

But higher levels?

Rob had hoped that the higher levels, dragon mind and above, would find it much easier. With the unity flowing to the land, and the way it was moving, Rob had hoped that the unity would allow them to understand that there was considerable power here and perhaps even be able to see it and subsequently use it. That combination was key and crucial to Rob's experience with essence.

"I don't think it means anything dangerous," Rob said. "The joining of our realm was for the best. We've done things that couldn't be done otherwise. We can move in ways that we couldn't otherwise. We have found people that we wouldn't know otherwise. Isn't that all beneficial?"

She frowned and turned her attention back to the tree, drawing essence through it. Rob was incredibly aware of how she was doing it and could feel that essence as it flowed up from somewhere deep, but he also knew she was doing something to the unity. He had not felt anything before, though he understood how she did it. She was pulling on an aspect of it, pulling upon life, and separating it so it would feed the trees.

But would the trees do better if they had unity?

"You think I'm making a mistake here?"

"I would never say that," Rob said. "This is your realm."

She started to laugh, glancing in his direction for a moment, the deep wrinkles along the corners of her eyes difficult to read.

"This was my realm, but now… Now it is nothing quite like it was before. It is your realm, I think. All of them are in your realm. And I wonder what will happen as you conquer more."

Conquer.

Was that what he was doing?

And if Maggie was saying it, did it mean that others felt the same way?

Rob certainly didn't want others to think he was trying to be some grand conqueror, imposing his will, as others already did in their lands, especially throughout the Borderlands. But what was he, if not a conqueror?

Rob wasn't even sure what he was. At this point, he wanted to be the one to serve the realm, and that was what he had tried to encourage others to do, but if he was trying to expand access, to link his land with Alyssa's, and to try to find a way to access another realm, maybe he was some sort of conqueror.

"Is that how you view me?"

"No," she said, with a hint of a smile, and turned away, striding to another tree. This time, she brought her hand upward, and he felt her using more of the unity, though there was still an aspect of life that was predominant in the way that she was pulling it up through the tree. "But I'm not the only one in these realms. Others will see you as they see you, so you need to decide how you'll present yourself and whether or not you can present yourself in a way that does not come across as conquering."

"I'm trying to free them," Rob said.

"You have freed our realm." She waved her hand, and once again, a bit of unity began to burn up through the tree, building in a way that stretched and didn't seem to alter the tree all that much. Rob couldn't tell, as he had never really focused on this particular tree before, but it did seem to him as if the power that existed within the tree was not altered dramatically. "But you have also changed it. And as you have seen and felt, change can be difficult for many people."

"My father said the same," Rob said.

"Your father taught you well."

Rob smiled. With everything he was doing, he hadn't spent that much time in the valley with his father. As far as Rob knew, he was still there, progressing, and perhaps he had reached dragon mind. Even if he had, there was still such a massive gap between where his father was and where Rob had gone.

What did that matter?

When it came to Serena, and her own progression, he had been telling her all along that it didn't make any difference to him and that her level of progression wasn't important, but even though he claimed that there was a part of him that felt otherwise. How could he not? There was a part of him that understood that progression, and an understanding of the power that they had, helped them understand each other better.

And he had been thankful when Serena had progressed to understanding the unity essence. He knew she needed it, not just for her, but for him — and the realm. At least, that was what he had told himself.

"Sometimes, I wonder if those lessons have been lost."

"You have to remember where you come from," she said. "Eventually, you will be challenged in a way that you need to rely upon those foundations. The foundations of who you are and what you are, are going to help define who you will become. I think that is why I have not objected to what you have done. Others..."

"Like the dragon queen," Rob offered.

Maggie smiled tightly. "Yes. She is one. I've been working with her to help her see the mistake, but she has proven difficult."

"I didn't realize that you were talking to her."

"She is unrepentant. She saw what she did as necessary to protect her realm, but I think she was too small-minded. And I've been struggling to help her see beyond that."

Small-minded. She had been traitorous, betraying her people and her realm, all because she had feared something more. And Rob didn't feel guilty about stripping her from her realm. Serena had been a part of that, but even if she had not, Rob still would've done it. It was necessary.

"Maybe I should also talk to her," he said.

"Perhaps," she said, and she turned to him, clasping her hands. There was something so amusing about how she moved, partly because Rob was fully aware that she was little more than a manifestation, but she had very human mannerisms. Maybe that was from her time spent among people her entire life, or perhaps it was that Maggie wanted to become human, or so it had seemed. "It is possible that she will gain insight, or even better, that she will forgive. But perhaps the greater question is, will those who have fought against her forgive her?"

"Forgiveness?" Rob asked.

"If you hold onto anger, you hold onto something that should not form the foundation of who you are. You're not an angry man, Rob. If you were, you would never have embraced the knowledge and the teaching that Arowend offered. If you were, you wouldn't know what you need to join the lands, and you would've never found this other unity essence." She paused and pressed her hands down before bringing them back up. Rob felt the unity stirring and shifting. Maggie had grown powerful with it. "But it's easy to hold onto anger. It's much harder to let go."

"Is that why you brought me here?"

"Not particularly," she said with a hint of a smile. "Actually, I brought you here because I want you to know that something about the unity essence, this new power that you brought to our realm, has begun to change."

Rob frowned. "The unity is changing. The unity is what's flowing through the land."

"It's not that at all," Maggie said, returning to her tree grove. "I can feel it, especially here. I have been pulling out certain aspects of the essence, teasing it apart to test it, and filtering it to get a better feel for its type of essence. I have found that some part of it is different than it had been a week before. The real challenge, especially for you, is understanding what has happened."

"It's probably because I linked to Alyssa and her power."

"Perhaps that is all it is," she said. "Or perhaps there is something else, but regardless, I think you need to be aware of it so that you can be ready for whatever it might bring to us."

"And what are you afraid that it's going to bring to us?" Rob asked.

"The same thing that we have encountered quite a bit of late. Change, Rob."

Chapter Nine

ROB

Rob felt the energy of the unity all around him, but now he had started to listen to what Maggie had suggested because he wanted to know whether there was any sort of danger that was out there, something about it starting to change as he didn't know if he had detected anything. But he wanted to believe that perhaps there was some aspect of the unity that had started to modify.

He felt drawn to the tower, as that was the most prominent source of unity, at least right now. As he focused on the tower and the power he could feel, Rob tried to make sense of whether some part of it was drawing differently than before.

As he neared it, he recognized that the tower itself seemed much larger than it had before, and there was a flowing sense of unity that worked within it, pressing in and out as if it were pulsing with some sort of heartbeat of the realm itself.

He hovered above it.

The tower from above looked as if it were a massive finger of rock that stretched downward, connecting to the realm. The tower's stone was pale white and impossibly smooth as if it grew out of the ground itself. It stretched all the way to the clouds, narrowing as it rose. There were no windows or doors, at least not where Rob could see. He couldn't tell if it was a manifestation or if this was simply something that erupted once he had freed the unity from the nexus. It was all possibly related, though Rob didn't know if there was some real connection he needed to understand or if anything here was more than what he had already covered.

He didn't spend a lot of time trying to make sense of the tower. Perhaps that was a mistake. He understood that the unity had created some aspect within the tower and generated a sense of energy here, but there was also a power he was not familiar with, a power that he needed to understand and perhaps even master.

It was going to take time to do that, and it was possible that Rob didn't necessarily have that time. He'd been so focused on other things and places, trying to make sense of what he might have to do, that he had not been spending the time that he probably should have been all along.

Power flowed from the tower, and he let it fill him.

When it did, he focused on his connection to the other tower in the other realm, using what he had to share with him about what had happened in Alyssa's realm. He thought the link between the two places should be enough to draw upon that power, but Rob couldn't tell whether the link between the two realms was solid enough to be useful.

He had to find other ways to link power, but the challenge was that he wasn't exactly sure how or where that would be, nor what that might look like. Given everything that he'd experienced and the danger of the heralds, subheralds, and now this other entity, Rob couldn't help but worry that the power that existed was going to be more than what he could withstand.

He drifted downward, feeling the activity within the tower, although he didn't know what he was detecting. Serena had said that the tower was key to helping others progress, and maybe she had brought others here.

He needed to connect to Serena.

He focused on the conduit between the two of them and felt a bit of resistance. He had shielded himself from her, so it was only fair that she'd do the same thing to him.

He stepped on the ground and approached the tower, looking at the massive archway that formed a doorway. It was the only part of the tower that had changed. It seemed to be made out of a gray stone that contrasted with the pale white. He didn't recognize the writing, though he did recognize the power within it. He could feel that essence trying to radiate toward him.

Rob had never attempted to force his way into the tower, even though he was connected to the unity essence, because it might not be possible for him to do so, regardless of how much essence he connected to.

He held his hand out, focusing on the unity that he possessed, and didn't feel any response to the tower the way that Serena described. How could he get inside the tower, then?

Aren't I connected to unity?

He was. He was the one who had brought unity into the realm. The power should respond to him because of that. Why was it not listening?

He strained it, but it still didn't make any difference.

"Rob?" Serena's voice came through the conduit.

Despite everything he'd been doing, he felt disconnected from Serena, despite the conduit. Although this bothered him, he didn't want to draw her into anything dangerous. And he didn't know if anybody else was going to be able to be a part of it. He was the one who was able to link the different essences, and because of that, he thought that he might have to do this alone.

However, each time he felt that way, something would happen that convinced him he could do more with others helping him, and he didn't necessarily have to fight alone.

"Where are you?" Rob asked.

"I went back to the palace," she said, and she sent him a series of images, which took Rob a moment to process what he was seeing. She was inside the tower. At least she'd been inside the tower; whatever she saw also came from there.

"The tower responded to you?"

"Well, the tower does respond, as it seemed as if there are some answers inside there, and something that power wants us to learn. I have the librarian working on it to find the answers, but I think that's going to take us some time. There *are* answers, though, Rob. We just have to be patient." He felt her hesitation, almost as if she were trying to decide what she wanted to say to him, or maybe she was trying to warn him, but then she went on. "I know that patience isn't necessarily something you're comfortable with."

"I can be patient," he said.

"Right. And where were you earlier?"

He was quiet. He hesitated momentarily, and then he felt a fluttering of power coming through the conduit.

It was Serena's way of manifesting, and when she appeared in front of him, she did so wrapped in a maroon cloak that reminded him of when her mother had first manifested to him. She practically radiated the unity essence and had a measure of control over that Rob marveled at. He felt a tugging sense of connection from her to the tower, and he realized that whatever she'd done and how she'd progressed had linked her to that.

He was not linked to that tower in the same way.

"The tower connected to me," Serena said as if knowing his thoughts, "and it seems to be trying to show us something. I don't know what it is, but I'm looking. Do you care to tell me what you were doing earlier?"

Rob breathed heavily and decided to share everything he had done, how he had ventured beyond, how it had drawn him away from Alyssa's realm, and what he had encountered. There was no point in keeping it from Serena. Not only would she be angry, but she needed that truth to help him in the fight against whatever was to come.

"So, you ventured off on your own again," she said. "And at what point do you think that this other entity might overpower you?"

"That's just it," Rob shrugged. "We don't know anything about this other entity, and I don't like this uncertainty."

"You don't like waiting," she said, rolling her eyes. "But you need to. Your people need you to. We all need you to be around."

He hated that she was right, but that was his same concern about everything he had been doing. When he ventured off, Rob didn't feel as if he was doing the wrong thing. He felt as if what he'd been doing, how he'd been fighting, and how he kept searching for information was necessary. And it was the kind of thing he wasn't sure anyone else could help him.

"I need to get inside the tower," Rob said.

"And what do you hope to find once you go inside?"

"Answers."

"I get that. The tower itself doesn't know what it can answer for us. You have to be patient, Rob."

"We don't have the time," he said, turning to her. "Maggie thinks the unity is changing a bit, perhaps because of what I've done by linking to other essences. And if that's the case, then we need to be ready for that change."

"I don't feel it changing," she said.

"Have you been working with the unity?"

"Maybe not the same way Maggie has," Serena said, frowning. "Because if Maggie felt it, then…."

Rob understood. If Maggie was feeling it, then it was probably real because Maggie had a very different understanding of essence than any of them did.

"I can talk with her," Serena said.

"I need to get inside the tower," he said.

"I can talk to the tower," she said, turning to it. "I don't know if it's going to listen to me when it comes to that or if it will be upset."

Rob smiled before realizing that Serena wasn't joking. "You talk to the tower?"

She nodded.

"And the tower answers. My father is still inside."

"That must be what I felt," Rob said. "I felt something inside the tower but wasn't exactly sure what it was. There's some stirring sense of unity." Rob closed his eyes, focused on the unity and the power he felt, and once again, he began to detect something there. He worried that he wasn't going to be strong enough to use it, but even if he wasn't strong enough to use it, he wasn't sure that even mattered. Not anymore. The only thing he needed to do was push inside the unity and pry past the power. "Talk to the tower, then."

She turned away from him, and he was aware of a vague trembling of unity.

The doorway opened.

Serena stepped over and held her hand out, looking inside for a moment. "I'm not sure where this is going to lead you." She glanced over at him, and she shrugged. "Sometimes, the tower does things. It changes. It can be hard to find where it's guiding. And…" She frowned. "It's possible it still might take you somewhere you don't want to be. I caution you to be careful."

"You aren't going to come with me?"

She shook her head.

"I'm looking for information, and you…."

Rob frowned. "I'm looking for information, as well."

"I don't think so," Serena replied, studying him. "I think you intend to take some sort of action. I'm not getting in the way of whatever you think you need to do, but I think you're planning something."

He came to the tower hoping he would have an opportunity to understand the unity here better, uncover the power, and find a way to link to it. If Serena were with him, he might be able to uncover more about it and feel something more significant. But even if she came with him, what might he uncover?

"I'm coming with you," a voice said.

Rob looked up and saw a cloud of essence drifting toward him. As it manifested, Arowend stepped free, landing next to Rob. He seemed more solid than before, and something about him and his manifestation left Rob wondering what he'd been doing.

He was troubled. That much was obvious from how Arowend radiated power through their shared connection, but Rob didn't want to push. Arowend was often troubled these days.

"We don't know where this is going," Rob said.

"I've been inside the tower once before, and I can transition between the levels much easier than you can. You'll need me if we can uncover something inside here. Unless you would like to do this alone?"

"I'll take your help," Rob said.

Arowend nodded.

Rob stepped inside, glancing over at Serena, who was still connected to him with the conduit, but she quickly drifted away, her manifestation fading. He distinctly sensed her leaving, as if she didn't want to linger long. Either that, or maybe she couldn't linger very long, especially as he stepped inside the tower. It might be that the tower separated her somehow, keeping her from staying with him.

Arowend followed, and the two of them stood side-by-side inside the tower. The energy had the essence of the unity pressing around him in a way that left Rob knowing that power but not understanding it. That was odd, as he felt as if he should be fully aware of the unity and what it meant for him or what it meant for his realm.

For the first time in a while, Rob was uncertain about his own land. He found himself looking over to Arowend, who was studying the room. Essence radiated from him, pulsing out as if he were trying to join it with the essence of the tower.

"It changed," Arowend said.

"What changed?"

"I'm not entirely sure," Arowend said, closing his eyes and focusing. "I can feel something different. I suspect that is why you came?"

Rob explained what Maggie had shared with him.

Arowend nodded. "We can try to follow the change."

"I think there is something else we need to do," Rob said, standing inside the tower and feeling the unity. "And it's something I don't want Serena to know." More than that, he was left wondering if the tower had already known what he had intended and whether the tower was trying to keep him from doing it. The tower obviously had some power and understanding. And more than that, Rob wondered if the tower was somehow conscious. If that were the case, it would make the tower incredibly powerful. "I think that we can use the tower to travel."

"Why would you say that?"

"I'm not sure," Rob said. "But if we link to the other places like this, linking to the other unity essence, then I feel like there should be some sort of way for us to follow it."

"You intend to leave?" Arowend asked.

"I intend to see where else it will lead," Rob said.

Arowend turned to him with a hint of a smile and shook his head. "I doubt you could do this."

"I don't know. I'm the one who is connected to the nexus and forced the unity out, and —"

Arowend raised his palms.

"'I'm not disputing all that you've done, Rob," he said. "What I am disputing is whether your current progression and your form are going to be enough for what you hope to accomplish. I simply don't know if that's the case."

"What do you propose?"

Arowend turned to him, and for a moment, his form shimmered as if he were losing control of his manifestation, though Rob knew that wasn't the case. Arowend had complete control over his manifestation, meaning he was doing this intentionally.

"I've been wondering whether there was something more for me and whether I was going to have any way of using what I can be. And maybe this is it."

"It would be dangerous for you," Rob said.

"More dangerous than you? You would be going as manifestation. I would be going as my entire being."

"Maybe we could go together."

"Do you really fear someone else doing something you think only you can do?"

Rob opened his mouth to argue but stopped.

Was that the case? Did he fear this?

He didn't think so, but maybe what Serena wanted for him, and asking that of him, was what he really needed to do.

He sighed, looking at Arowend's determined face.

"Be careful," he said.

"Always."

Chapter Ten

AROWEND

Arowend was surprised that Rob was willing to let him do this. Arowend wasn't even sure that he wanted to try to do this, as he didn't know what would happen if he connected to the other essence.

Rob had always done this kind of thing, and now it was him.

But *shouldn't* he be the one to do this? He wasn't lying when he told Rob that it might be more dangerous for him as manifestation than it would be for Arowend because essence could flow while physical forms could not. And a manifestation was not nearly as potent as Arowend's essence form. He had to believe he could draw through the tower.

But would it work?

That was something that Arowend didn't have an answer to, and as he looked at Rob, he had the distinct sense that Rob didn't know, either.

He had attempted to do many things in the past

where he didn't know the outcome. When he was alive — or, traditionally, alive — Arowend had certainly attempted many different things. He tried to link the types of essences and had hoped for some sort of binding of the realm that would negate the need for the different artifacts. And he had experimented with different types of essences, trying to bridge and link them to form something more.

Should he try to do that now?

He looked at Rob, nodding. "I'm going to try to disperse. I don't know if it's going to work, but I want you to be ready to call me back if something doesn't go right."

"I don't know if I could call you back," Rob said.

"We share a connection," Arowend said. It was true. They had initially fought that connection, but over time, the more they worked together, the more the connection continued to form, though it might not be nearly as strong as the one that Rob had with Serena, nor as strong as the one that Arowend had with Tessatha. Even though that was the case, he still thought that he would prefer to have Rob here with him, working to help him with his essence, trying to make sense of the type of power that he was able to summon and trying to draw that through him in a way that would allow them to call upon more than they had already done. "You have command over a different kind of essence, and you understand the link that has already formed, so I am confident that if anybody were able to call me back, it would be you. I'm going to try to use this connection, and the connection I already felt, and travel. If it doesn't go well, I want you to call me back."

Maybe if it didn't go well, Arowend could bring *himself* back. It would take a little longer, but he could recreate his physical form, manifest once more, and return.

He focused on the essence around him.

He could feel the pulsation. It seemed as if the unity was pressing outward, along with downward. Rob wasn't exactly sure why the essence flowed the way it did and didn't know what it was that he detected, only that he could feel some trailing of it working around him. And if there was something like that, Arowend believed he could follow that and link to it.

He focused on the pulsation and the power he felt, then flowed.

Dispersing, in essence, a form was a fairly straightforward process now, and Arowend could do it easily and quickly. As he did, he allowed himself to blend briefly, nothing more than that, with the essence of the tower itself, and he felt the unity flowing around him. It was not the same as his essence, which momentarily startled him.

He knew that some part of the unity and the essence had started to change, but he hadn't known how profoundly it happened. Now that he could feel it, now that he could feel the way that the essence was blending and shifting, he realized that it was altered more than it had been before.

This had to be the reason that Rob was concerned.

He almost pulled himself away.

Almost.

Arowend suspected that if he were to do that, Rob would not want him to go. It was a bit of a victory that Rob even permitted him to come in the first place, and Arowend wasn't going to give up that victory. He was going to do this.

He was going to be helpful.

Wasn't he?

He tried not to think about that. He tried to resist the urge to talk to Tessatha and tell her what he was going to do. He wanted to warn her about how much he might risk, as she might tell him no. If she did, Arowend knew what he would do. He would withdraw.

But withdrawing was not what he needed to do. He needed to push.

He needed to be more. He needed to be…

He needed to be the essence.

And there might have been only certain things that he would be capable of doing. He couldn't help but feel that way, and he didn't know if Rob, or the others, would believe him. In this case, going as essence felt like it was something that only he could do. He had been the one to help with the heralds, stripping their essence and changing them. Had he been unable to do that, they wouldn't have survived the fight. It was because of Arowend and what he had become.

He pushed again.

This time he felt the pressure of the tower propelling him upward. He resisted the urge to come back together and return.

He followed the flow of the essence.

It guided him. Pushed him.

And Arowend could feel the way that it was sending him. He was nothing more than an essence cloud. He held himself together, but increasingly, he felt some part of him was stretched as if it were trying to tear him apart. It took concentration, experience, and familiarity with the unity to hold onto his form so that he wasn't stripped of everything he knew. He maintained that connection.

Then he drifted.

He lost track of how long he drifted. It felt odd because he could feel things and parts of him that had been lost. He struggled to keep those memories together, to keep some part of him from drifting off into the nether, losing everything he had become. He didn't want that.

And as he held himself together, he began to feel something else grabbing him, targeting him. For a moment, Arowend began to pull himself together and thrash, fearing that there was some sort of attack.

Whatever it was, it didn't feel as if it were trying to assault him in that way. He felt as if it were just drawing on him, pulling upon him in the same way the essence had been drawing on him as it pulled him along from one tower…

To the next.

He was drawn to the other tower.

This one was not nearly as large as the tower in his realm, but there was still a sense of essence within it, and a sense of unity. Arowend could feel it, but there was also a part of that unity that didn't feel quite natural to him. And he realized why. This was not *his* unity. Though it was still unity, it was different. He was modified in some way. Maybe he could focus on it and understand it, but he wasn't sure what that was going to entail.

Still… It had worked.

Something seemed to be aware of him.

He began to feel power pushing on him, drawing on him as if trying to assault him. Arowend resisted the urge to come back together, as he didn't know what would happen if he were to do so. It might drag the others into a battle.

Instead, he focused on the pulsation of the tower, the same pulsation that he felt from the tower in his realm, and he let it propel him upward. He had flowed down into some deep space until he felt the blending and blurring of the power. He has then pushed upward once again. It left him feeling the connection to the unity.

And Arowend realized that he recognized some part of the different connection. It was strong enough that he could focus on it and pull that power, but he also didn't know if there was anything there that he might be able to use.

Rob could use the other unity. Could Arowend?

Now wasn't the time for that, though. As he allowed himself to be propelled, he still felt something working against them, some way that power to push, as if it were drawing back, trying to drag him down once again.

Was Alyssa aware of him?

"Alyssa," Arowend sent.

It was faint, a faded sort of connection, one that Arowend wasn't sure that he could command, especially as he was not in his full form. He was the essence and nothing more than essence at this point. Attempting to hold onto this power, and attempting to maintain his form, made it difficult for him to do much of anything.

Still, that drawing on him and resistance against him began to fade to the point where Arowend was released and propelled upward. The tower once again pushed him.

It was a different sensation.

There was part of Arowend that began to question whether he was going to flow right back to his own realm. Instead, he drifted. He followed a flow of essence, following a link of unity, until he felt something even more unfamiliar. He knew the other two types of unity, as he had dispersed into them enough that he was aware of them, but this one…

This one seemed to draw him differently.

He resisted the urge to fight.

That would be dangerous, he suspected. If he were to fight, and if he were to follow that trail in any sort of way, it was possible that he would draw the attention of the subheralds. He had to be careful of that, as Rob had warned him that they had some way of detecting and would attack. Arowend understood that, and he knew that he needed to fight and counter anything that they were capable of doing.

Instead, he let the power drag him.

The connection was a little more tenuous than when he went from his realm into Alyssa's. That was a strong pulling like it was going to pull him apart, ripping him free, but it required that he maintain some part of himself as well. In this case, there was nothing like that.

It was a gentle trail. He followed it, feeling the essence dragging him from one place to the next until he felt a pulsing of another unity.

This one was different, much like the last one had been, but this one didn't feel as if there were anything trying to drag or assault him in the same way.

Arowend allowed it to call him down, and he flowed. He was vaguely aware of another tower, though he wasn't sure what it looked like, only how it felt. Had he manifested more, he might've been more aware of it, but he had avoided doing that, wanting to be nothing more than the flow of essence.

Then he felt the unity around him. It blended and blurred inside of him, forcing Arowend to take a moment to try to hold onto that sense of self so that he did not lose aspects of himself. He managed to hold on and keep himself from dispersing even more, but even as he tried to do that, he could feel something attempting to work against him, something blurring against him, and he was worried.

But he waited.

The blurring and pain began to ease until Arowend felt himself once again.

He needed to know more. He learned he could travel from one tower to the next, but now the question was *where* he had traveled.

That would be significant for Rob, at least for them to be able to understand whether there was another tower or other places they could link to, but until he understood more about it, it might make no sense for him to call Rob.

Even if he could.

Could I?

Arowend didn't know if there was a connection there for him, but he started to focus on the power that he felt within himself and the unity that he had experienced, and he realized that there was some link to it that he could uncover. It flowed around him, and it seemed as if it drifted on that same connection that had brought him here in the first place. He might be able to use that for him to communicate.

He flowed outward. It was the only way that he was able to describe it. It seemed as if he stepped free of the unity, and then manifested.

Unsurprisingly, he was inside a tower.

At least, it *felt* something like the tower. He could feel the essence around him, though it was dark, with little more than a cavern swirling with power near him. He tried to test for any dangers but felt nothing.

He checked the walls, didn't see any writing, and didn't see any essence manifestations, nor any essence users, waiting to attack him. Thankfully.

He decided to drift upward.

He separated, the advantage he had of his own form allowing him to do that, and found his way free. He followed the contours of the tower itself until he erupted from what he believed to be the peak of it. Once he did, he hesitated before starting to come together. There was power here, and Arowend could feel that power, but he also wasn't sure about the source of it.

It was unity but vague and faint and little more than a trickle.

As he manifested, he braced for an attack.

One didn't come.

He looked around.

The land was vast but empty. It was bleak and broken, little more than dark rock, with no sense of life. It was almost as if everything had been drained from it. There was still a hint of unity, enough to link the towers together, but there was no other essence.

This was what it had been like when the other had attacked.

He drifted, heading back toward the tower. This had been a test. Nothing more. He had proven that it worked. And now it was time that he returned.

He flowed toward unity.

He could feel that flow of unity but couldn't follow it. He reached out for Rob, trying to open the connection, but there was nothing other than emptiness.

Arowend was trapped.

Chapter Eleven

ROB

Rob approached the cave entrance carefully, especially after what he'd just been through. He needed answers, but he wasn't sure whether the heralds — including the Eternal—would even provide him with anything. Before he risked anything going after Arowend, he needed to know.

It was time that he stopped taking things lightly.

He stopped inside the cave, focusing on the Eternal. He looked up at Rob with amusement gleaming in his eyes. He looked haggard and worn, but at the same time, he also seemed like he'd been waiting on this moment, like he knew Rob would come.

"You saw him, didn't you?"

Rob stopped across from the Eternal. He wanted to lunge through the protections he'd placed, grab the Eternal and make him talk, but that wasn't the right strategy. And without Arowend, Rob wasn't sure that they would have any way to rip through the Eternal and force him to talk, anyway.

"What is this thing?"

He needed to get answers while Arowend was away, but he feared he didn't have enough time.

"It's what you've long wanted," the Eternal said.

Rob shook his head.

"I don't want power."

The Eternal laughed.

"He is everything. He is the Dragon."

Rob stopped. "The final form?"

"He is."

"But he can be stopped."

"Can one so small as you stop the Dragon? Can a raindrop stop a storm? Can a snowflake stop a blizzard?" He laughed again. "You're but a part of a greater whole, and he will consume you. He will have everything that you've taken. He will be one again."

Rob raised his fist.

"I'm going to stop him."

"You may try, as so many others have tried, but you will fail. Your better option is to beg to serve."

"I'm not going to beg, and I'm not going to serve."

"Then you're going to lose, and everything that you are, and everything that you have with you, will be lost as well. It's a shame I won't be there to watch. Perhaps he will save, free me, and permit me to serve that way again."

"You would still beg for his forgiveness?"

"Not forgiveness. An opportunity to continue to serve.

Without that opportunity, there is nothing. *You* will be nothing."

Rob wanted to say something more, to force the eternal to talk to him, to tell him to provide answers, but at this point, Rob simply didn't know how to do that. Without Arowend, Rob couldn't.

He sent a burst of unity at the eternal, feeling a dark satisfaction at the slight grunt, and then spun, heading out of the cave. He had to go after his friend.

And that was how he saw him now, didn't he?

Somehow, he was going to have to get to him, and he was going to have to get answers. A burst of essence carried him back to the tower, where he hurriedly found his way back to the room where Arowend had disappeared.

Rob waited. Pacing.

It was strange for him to be waiting on somebody else, especially Arowend, but Arowend was the one who had brought him here in the first place. Arowend was the one who had helped him understand that there was something more to the kind of essence he was using and helped him understand how to bind those essences together and create what he called unity.

All around him, Rob could feel the sense of unity, and he could feel the way that it was pressing toward him as if it were trying to swirl around in a way that would begin to connect to him. He needed to understand that unity better.

He paced the room, waiting, but time passed, and Arowend didn't return. He felt a faint trailing of him as if some part of Arowend had been left behind so that Rob could track it, but beyond that, nothing.

He felt something else inside the tower.

Raolin was here, but he seemed to be busy, which Rob remained curious about as he wondered what the tower was doing with him.

He closed his eyes and focused on what he could feel of Arowend.

Rob strode through the hall. Maybe it would've been easier if he had manifested here so that he could be here, in essence, form like Arowend. But he was fully present in his physical form, which gave him a better understanding of the tower and the energy that was here.

There were no markings on the wall, no sculptures, no paintings, and no sign of artifacts. That didn't surprise him, as increasingly, Rob believed that this was purely a construct of the essence, and not truly an actual tower, even though it felt like a physical construct.

The essence flowed through the walls. As he made his way here, he tested for anything the unity could tell him. The unity, like essence in general, should connect him to something greater, something more that would help Rob understand the kind of power that existed in the world and the kind of power that Rob could link to. And if that kind of power existed, Rob didn't know what to make of it.

He found himself at the end of the hallway, with the unity pulsating around him. He found that intriguing, as it felt almost like the essence was alive, which he had felt before. And in this case, Rob wasn't sure why he felt the essence like that, only that it seemed to him that the essence was trying to guide him toward some aspect of that power.

Vaguely, he felt a shuddering of energy.

That was odd.

It wasn't from the tower.

Rob was only aware of that power inside the tower and could feel the unity flowing out into the land the way Serena had described it and back into the tower. He was also vaguely aware of Alyssa's tower, but only because he had linked to that power, and he felt as if there was some part of it that was bonded to him, even though Rob was not native to that unity.

He still wondered what would happen if he could link the different towers that he had uncovered. Rob didn't know if such a thing would be possible, and if so, what would happen to his own connection to unity. Perhaps nothing.

There was another shudder. As before, it felt as if the trembling of energy came from essence, but what kind of essence?

Unity?

Perhaps it was his unity, but why was the unity trying to call to him?

It felt like a warning.

He focused, using the tower itself, and wondered if he might be able to link that essence the same way that Serena had. He didn't have the same control over it or the same connection to it.

Another shuddering came.

Rob latched onto it.

Rob worried about any new power that appeared. He

didn't think that any of the heralds had managed to escape, and he didn't think that the dragon blood was reaching for him, but something surged around him.

Not this other entity, though. *The Dragon, as the Eternal called him.* Rob had felt that even if he didn't fully understand it.

What he felt now was Arowend. And there was a call in it. The unity he was speaking to Rob through was twisted. Different.

It wasn't the same unity they had here.

Which meant that he had succeeded.

Why would Arowend have been calling out to him if he had managed to reach another place? Unless Arowend was stuck.

That was a possibility if Arowend were to extend beyond the boundary of their realm and put himself in danger. He wouldn't be able to do anything. He would be trapped, and calling for help was his only option.

Rob needed to find him.

Better yet, he needed to *go* to him.

Could he help him?

He focused on that essence and began to use the unity within him, trying to draw upon what he felt all around him, but it felt like the tower wasn't permitting him to draw upon as much as he wanted. It wasn't that there was much resistance, though there was some. It was that the tower seemed to push *against* him.

Rob wasn't sure why or what the tower was attempting to do, only that it felt like it was squeezing.

"You won't be able to do it that way," a voice said from behind him.

Rob spun, ready to fight, but it was Raolin.

"What do you mean I won't be able to do it like that?" Rob asked.

Raolin looked around and up at the ceiling. His eyes seemed to go distant, and as far as Rob could tell, a different power emanated from him than what Rob was aware Raolin possessed. Had he manifested more energy? Or better yet, had he progressed? As far as Rob knew, with Raolin, there was always a hint of resistance to progression, though Rob didn't know if it was because of Raolin's fear or something else. Whatever it was, Raolin had been reluctant.

And Serena had not pushed.

This was her father, and she didn't want to push him into doing anything he didn't want to do, even if she was concerned for him and his safety.

Rob also knew there was more to it and that Serena was more concerned about her father and his connection to her mother and whatever her mother might be able to do to her father, given the strange and strained relationship between the two of them.

But maybe now, Raolin had finally seen it fit to progress.

"What I mean is that I don't think you'll be able to find what you're looking for. I can feel it, as well." He settled his gaze on Rob. "I'm not sure why I should feel it so strongly, but it's there. You can feel it, as well, I suspect."

Rob nodded. "It's the unity, but it's not the kind of unity I'm normally connected to. I can't tell what happened to Arowend."

Raolin's brow furrowed. For a moment, Rob worried that he might not offer to help, especially as this was Arowend, but then the essence that he used pulsed out from him, pulsing in time with the tower itself, almost as if he were connected to it the same way that Rob suspected Serena was connected. And if he had progressed and used the tower to do so, he likely connected in the same way.

"I can't tell if anything happened to him, but he is still there, isn't he?"

"He is."

"And you would go after him?"

Raolin studied Rob for a long moment.

"I'm trying to understand what we need to do for us to defeat this other entity," Rob admitted. "The Eternal called it the Dragon. And I don't really know what that's going to entail, but I do feel like there has to be something we might be able to learn. So far, I've not discovered what that might be. If you've learned anything here, I would appreciate you sharing."

Raolin pressed his lips together into a tight line.

"I've learned several things about the tower, but it does seem as if the tower itself is trying to limit what we learn about it. Serena might know more, as she has a better mind for this sort of thing than I do." He started to smile. "As she should, though. I did spend quite a bit of time trying to convince her of the need to master everything that we've been talking about over the years. Thankfully, it seems as if those lessons did not go to waste."

"Raolin?"

He shook his head, and then he focused on Rob for a moment. There was another pulse of essence that seemed to be coming from all around him. The tower reacted as if pulsing in time with whatever Raolin was doing.

"Yes. As I was saying, there is a place I think you need to go, which will help you understand more. But there's also the place I think you can be so that you can follow him. You intend to manifest, I imagine?"

"If it works," Rob said. "But there is danger in it."

"There is always a danger with essence," Raolin warned. "That's something I've tried to instill upon Serena from a young age, but it's one that I think that her mother tried to change, as she wanted Serena to chase essence, to chase the danger, and to feel like she didn't need to fear it. Perhaps she didn't. Given that she is the dragon queen's daughter, her understanding of the essence and everything she was connected to is certainly greater than anything I was able to offer her. But you don't need to hear those stories."

A part of Rob wondered if he *needed to hear those stories to help him understand Serena and her relationship* with her father and mother. He knew Serena struggled with her mother and that she had had a hard time with her father's return, and there was more to what happened to him in the interim than Rob even knew, more than Raolin wanted to share.

Had Serena learned what she needed?

"Come along," Raolin finally said.

He walked down the hallway, with Rob following

behind. They reached a large stone door with a series of symbols etched on it.

There was another pulse of the essence, and Raolin tapped on several of those different symbols before the door rolled open. It revealed a circular room inside, which towered high overhead, but even that wasn't what caught Rob's attention. It was the markings on the walls, markings that seemed to be filled with knowledge and power. They drew upon the essence around him differently than he'd felt before. These markings were there to help direct things.

Rob felt the essence and the way they were linking in some manner, even if he didn't know what it was, nor did he know how it was connected or what it was connecting to. Those markings seemed significant, but Rob couldn't tell why.

"What is this place?"

"You'll be safe here," Raolin said, standing in the doorway.

"Safe?"

"When you manifest," Raolin explained. "The tower will protect you."

Rob frowned, watching as Raolin stepped back and did something with a pulse of essence that triggered the door to roll back into place, sealing Rob inside.

"Where did you go?" Rob asked, connecting to Raolin through the dragon mind connection.

Raolin was distant. He was still there, but as Rob attempted to connect to him, he could feel something interrupting it. The tower was intervening on Rob's behalf so that Rob couldn't get to Raolin the way he wanted. There was some part of the tower that was stepping in between them, limiting him, but it also seemed to guide him.

As he focused, he realized that while he couldn't feel Raolin, he could feel Arowend.

And it was distant.

A cry for help.

He tried to make sense of it.

Rob learned how to manifest as well as any and had begun to use it in ways that allowed him even to have a certain physical presence when he did, but what he needed was beyond what he had done before.

He pushed, using unity. The tower's power began to constrict, but rather than trying to fight him as before, it seemed like it were drawing him.

Rob felt propelled in a way that he hadn't before.

At first, he fought it and attempted to reach back for his body, his physical form. But then he stopped. He could feel the presence, the pressure, and the power, as it was trying to drag him along.

When he was tossed free of the tower, he felt propelled. He felt the unity above him. Rob began to feel another stirring of unity. One aspect was familiar to him from Alyssa's tower, but there was also another mixture of unity, another strange and foreign kind of essence. And have they been combined in some way? He didn't know as he let it drag him forward.

And he flowed.

There was no other way to describe what it was other than he was pulled. He whipped faster than ever moved, faster than he could when he was using his own unity essence, feeling as if the essence itself were dragging him — and attempting to pull him apart.

It was something that Arowend had mentioned to him, a warning that he'd given Rob about how he'd been pulled apart back when he was destroyed, and that turned him into the Netheral.

Rob wasn't sure if that was the only reason or if it was more about the rage and anger that Arowend had felt in having been betrayed by people he thought cared about him. But now, Rob could feel something pulling on him, and he felt a power greater than him. It took focus, concentration, and a will to stay within it, to hold together, and try to master what was happening to him as it dragged him.

And it *did* drag him.

That essence continued to propel him until he felt another essence begin to tug at him and his awareness. Rob struggled to hold onto himself.

Rob feared what would happen to Arowend if he lost that bit of himself. Would he lose the fight before it had even begun?

Chapter Twelve

SERENA

SERENA STOOD OUTSIDE THE EARTH'S REALM, FEELING THE essence inside it. She didn't come here very often because she didn't know Gregor the way that Rob did, though she did know him to a certain extent. Then again, Serena didn't know any of the other dragon blood like Rob did.

That was something she needed to correct. If she had time, and perhaps if she had more motivation, she would do that, but at this point, the only thing that Serena knew she needed to do, was to continue to connect to the unity.

Out here, close to the northern ice realm, she could feel the pulsations of unity and the way that the nexus propelled power outward, mixing from the ice into the earth and blending powers in ways it hadn't done before.

Serena wondered what Rob felt when he came here and wondered how he saw it and whether it bothered him that so much of his land changed and blurred into the boundary of the earth realm.

What am I thinking?

This was Rob, after all. He wanted this.

In fact, as far as Serena knew, Rob was probably the one who demanded that this happen. He may have pushed the unity here himself, as she had felt the way that the unity flowed and continued to progress, moving from one place to another, with increasing pressure and pulsations of energy that left her feeling as if there was a lack of control.

She stepped forward and saw an arctic cat waiting.

She paused.

"Eleanor?"

The former Nelah stepped forward, practically gliding on the ice. The power that she felt around her continued to shift and change, blurring as more and more people she encountered and worked with became connected to the unity. With someone like Eleanor, who progressed enough with her connection to essence, she wasn't surprised that the effect of the unity was changing her.

"It's surprising to feel your presence here," Eleanor said, stopping before her.

"I'm looking for answers," Serena said.

The arctic cat's tail swished.

"Answers? Without Rob?"

"Rob is looking for a different set of answers," Serena admitted.

"And what are yours?"

"The purpose of the unity."

There was no point in lying to Eleanor, as Serena felt like she might be able to provide her with some insight. Much like Maggie, Eleanor had served as a dragon soul for an impossibly long time. Long enough that Serena wondered if her experience could give insight that would help them. She never had the opportunity to visit the former Nelah before, so she wasn't sure if working together was possible. There had to be something, though.

Rob certainly trusted Eleanor and believed there was more to her, especially since she came back through the nexus.

"Things have been changing, and I'm trying to make sense of it, to understand my purpose and whether there is anything more I can do or be. I suppose that's no different than anyone else."

Eleanor tipped her head, nodding.

"No different, and no differently expected. You're searching for purpose. All should seek to do the same."

"All?" There was something more to it, something that Eleanor wasn't saying, but it left Serena wondering, and she couldn't help but worry that she was missing something.

Had Rob come to her?

She didn't think so. For the last few weeks, Rob had been so focused on the heralds, and trying to understand the Dragon, that he spent time either there or testing the perimeter of the border, searching for any flaws that might exist, as if he alone was responsible for sealing them off. He didn't uncover anything, but at this point, she wasn't even sure if she knew because Rob didn't reveal such things to her. He had the conduit, and she could feel what he was doing and the things he felt, but there were other aspects he shielded from her.

"The one known as Arowend came to see me."

That shouldn't surprise Serena, but for some reason, it did.

Then again, her experience with Arowend was one of conflicted feelings. From everything she knew about him, he was far different from the Netheral. Arowend tried to make amends, though Serena wasn't even sure how sincere they were. It was something she didn't want to share with Tessatha, fearing that if she were to reveal too much, her friendship with Tessatha would suffer.

But she suspected she knew, nonetheless.

It came from the innate connection that they had. The two of them worked together long enough that Serena couldn't help but feel as if the other woman recognized what Serena was doing, how she was struggling with what Arowend had done, and her fear that he may eventually return to the Netheral.

Not only that, but the Netheral might be some true aspect of *who* he was.

"You question him," Eleanor said, striding over to what had once been the boundary of the northern ice realm. It was no longer, as there was so much blurring now, but Serena was aware of an essence memory that existed here, a link of what Rob had placed. She could feel it, but she wasn't sure why she would be so attuned, only that the sense of it was here.

"I've questioned him," Serena said. "And the hard part is that I'm unsure what to make of what he's done or who he is. My father thinks I need to find forgiveness. I've been trying, but it's hard."

Eleanor snickered, but it was an odd sound for an

Arctic cat to make. However, she was an essence memory, a manifestation of power, and...

And she was no different than Arowend.

"He came out here because he wanted to understand you, didn't he?"

"I think he's searching for his own purpose as I have been, to be honest. Ever since Rob brought me back, I've been trying to understand what purpose I might have. When I was the Nelah, it was easy. I knew that I was to serve my people, and in doing so, I could help them find a path they wouldn't be able to find on their own. I always hoped for enlightenment."

"You didn't want to help them progress," Serena said.

"No," Eleanor replied. "Not the way that Rob does. I didn't hold them back, either, but we were limited on what we could access and the kind of power that existed in my realm, so I felt as if we needed to use that energy judiciously, granting only those who had the necessary potential and resources to reach it. I realize now that was a mistake."

"My mother never wanted others to progress," Serena said. "Well, maybe that's not quite true. My mother wanted people to progress, but she wanted them to fight for essence, and supremacy, to prove that they were strong enough and worthy of it."

"So much has changed. I can feel it."

"Can you feel the unity shifting?"

Eleanor growled softly. "I can feel something," she said slowly, "and I understand that you blame Rob for this?"

"What?" Serena looked over at her. "I don't blame him. I'm just…."

"You're looking for answers and trying to make sense of what has happened and how this power is changing. But you have doubts. I can see it in you."

"How do you see it?" Serena asked, thinking she'd close herself off to the dragon mind connection she might have with Eleanor, but perhaps she hadn't. Maybe there was something that Eleanor was capable of doing, some way that she could link to power, that Serena couldn't counter.

She was an essence construct, essentially, and that gave her a way of reaching the world, and reaching essence, that Serena simply did not possess. If she was able to draw upon that and draw through Serena, then she had to be especially careful.

"I do not see your mind," Eleanor said softly, though there was a hint of amusement in her tone as she did. "But I can see your intention. I can see your heart. I can see the way that essence flows around you."

She swirled.

It was strange to see, as any time that Serena had seen Eleanor, she'd always maintained a steadfast connection to her essence form. There was something quite distinct about it. Power, the kind of power that continued to concentrate into the form of the Arctic cat. The form of the Nelah.

Now there was something else about it. There was a different part of it, and it began to blur ever so slightly, as if Eleanor were losing her form, or perhaps she was willing herself to lose a measure of her form. But why?

"You see it all?"

"That is my gift and my curse," Eleanor said. "Ever since I returned, I have been able to see the essence in a specific way, but it's different."

"Rob has always been able to see the essence, as well," Serena said.

Eleanor nodded, her essence swirling again, almost as if she were taking on a human form, but then she coalesced into the arctic cat again, and there came a steady kind of growling from her. "Interesting, I think. Somebody like that, somebody who has that kind of power, for him to be able to see essence suggests that he has a different connection to it."

"I think it stems from how he was injured when he was first progressing," Serena said. She remembered that time all too well, remembered how they had nearly lost Rob. She was intrigued by him at the time but had not really felt the same connection that she had now. Now she would be devastated if she had to bring him back from that same kind of attack.

But there had been no further attacks, nothing like that, nothing that could harm him. At least not in this realm.

There was danger in other places, a danger that Serena knew that only Rob could counter if he continued to chase the knowledge and the power that she'd seen him attempting to do. Rob was the only one who might be able to survive. But he was working to ensure that others had that same possibility, working to help them find the essence.

"I can see you. I can see your heart, and I can see what troubles you. It's all this change."

Serena shrugged.

"It's actually not the change," Serena said, and she tried to make sense of what it was, as she wasn't even sure how to explain it to herself, let alone to Eleanor, but perhaps what she needed to do was just that. If she could find a way to explain it and find a way to help her see what she was dealing with and the kind of power that was flowing through the world, a power that continued to shift and change and left Serena thinking that there had to be something more taking place here, maybe Eleanor would understand. "It's the way that it's changing. We're starting to add aspects of unity to our essence that is from outside of our realm. What happens when our essence becomes unusable to us?"

"You fear that we are getting… infected?"

The question was an odd one, and the way that Eleanor pitched it left Serena feeling like she was a bit ridiculous in it, but at the same time, wasn't that what she was actually worried about? She feared they might be losing their power and connection to the point where they wouldn't be able to do the things they needed to do.

It was subtle, at least right now. So far, there had been only a few small changes, a bit of unity blending and blurring, as Rob had linked them to Alyssa's essence. If he were to continue to link other realms — something that Serena wasn't even sure was possible — what would happen to the essence?

"Is it an infection, or is it blending that essence, which becomes unstable for us?"

"You fear losing what you've gained," Eleanor said. "That's something I understand. It's something that I felt for so long, to the point where I fought against it. But once I realized that I wasn't going to succeed, I found a way to pass on what I could, allowing others to gain. And if I hadn't, think of what would've changed."

Serena knew that it would've been more than they could ever imagine. They would've lost Rob. And that would've been more devastating than she could even fathom. Rob had been pivotal for everything, not only for the realm but for her.

"I fear not understanding," she said softly.

"A worthy reason to fear." Eleanor solidified her form, and for a moment, there was a pulse of essence that radiated outward, and it connected to the unity in a way that Serena could feel. Essence seemed to emanate from deep inside of her. "We all need to fear not understanding, and we all need to chase what we fear."

There was something more to that than what Serena had asked, but she heard the message, nonetheless.

"I'm going the wrong way, aren't I?"

"Only you can say," Eleanor said.

The arctic cat then slipped away, drifting off into the cold, and if Serena weren't mistaken, she simply vanished, dispersing on the wind. Had she ever really been there? It was possible that she was nothing more than essence manifestation, or she might have floated in, using her own unique ability to appear, giving Serena the opportunity to have the conversation with her as if Eleanor needed to provide some measure of advice.

And perhaps she had.

It was no different than the advice that Maggie had given, though the way Eleanor presented it was. Eleanor was wise and experienced, and she had seen parts of the world and experienced things that Serena couldn't even fathom, in ways that Serena wasn't even sure that she could ever understand unless she were to move on from this world and then be brought back as an essence memory.

Her initial plan was to talk to other dragon blood, Gregor, storm cloud, and maybe even to Oro, but now, she knew she couldn't because what she needed to do, was what Eleanor implied, which went back to where she came from.

Serena flew up with a blast of unity essence and landed in her own realm atop the palace. The palace was familiar to her, seemingly carved out of obsidian, and created along a ridge line that overlooked the city. It was filled with essence, and there were times when Serena could feel that essence pressing up against her.

Such as now.

She paused momentarily, feeling the surge of fire essence all around. It was familiar and comforting, tainted ever so slightly by the new pressure of unity essence all around her. She could feel it flowing and began to wonder if there was going to be something in this essence that would be a problem for them, but even as she focused on it, she couldn't tell what that was, nor could she tell whether there was anything for her to be concerned about. That unity continued to flow through here, and as far as she could tell, the people who needed fire could still reach for fire. There was nothing that limited them.

She smiled and strode down through the palace until she reached her mother's quarters. She paused at the line of soldiers that were in the hall, all of them changing, as well. The soldiers were made from the essence of the palace, and each one was identical. It was as if the palace had duplicated a singular soldier, leaving her wondering which soldier was the baseline and why that one was chosen. They all took on aspects of the unity essence as they blurred, blended, and gained additional power. For a moment, Serena focused on that essence and could feel how the soldiers were linked to the palace and the way that the palace was linked to the tower. And Serena was linked to both.

The palace first, but now it seemed as if her connection to the tower was more profound. Rob was still there. She could feel him, and could feel him pacing, and could feel…

She could feel where he was.

Was the tower trying to give her some reassurance about him?

Maybe it wanted her to know that he was safe. Maybe the tower was somehow sentient in the same way that the palace had been sentient. The tower obviously wanted to communicate with her, even if it didn't understand what purpose it had. Rob was safe.

As was her father, though they were both in the tower, they were not together.

Serena breathed out.

What she needed to do once she finished this was to

go back to Tessatha and try to figure out what they would do next, if anything. Serena didn't know how to react, nor did she know what she was going to need to do with all of this, but she wanted to do it with her friend. And she wanted to do it with Rob.

She reached the door outside of her mother's quarters, and she hesitated for a moment. There was a sense of essence inside. It was weaker than she had believed. Her mother might have been dragon blood, but she had not progressed the way others had, so she was stunted.

When she pushed open the door, a burst of fire essence came out, but Serena grabbed it with her own essence, absorbed it, and then redirected it, pushing it out into the tower.

"That's enough," Serena said.

Her mother staggered back. She was dressed in a maroon gown, heavily embroidered with long sleeves and a neckline that showed a series of dragons, depicting them dancing along the embroidery. She looked up, rage fluttering in her dark eyes, a hint of flame burning there momentarily before it tamped down. Serena didn't have to do anything.

But I can.

It was a strange thought for her, knowing that she could easily push down on her mother's essence and counter anything she did to her.

"Did you come to taunt me again, Daughter?"

"Have I taunted you at any point?" Serena asked.

"Your man did."

Serena had a hard time thinking that Rob would've

taunted anybody, especially her mother. Knowing Rob, he may have questioned her and…

And he most likely had. Maybe not in his physical form, but as a manifestation. Maybe even directly into the dragon queen's mind. Rob would've wanted answers. He would've liked to know who Serena's mother had been working with, though Serena suspected that it was the Herald — and the Eternal — to try to give them an idea about what more they had offered her.

"Rob was here?"

"Not recently," she said, standing in front of the hearth, a flame crackling suddenly inside it. Heat radiated outward, and her mother drew upon that heat as if trying to control and manipulate it, giving Serena more reason to smile. "What reason are you here, Daughter?"

"Are you well?"

Her mother flicked her gaze over to her. "You do not care if I'm well."

"I care, and if I didn't, you'd already be dead."

The words were harder than Serena intended, but they were no less true for that. It would've been a simple thing if she had wanted to harm her mother. She could drain the essence off — or have Arowend do it, as now they understood that he had that ability — she could simply have destroyed her mother and made sure that her essence had been dispersed so that she was not able to come back as an essence memory.

"You think that you could kill me?"

Serena drifted toward her. She focused on the unity essence and felt it was burning within her. "You know that I could," Serena said. "And you know you've been stunted because of what you've done and who you've become. But it doesn't have to be that way."

Her mother stared at her, hands clasped in front, watching Serena as if trying to gauge whether she could gain some advantage. Under other circumstances, when Serena had first come to her mother, that might've been possible. She had been afraid of her, and for a good reason, she thought. Her mother was a very skilled essence wielder, to the point where she was one of the most powerful, even as a dragon soul.

"Why are you here?" Some of the rage had seeped from her tone, and now she looked at Serena with a different expression. It wasn't fear. It was resignation.

Serena hated seeing her mother without expression and hated that she had to be the one to push through it, knowing that there was nothing different that she would do, especially given that her mother had already proven all that she was willing to do and everything that she was willing to harm, for her to do what she thought that she needed. Her mother wanted to keep the status quo, something Serena had rapidly begun to realize was impossible or unnecessary. Her mother had a hard time with change, though.

"I'm here because I want to talk."

"Just talk?"

"I think that's enough, don't you? We have not had an opportunity to talk, and I thought we might learn something about each other."

"Why do you want that, Daughter?"

Serena took a deep breath. She had been trying to find a way to understand what she needed to do, but perhaps the first thing was to find forgiveness. That was something that Rob would appreciate, she suspected. And even if he didn't, it was something that Serena *needed*.

"I want it because you are my mother. I want to because it is necessary. I want to because I don't know what's coming and want to leave this world without having answers. Do you?"

The words hung in the air for a long moment, and in that time, she wondered what her mother might say and how she might react.

She finally let out a heavy, irritable sigh before turning to Serena. "What do you want to ask me?"

Chapter Thirteen

ROB

It was hard for Rob to hold onto this form and maintain a shape that he was familiar with, as every passing moment left him feeling as if he were stretched, strained, and twisted. What must it have been like for Arowend? Maybe it was easier, as Arowend didn't have the same limit as Rob did as manifestation.

Manifestations were odd, drawing upon the essence around him for him to hold them together. It was part of the reason that he could manifest more easily in places where his essence existed. Although he was able to manifest beyond, it did take more out of him and required constant maintenance from his physical side to the point where Rob could feel that essence draining, straining, and making it harder for him to hold onto.

In this case, though, Rob tried to draw upon the essence around him, but it was even harder than it should be. A bit of foreign essence began to mingle into his manifestation. He was aware of his own essence, that unity that came from his realm, and he was aware of the unity that came from Alyssa's realm, but beyond that, there was something more. How was he going to hold onto himself long enough to be able to pull himself together once he reached Arowend?

Arowend.

That was the thought that came through to him. It was wispy and thin, and it felt as if he were losing some aspect of his own thoughts as he floated, pulled upon the essence, and pulled apart. He pulled himself toward what he detected, using what he could feel of Arowend and letting it drag him.

Something painful pulled on him. It reminded him of the subherald and the way that they lashed at essence. Maybe there were subheralds trying to disrupt this unity flow, to sever it from him, but if that were the case, was there anything that Rob would ever be able to do?

Not in this form. Not until he was linked to other essences.

Could I do that?

It might be possible if he were physically present, but he didn't know if he could hold this form long enough to find the answers. Power was draining and pulling on him as if it were trying to separate him.

The longer that pulled upon him, the less intensity it used. That seemed to be significant, though Rob wasn't sure what it meant.

"Arowend," Rob tried to send, though he wasn't sure that the dragon mind connection was even there, nor did he know if it linked to him the way it once had. He needed to find a way to hold onto that connection and tap into what he could find of Arowend, but could he?

If it worked, he could use him as some sort of a beacon to follow.

"Arowend," he repeated, pushing out with essence and sending it outward with as much force as he could. Foreign essence mingled within him, mingling within his manifestation, to the point where he began to feel it was pulling upon him and dragging him.

Rob allowed it to pull him.

He couldn't fight it, even if he wanted to. He didn't know if he had enough strength to do so. He didn't know if there was going to be any way that he could overpower what was happening. Even if he could, he didn't know that he wanted to. He needed to know where this was going to guide him.

Could he disperse his manifestation?

Sending a manifestation of essence required a part of himself and a part of the essence that existed within him naturally. If Rob were to try to disperse, would he lose that? He had sent his awareness through this manifestation, followed it, flowed along it, and used that to find answers, but he didn't know what those answers were even going to be. The longer he focused and the more he had that manifestation, the more Rob could tell that there was something else out there for him, but he couldn't tell whether he could do something more or different, only that there was power.

Then he began to feel something more—a familiarity.

It took Rob a moment to realize what it was. Once he did, he latched onto it with every bit of essence he could.

It was Arowend.

Arowend was trying to reach for him, grab onto and connect to him. Rob used all the power he could and every bit of essence he had to spare to strain for Arowend.

There was something there, but what he could feel was vague.

"Rob," the voice said, connecting to him and pulling on him.

Then he was pulled even faster.

And he was pulled *down.*

Rob had been drifting high in the sky for long enough that the sudden shift to pulling downward left him with an uneasy sensation. What if Arowend was pulling him into a trap?

Hadn't Arowend already gotten trapped, so if Rob were to go with him and to flow down into that essence channel, there was the possibility that Arowend might pull Rob into the same trap and that they would be trapped together. It was too dangerous. Rob knew better than to allow himself to get pulled into it, to be sucked up by it, but at the same time, he also felt like this was where he needed to be and what he needed to be doing.

And then he felt a warmth flow around him. It was a swirling of energy, and it seemed to gather parts of him together that had been faded and distant.

But then he was pulled back in.

Arowend suddenly manifested in front of him, and Rob tried to pull upon his essence and found it much easier to do now that Arowend was here, and it seemed as if Arowend had summoned the essence that Rob nearly lost back to him.

Arowend breathed out with a heavy sigh and looked around, focusing his gaze on Rob. "You came."

"I heard your call. I wasn't sure what it was, but the tower seemed to guide me, and... Well, I wasn't even sure this was going to work. Thank you, I suppose I should say, as I don't know what would've happened had I not had you pull back together. I don't know what happens to a manifestation that gets lost in that way."

"I don't either," Arowend said.

It surprised Rob. With everything he had experienced, all the research he had done before, and the fact that he was the essence in general, Rob thought that would've helped Arowend understand what happened.

"Where are we?" Rob asked.

He could feel something around them, but his vision in this realm was hazy.

"We're in another place, another realm, and this other entity has targeted it," Arowend said." Can you feel it?"

"I can feel... Well, I'm not sure what I can feel. There seems to be some memory here," Rob said, focusing on what he could feel around him. He tried to make sense of it, thinking that maybe there was something here that he could understand, but even as he focused, he couldn't tell what it was, only that it did seem that there was some other aspect of power here that was trying to push on him, trying to connect to him, and trying to make it so that he could not reach it the way that he wanted to and the way that he should. Essence was here. Given that Rob had been drawn down by unity through Arowend, he believed that unity essence was here, but it was a different kind of unity than what he'd experienced before. This was something less profound. "I can't tell."

"Perhaps you haven't manifested strongly enough," Arowend suggested. "That can happen, especially since we're so far from our realm. I might be able to help."

Rob wasn't aware of what Arowend was doing, only that he felt a sense of familiar unity. For a moment, Rob thought that Arowend was trying to mingle his own essence with Rob, but that didn't seem to be the case. Arowend called some essence down from high overhead and drew it into Rob. When he did, gradually, Rob began to feel more like himself. He began to feel more essence, and he began to feel the unity flowing into him. His vision cleared, and he saw the landscape nearby. It was all bleak, black, and broken. And as Arowend had said, there was a bit of essence memory here, but it was stunted and twisted.

It was shattered.

Shattered memories?

That seemed impossible, but then again, given what Alyssa had claimed about how the Dragon had targeted the essence and how they had used it against her people and her realm, he couldn't help but believe that such a thing was possible. If so, what did it mean?

"Where did they take it?" Rob asked.

"I don't know," Arowend said. "I can't feel anything. I can just feel this unity. It's different, but it's also similar." There was confusion in Arowend's words, and Rob understood it. Arowend didn't have the same connection to unity as Rob did, at least not to Alyssa's realm and the bridged way. Could Rob use his connection and try to find some way to link to this unity?

"Did this one call you here, or did you follow it?"

"I think I followed the flow of unity," Arowend said." It was hard to hold onto myself."

"It was hard for me, too. You did a better job than I did."

Arowend laughed and took a few steps away from Rob, out over the rock. Rob followed, and when he did, he could feel something beneath his feet, some part of the essence that was there, as if it were more than just a memory. He could feel the unity, but it was buried — and it was deep.

"Well, I do have a bit more experience with it than you do," Arowend said. "I'm impressed. I wasn't sure how well you were going to be able to do with that or whether you were even going to come after me."

"I wouldn't leave you," Rob said.

"I would've understood if you did."

Rob shook his head.

"You only came here because you thought that you needed to, and we needed the answers you might find here. I wasn't going to leave you."

"Thank you," Arowend said. He took a deep breath. "I might be able to keep helping you and drawing more essence down, but it is difficult. To be honest, I don't know what's going to happen if I do. I worry that we're drawing attention to ourselves."

"Have you been attacked?"

Arowend shrugged.

"Not exactly," he said. "But I have felt a presence here. At least, a presence that's somewhere nearby. It might actually be here." He frowned, and for a moment, he lost his form before it came back together. Rob was tempted to follow Arowend, wondering if he could lose his form that way and put it back together, but he was not an essence memory in the same way that Arowend was. He was only a manifestation. If he let himself flow out like that, he was more likely to lose it altogether and have himself drifting off into nothingness. "I can feel it. It seems to be trying to make sure that I'm aware that it's there and wanting me to target it, but I've been careful to stay here."

"But you can't leave," Rob asked.

"No. I can call essence down, and I can feel that power flowing into me and now into you," he said, arching a brow at Rob, "but I'm not able to travel out again. When I visited Alyssa's realm, I was able to go down into the tower and use the pulsation to propel myself back up."

"The pulsation," Rob repeated, mostly to himself, because he understood what he meant. It was the same pulsation that Rob had felt, and he understood power, even if he wasn't sure what it was doing, only that it did seem to be pulsating, sending, and emanating a surge of power that radiated out beyond. If there was something that he could do to follow that, shouldn't he? Maybe he could find the pulsation here, and he could follow it. Maybe both of them could, for that matter.

He wasn't sure if that was going to be possible. He

strained, struggling with it, hoping that there would be some way for him to find it, and attempting to test for that pulsation, that same kind of power that he thought might be necessary for them to use to escape, but any time the attempted to do that, he felt that he was drawn downward rather than upward.

"What do you feel when you try to draw on that," Rob asked.

"I don't feel anything," Arowend said." At least, nothing is similar to what we have in our realm or Alyssa's realm. You would probably better understand what is there, not only in her realm but in ours. But I've been feeling the unity pulsing out. It started once you link to the nexus, pressing outward, changing things, so…" He shrugged. "So, I don't feel that now. It's easy to pull power down, though."

"Well, we know that this other entity is trying to siphon power in some way, right?" At least, that had been their experience and what they both believed, to the point where Rob thought they might be able to use that, but how could they use it? And better yet, what would it permit them to do? "What if this was all some massive technique that they've used for them to continue to pull upon power?"

"Well, if it is, it's working," Arowend said.

"You think we could counter it?"

"We?" Arowend asked.

"Well, maybe if we link to the other realms, we can draw it the other way."

"I'm not so sure that it's going to work that way," Arowend said. "Given everything that I can feel, everything I'm sure you can feel, you have to know the power."

"We can feel it pulsating outward," Rob said.

"Well, it's pulsating outward now, but what happens if this other entity can reverse that? What if it can pull it down, draining it inward?"

"And claims it like it has claimed the essence in other places," Rob whispered.

Arowend nodded.

Rob didn't have an answer. And that bothered him. He wished that he did, wishing that there was something that he might be able to say, something to do, something that might make sense to him, but maybe there wasn't going to be anything.

Instead, he focused on the unity that he felt here. He had traveled through that unity, and he had felt the way that it was different, foreign to him, and he had felt the way that it was separating him, pulling upon him, but there had to be something that Rob might be able to use with it. Could he draw on something, some form of it, to make sense of that essence? And better yet, could he link to Alyssa, to his realm, and pull some of this power back out?

If he did, what would it do?

There were dangers in it, Rob knew. Any time he had linked around his overall realm, adding fire, earth, storm cloud, or even life to his own, he had felt that there was a blending of power, changing what he was already able to access. Over time, that blending had become something stronger. It had truly become the unity.

And now Rob felt unity elsewhere. An essence that

had blended and blurred together seemed as if it belonged to something greater. If he were to continue to call upon that essence, would he be able to help it, or would he only end up harming, perhaps, his own realm by linking and blending it?

"Do you think we will do more damage if I use this?" he asked Arowend.

Arowend watched him for a long moment, and there seemed to be a deep, serious consideration from him. Rob wondered why, but when he started speaking, he immediately understood.

"Others thought the same when I wanted to link the essence in our realm," Arowend began. "I felt it was necessary, even though I didn't have any proof. I still feel like it was necessary, even with what happened to me. But I wasn't sure. And there's a real possibility that what you choose to do here may cause danger. We've already seen a change of the essence in our realm. I could feel it. It was blending, but it was subtle and slow, and perhaps it will take time for that blending and blurring to become something more significant. But it is definitely there. It links our land to the other, and if you do this, I suspect you will link our land and the other to this one."

The implication was clear. Was that what Rob wanted to do? More than that, was it what Rob should—or could—do?

"I feel like the connection is the key," Rob said. "With everything that we've done, everything we've seen, the connection seems to be crucial. And if I don't do this, I fear we will lose power."

Progression.

That's what it was about.

Do this in the right way, and they run the chance of progressing in a way they hadn't yet identified. But if they did it wrong, or if Rob was wrong about it, then it was very likely that he could corrupt his land. Maybe that was exactly what the Dragon wanted. Perhaps it wanted Rob to find the unity and try to link it, connecting so that it could join that power and perhaps even steal it.

But if that were the case, why had the heralds come?

Rob focused on this essence, making a choice.

He knew what he needed to do. It was all about making connections. It was all about gaining power. It was all about progression.

That was the only way they would survive.

Chapter Fourteen

ROB

Rob focused on the essence all around him. Though he was here only as a manifestation, he tried to use what he felt to reach for something more. And every time he attempted to do so, he found it more difficult than it should be. He was not connected to this essence in the way he needed to be to find the kind of power he wanted. There was energy here, which he felt vaguely, but it wasn't the kind of energy he would've detected somewhere that essence was more prominent. Every time he thought that he had an opportunity to try to detect something else, he felt Arowend beginning to swirl around him, adding a bit more of himself to the essence that Rob was drawing upon and trying to hold Rob in place.

"We have to find a way to move," Rob suggested.

"I've told you I'm unable to find anything, and it doesn't seem as if the essence is letting me move. I can travel downward, but I'm not able to follow the flow upward. I can pull essence from above, though," he went on, "but I'm not able to use it in any other way, nor am I able to draw it the way that I think it needs to be done for us to find the kind of power that exists."

Rob could feel the pulling of that essence, and as he did, he wondered if maybe there would be some way for him to draw upon something more. Even as he attempted to feel it and focused on that strange unity essence, he began to recognize that he felt something more.

At first, he wasn't sure about what he was detected, but the longer he felt the Dragon, the more he became aware that what he was detecting was another source of unity essence, something coming toward them, though it did not do so rapidly. It was slowly beginning to sweep in their direction, making Rob think he had time — but he didn't have that much time. There was a real danger here for them because he didn't know what would happen if they were to be stuck.

And unfortunately, it *did* seem as if they were stuck.

He tried to follow the flow of essence upward. Normally, such a thing should be easier. He could allow himself to simply follow what he detected, to let the essence guide him, but for whatever reason, there was a directionality to the essence as if he were stepping in the current of a river that kept him down, attempting to sweep toward him and hold him in place. As much as Rob wanted to try to fight through that, he didn't think he could.

"You can't do it, can you?" Arowend asked.

Rob shook his head.

"I can feel something," he started and looked up,

trying to make sense of the flow of essence. He could feel it, but that was all he could do. "I can't see the essence like I once did."

"It's because the essence here is different, and your connection to it is different, so it doesn't work for you how you expect it to. If you were to use more of a physical presence, you might have a better chance of doing this, but for whatever reason, it won't work for you. And it doesn't work for me. The only way that we might be able to do it would be to —"

"To link to this land," Rob finished.

Arowend watched him with a frown.

"I know there's a danger to it," Rob said.

"How much will it change?"

"I don't know. When we linked to Alyssa's land, I knew something had also changed in our realm. Serena has been following that change, trying to make sense of the difference, and I think it bothers her that so much has changed, but I don't know that I have an answer."

"My only concern is that others in our realm might suffer," Arowend said.

"I'm trying to do it in a way that no one else suffers by linking to this essence, and all I'm trying to do is to give everybody an opportunity to draw upon it in the way that they need to so that we can call on the power in a real and meaningful way. I feel like everything that we've encountered so far suggests that the connections are going to be key. I feel like if we can understand those connections, we can forge new ones, and we may be able to stop this."

"What if the connections are not going to be enough?" Arowend asked.

"This is the same thing you wanted," Rob reminded him.

"I know," Arowend said, his voice trailing off and becoming a bit distant. "And I don't have clear memories about that, but I feel like I need to, and I feel like there's something there that I was supposed to remember, only...." He frowned, taking on a bit more of a solid form before he lost it, swirling away as if he were trying to separate once again.

"There are times when I can't remember everything that I need to, times I remember what it was like when we were attempting to make sense of the power in our realm before everything was lost. I just remember the others, what they wanted, and how they sought to keep us from reaching for more. I feel like all of that is important to know, important for us to remember, as I feel like there are lessons that we can learn from the past for us to understand the future better." He watched Rob. "But the problem I have is that I don't know what those lessons are or what role I'm supposed to have in them. I just know that I can feel this power, I can feel what you intend, and I can feel... Well, I can feel the same thing I think I felt before."

Arowend turned his attention off in the direction that Rob was detecting that strangeness, the energy that suggested to him that they were going to be targeted. Rob knew that they probably didn't have long before that power reached them. At what point did they need to worry about what it was and what they were going to face? If that power came and it overpowered them, they may not be able to escape. Given the drawing of the essence here, Arowend would likely be held. Rob thought there was a possibility that, in his manifested form, he may be able to escape, but even that was not a guarantee, as he didn't know if he would be able to get free of this power. He may be trapped, and then what? How much of himself would be lost if he were held like this?

"If you don't think I should do it, let me know," Rob said softly.

"I'm saying that I don't know," Arowend said. "If you feel this is crucial, I'm here to help. I don't know if there's anything I can do that would help, as I do feel like this is something that you are most familiar with, but...." Arowend let out a breath, though he was, in essence, manifestation, so he really didn't need to breathe. "I'm saying that you will do what you need to do, and I will defend you."

"Defend me?"

"You have to be able to feel it, can't you?"

"I can feel that something is changing," Rob said, "but I don't feel like I need to be defended. I don't know what's out there, nor what's coming at us, but...."

"But you may need me to keep an eye on you, at least for now. And if we don't work quickly, there's a real possibility that this power may begin to build too quickly for us."

Rob knew he needed to work quickly. He only had a vague sense of that external power coming at them, not in the same way that Arowend obviously did. Then again, in his essence form, filled out as he was, it might be that Arowend was far more capable of detecting things than Rob was. Given everything that he was and had become, Arowend may feel things so much better than Rob could.

So, Rob had to try, but he wasn't sure how that was going to work.

Link the essence.

When he had done it before, there had been a distinct sense of somebody else there, a distinct sense of the essence, and an understanding of who that person was and how he might be able to join it to his own essence. In this case, the only thing that he had was…

The familiarity that he had from traveling.

He had mingled with that unity, hadn't he?

Arowend had pulled him back, reuniting him and his form, but Rob had also gained an understanding of that essence in the time that he had been traveling. That would be enough. It had to be. He could focus on that power and let it fill him in a way that might help him bridge and use the power he detected.

That was what he needed to do.

Rob started to disperse.

Arowend looked at him, and Rob sent an understanding to him, using the dragon mind connection to try to fill Arowend in on what he planned, hoping that the other would understand and that he would be ready for the possibility that Rob might need Arowend to pull Rob back together.

Arowend relaxed but began to call upon essence from above, readying for whatever Rob might need from him.

Rob continued to disperse.

He didn't do it in the way he had before, not wildly, not trying to travel, but merely trying to understand the essence he felt around him. There was unity here, and Rob thought that he might be able to let that unity join in with his own essence to bridge the two of them. This wasn't even his form, though. Maybe this was the mistake. He had done it with Alyssa because he had been there in his physical form but in this manifestation...

Would it even be enough?

Could it even be enough?

There was a real possibility that Rob may not have enough power to make such a thing effective for him. And if not, what would he be able to do? He didn't know whether there was something that could be done here. The only thing he knew was that there was power out and around him, the kind of power that Rob could feel and that mingled with his own essence.

But he was here in a different form than what he thought might be necessary, but even that might not be too much of an issue. Given that Rob had come so fully, that his manifested form was so extensive at this point, he hoped that he could press part of himself outward, embrace the essence here, and let it flow in a way that allowed him to pull on that power.

So, he dispersed even more.

It was hard for him to do that as he began to feel some tenuous connection to the essence within him, as if some part of him were starting to separate and he was going to lose himself. He didn't want to lose everything that was himself, but he also felt like he needed to do this, primarily so that he could connect to this other unity.

"Rob," Arowend said, his voice a bit urgent as it came through the dragon mind connection.

Rob was separated, drifting and distant, and he wasn't even sure that he would be able to pull himself back into that Rob form, not without more power and not without more focus, so he wasn't sure if what Arowend was trying to say to him was because of fear or some other reason.

But he felt an urgency.

More than that, he began to feel something else. Whatever Arowend detected was near enough, a power that was building.

This other entity. The Dragon.

And maybe not the Dragon in full, but enough of it, and enough power from it, that Arowend grew concerned about what it meant.

Rob worked quickly.

He continued to let himself stretch. This was the risky part. He may disperse if he stretched too far and lost control of himself. He had to hope that some part of himself would return to his physical body, but having flowed on the essence, allowing the unity to carry him, he lost the same sense of his physical form that he had before. It was there, distantly, he thought, but it was not so prominent as to be detectable to him.

Rob could feel that energy stretching and straining, and he allowed himself to flow outward until he could feel a different sort of essence beginning to mix and mingle with what he had out and beyond him. There was some part of that that he could feel, some part of that, which began to swirl, and some part of that that was foreign enough that he knew he needed to try to find some way to incorporate inside himself.

And as he felt that foreignness, Rob started to pull it back. He started to pull himself back. He started to manifest. And rather than expelling that strange and alien essence, Rob brought it inside of himself this time, holding it and trapping it and hoping that there would be something more he could use it for. He had to find it because he had to find that power, and he had to understand whether there was going to be any way he could use it.

It wasn't just using it. It was a matter of trying to pull it in and storing it.

Linking to it.

That power started to rebel against Rob.

It seemed as if the essence recognized what Rob was trying to do and wanted to counter everything that he attempted, but at the same time, Rob needed to keep pushing, trying to absorb as much of that essence as he could so that he might be able to let that build within him. The more he felt that pressure against him, the more he began to release it before realizing it was a mistake. It wasn't about releasing that essence so much as trying to push them together to allow the unity essence to build a connection.

The essence started to bulge.

There was a part of him that fought.

He had to use his realm, Alyssa's realm, and try to share.

It wasn't about overpowering. It was about sharing.

Wasn't that what Rob had always done?

This was the unity, after all, and it wasn't about destroying so much as it was about trying to make the necessary connections for the kind of power Rob wanted. And the more he pushed, the more he felt that energy, and the more Rob started to think that he had to have some idea about what was here and what he was going to need to do.

And he felt it.

His essence seems to know. They began to connect with this other essence, not only his but Alyssa's essence. It was slow, but it was effective. More and more of it was starting to swirl in a way that felt like links were beginning to form; connections were there.

Then he began to feel that some part of that essence was pulled into the essence that formed his manifestation. No longer was the same pressure pushing against him. No longer was there that pain as Rob attempted to hold himself together. Now that essence started to settle, as if his essence, his own unity, and that of Alyssa's realm guided this other foreign essence on how to settle for him and how they could work in unison. Gradually Rob began to retreat, withdrawing, feeling that form settling until he was himself once again.

He closed his eyes, feeling the different essences inside of him. This essence had become a part of him, no different than Alyssa's essence and his own. He may be better connected to his own essence, but he felt that power, and he felt the way that it was there within him and bridged in such a way that he could use it.

"Rob!"

Rob realized that Arowend was calling to him, and

he had ignored it. He had been so focused on what he was doing and the power he was pulling upon, that he had allowed himself to look past what else he needed to do. And he could feel the way that Arowend was trying to call to him, could feel that essence flowing through him, the way that Arowend wanted to draw on him.

And Rob needed to help.

He immediately pushed outward.

Now the essence seemed to work.

It flowed, though it did flow with some resistance, as if it was naturally attempting to flow downward rather than upward and as if some pressures were pushing against him, something that Rob had to fight against. He strained with it but didn't know if he had enough control.

He recognized Arowend's concern. He couldn't see anything, but he felt it.

It was like a massive hand pressing down upon them.

Maybe that was what he had felt before, the way that the essence had been flowing and starting to cause problems for them, and maybe that was why he had come to know that he could not follow the unity back up.

Arowend began to swirl around Rob, adding strength to him. Between the two of them, Rob felt a surge of energy and an explosion of power that worked through him. Then they were able to move.

"Did it work?" Arowend asked Rob.

"A part of it did," Rob said. "At least, enough of it worked that I feel like I can follow it. Are you ready?"

"Ready for what?"

"I think it's time that we return, figure out what else we can do, and then prepare."

Arowend stared, swirling long enough that just a hint of his head had remained focused, the rest of him little more than essence swirl. Finally, he looked around Rob and then formed his manifestation. He nodded. "Let's go."

Rob used what he could feel of the essence here, having that to augment him. He blended it with Alyssa's realm and that of his own. The combination gave him enough power that he could push upward, and so they did, surging higher and higher, fighting through that pressure that was bearing down upon them, the hand that attempted to squeeze, until…

Until they were free.

Then he felt the essence pull on him.

He tried to push themselves back toward his realm, letting it guide them, but another power latched onto them and tore them forward.

Chapter Fifteen

ROB

THE ESSENCE WAS TRYING TO SEPARATE HIM, BUT THIS time, he had more than one realm helping him hold himself together. And if that wasn't enough, Arowend was there with him.

The pressure was significant. It was more than what Rob had felt getting dragged to the last place, so it took every bit of concentration for him to hold himself together.

But there was something different about it.

When he had gone the last time, he was aware of the strange, foreign essence, the way it worked through him, and how he needed to fight past it. In this case, it wasn't a matter of fighting past it. Rob tried a different approach and incorporated that essence into him and into what he was doing.

He pulled it inside of him, solidifying his manifestation long enough that he could use that essence and form another linkage. Something shifted.

The pressure on him began to fade, and he was able to maintain his form better. Rob had no idea what he was doing, nor did he know how he was pulling on that essence, only that it seemed to be effective. He was more aware of Arowend now, as well.

Arowend was near him, twisted, stretched, and strained, as some part of him started to separate. Rob added a bit of essence to hold him into form. When it happened, Arowend looked over to Rob, his eyes wide.

"I don't know what's happening," Rob admitted. "I can feel the essence trying to drag us, but I don't know how to slow it."

"That was my fear," Arowend said. "I can feel the way it's dragging you and me. If we lose control of this, what's going to happen to us?"

"It's going to keep pulling us away from our realm," Rob said.

"But pulling us where?"

That was Rob's concern, as he didn't have an answer. The essence was pulling and drawing on them, but it was a form of unity. At least that much was clear to Rob. As he focused on what he was feeling, the way that the unity was drawing upon him, he thought that all he needed to do was find some understanding about this essence, and maybe he could blend it, link to it, and give him an opportunity to get free.

He didn't know who and what he was connecting to. That was part of the problem. Though he knew that he could link to the essence, having done it now a few times, he also worried that if he were to link to a more potent and powerful place, there was a real possibility that he might harm his own realm.

The way that the essence was drawing downward, pulling deeper and deeper into the land, he recognized that something about his own realm and Alyssa's realm was different. It did not pull downward. It pushed upward. It was like a beacon.

And perhaps that's what the Dragon didn't care for. It didn't like what Rob had done, freeing the unity for it to find a way to send out whatever signal was there. There had to be something that Rob could do, some way for him to push that power, some way for him to allow that energy to flow, but he didn't know if it was going to be enough.

And even if it was, what did it mean?

Rob looped essence around himself, trying to add some of the unity to hold himself together as this power began to pull upon them more rapidly.

Everything around them was a swirl of clouds, sky, and energy. The only concrete entity he had near him was that of Arowend, and between them, they were drifting, pulled on the unity, pulled on that essence, and dragged away from everything they had known.

It was dangerous.

That was always Rob's problem. He was always willing to explore, test, and push and had always managed to come back. What if this time he could not? What if, this time, he ended up being ripped apart and becoming nothing more than an essence memory? If he were expelled from his physical body, he had no idea what would happen to him, nor did he know whether he would be able to return, drawing upon the essence for him to take on some sort of semblance of power the way that Arowend had.

What he needed was to hold onto what he was.

He pulled more of the essence inside of him. It was still that same foreign essence, and despite Rob knowing that it was dangerous, he began to link to it, making it a part of himself. It blended until Rob could feel something bridging, and he gained greater power and a connection than before.

That power allowed him to hold onto the essence and send it out to Arowend so he could also stabilize. At least they were what they were supposed to be and who they were supposed to be, but for how much longer?

There was a real possibility that that essence would begin to change again. If it did, how many times could Rob link to other essences, and how many different types of essences could he bridge into himself before everything that he was began to change in a way that it was not the same? He was just a manifestation here.

"Look," Arowend said.

Down below was a vast expanse of land. Rob could see a darkened, broken stretch of land with no sign of life. There was no sign of essence, either. He had found other places like that, having traveled with Alyssa and then beyond, and knew that there was likely going to be some bit of essence there, even if it was distant and difficult to reach. He focused on that land, whether there was going to be anything that he might be able to draw toward, whether that was the key to the unity, but it didn't seem to be. Every attempt he made to try to pull himself toward that land left him feeling as if he were drawing some part of himself apart. He could not feel any essence. He could not feel any unity.

"They stripped it," Rob said.

He and Arowend managed to hold onto a bit more of a manifestation, but they were still caught in some sort of unity flow, as if there was some higher power here, bridging from one place to another.

"I can't feel anything," Arowend said.

"Alyssa said there were places like this."

"Why would they do that?" Arowend asked.

"I don't know. There should be essence there, and maybe there still is, but it's distant."

Rob continued to focus. He was able to blend the different types of unity, and through that, he had hoped that there might be some way to tap into a greater sort of power.

"They took it all," he said softly.

"Then we should be careful," Arowend said.

"I don't get the sense that there's anything there. No unity. Nothing that would be a danger to us. There is simply an emptiness there."

"Again," Arowend said, looking over to Rob and still holding onto his form, though there was a part of him that seemed to be separated in a difficult way for Rob to watch, as if some part of Arowend was getting pulled into the essence flow. "If that emptiness begins to swallow us…."

"I don't think that's how it would work," Rob said.

"We don't know enough about how it would work, only that the power that's there, the power that I can feel, is certainly enough that it has the potential to draw on us. And if it does come and it draws us down, then…."

Rob understood, and he also understood that they certainly didn't want to be drawn downward like that, at least so they wouldn't have to feel the power pulling upon them and possibly pulling them apart.

But he didn't feel like that. It just felt hollow. It felt like something was supposed to be there, but now there was not.

What had happened here?

The parasitic effect of the Dragon had swallowed that power. If there were others still here, or even a shred of essence, he might find unity. There was none.

And so, he drifted past.

As they did, he began to feel Arowend relax.

"We need to get back," Rob said.

"I thought you were going down there to see if you could link to it, too."

"Well, I considered it," Rob said, sharing his thoughts with Arowend. "If there was another pulling, we might lose what we already gained. I think we need more pushing if that makes sense."

"Well, it makes a little bit of sense."

"There has to be something else," Rob said, and he opened himself, spreading the manifestation outward and losing some semblance of his form until he could feel the other essences there. "I can feel this fourth unity, even though it's distant. It has become a part of what I am doing, but I don't know where to find it, and I don't know how it connects. I think that if we can pull that other unity in, we might find another place that could help us."

"How many more do you think we can uncover before returning?"

That was the real question for Rob, as well. He didn't have the answer, as he could feel some kind of power pressing on him, beginning to build in a way that was squeezing out against him. He recognized it, but there was too much strangeness.

"I don't know," Rob said. "But eventually, I think we're going to find a way to fight past what is there, for us to find a way to escape the essence that is pulling upon us. That's going to be the key, I think. We're going to need to push against it and find a way to escape so that we can return."

"Return, or…"

"Again, I just don't know."

They were drawn and drifted across other lands, this one larger than the last, rockier, and mountainous. Rob sensed that there were once trees, grass, flowers, and rivers, everything that would've been familiar to his own realm, but now there was nothing. It was almost as if the loss of essence had changed the realm. Much like the last one, he focused on whether there was any essence that he might be able to draw upon, but as before, he felt nothing. Just more emptiness. The longer he focused, the more he began to question whether there would be any way for him to find anything more than he already had. He focused on that power, continuing to feel for anything else, but there was nothing. That extra unity essence wasn't coming from there or blended through that land.

Arowend manifested as they neared that land as if he were questioning what Rob might do. The fact that Rob did not change his own form, and did not attempt to probe down, gave Arowend a moment of relief.

But it was more than just that which bothered Rob. It was the power that he felt, a power that he recognized, and a power that he could feel flowing through and around him in such a way that he knew he couldn't do anything more with it.

They were drawn. The current of essence continued to pull on them, unity dragging them forward. Rob attempted to link more into that unity, trying to find something that would help him understand that power, but every time he attempted to do so, he felt as if the unity was separating him in a way that he could not quite grasp.

He focused, and when he felt the unity swirling, he started to draw into himself. This one was a fifth form. It wasn't quite as prominent as the fourth one, which was more prominent than the third one, but it was less than either his or Alyssa's essence, though both of them had become more and more distant the further they went. Rob knew that he had to work quickly if he wanted to link to that unity to maintain some control over it, for if he didn't, there was a real possibility that he would lose control over his essence altogether, and then he had no idea what would happen. He was holding onto it, trying to make sense of that essence, trying to draw upon it, when he started to notice something, some part of it, that began to push, pulling on him, and dragging power downward. The more that he focused on that, the more certain Rob was that he could feel that essence fighting him.

"Rob?"

"I can feel it," Rob said.

"I can feel it, too, but what is it?"

"I don't know," Rob said.

Unity began to surge within him, and it was almost as if it were pushed.

And this time, it seemed to be controlled in a way that the other unity had not been. This fifth unity essence was slithering through him, starting to solidify and trying to disperse the other unity essence. It was almost as if it were countering everything Rob was trying to do.

Arowend swirled around Rob, trying to help him hold onto some semblance of form, but even Arowend's control over this wasn't enough. The more that he swirled and the more that he worked, the more that Rob felt the essence trying to fortify and combat everything that Rob was doing. The combination of the two was not enough.

He had to link, didn't he?

But anytime they tried to link this essence, Rob felt the essence combating him.

And with a growing understanding, he realized what was happening and who was responsible for it.

It was the Dragon.

He had never felt its touch directly. It had always been the subheralds and heralds, incredible powers but powers that Rob thought he could counter. In this case, what he felt, he suspected, was a direct touch. It was unity, but it was a unity that was so profound and so potent that Rob wasn't sure that he could counter it.

That energy and essence were pressing through him, to the point where it was going to unmake him.

Worse, he could also tell what was happening to Arowend.

With every passing moment that Arowend was swirling around Rob, it seemed as if the other essence was beginning to work inside of Arowend, as if it were starting to focus on him, trying to peel him away, and trying to add to Arowend in a way that would change him just as much as it had changed Rob.

The only way that Rob thought that he might be able to do this, and stop this, would be to expel that essence.

Everything that he had done so far was about bridging essence and linking to it, so that he could find understanding, but in this case, it felt as if linking to that essence was going to be the most dangerous thing he could do. If he were to do it, he feared what would happen to him and Arowend, and whether they would be ripped apart, and lost for all time.

"I'm sorry," Rob said, looking to Arowend.

For a moment, Arowend swirled, and he took on a more solid form, looking over to Rob, and there was a burst of understanding between them.

And then Rob pulled on the essence all around him.

Chapter Sixteen

SERENA

SERENA SAT NEXT TO THE FIRE, FEELING THE CRACKLING warmth, and wondering how much of it was real and was simply essence manifestation, but the two of them could look the same, oftentimes. She could feel the heat and warmth, but she could also feel the essence that had gone into its creation. She was tempted to reach out to the palace and ask for understanding, but she didn't know if it even made a difference or if the palace would answer her. It was possible that it would not, that the palace did not care enough to share, and that the palace didn't even know.

Her mother was sitting next to her quietly. Her hands rested on her lap, as she stared at the fire, the flames reflecting in her eyes. There was a surge of essence ever so often, but Serena felt nothing more within that surge. There was certainly no sign of the dangerous woman that Serena had known her entire life, nothing that would suggest that she was going to harm Serena anyway, not that she actually thought that her mother would actually do that. This was her mother, after all, and though she was the dragon queen, she didn't think she wanted to hurt Serena.

In fact, everything that her mother had claimed she was doing had been to protect the realm and Serena. At least, that was her claim.

Serena decided to use her dragon mind connection.

She pushed.

She didn't push so hard that she would overwhelm her mother, though such a thing was possible, she suspected. She never tried to overwhelm her mother or harm her, unlike her mother, who did try to harm her. Serena wondered if she should follow in her mother's footsteps, this once.

No. I'm not going to be like her.

That was the way toward failure, Serena knew. She had to be more than her mother, and she had to be better than her, if she could find a way to do so. Serena didn't know what that might entail, but she knew it didn't involve acting like her, and letting anger get the best of her.

"You're just going to sit there silently?" Serena asked.

"You're the one who came here," the dragon queen said, looking over Serena for a moment before turning her attention back to the fire. As she stared at the fire, there was a vague sense of energy that radiated, but it was more than just the energy that was radiating. There was some energy that was radiating from the dragon queen. It was going through her. She was touching upon the fire using her essence. "I thought that you had something that you wanted to accomplish in doing so."

"I was hoping we could have a conversation," Serena said. "I want to understand what you did."

Finally, her mother turned to her, and when she looked at her, there was a bit of confusion in her eyes. "Why do you care?"

"Because you're my mother."

"Your mother," she scoffed, "if you cared about your mother, you would have followed my guidance."

"Just because you're my mother doesn't mean you're right. You had limited exposure and refused to see anything beyond the boundaries of our realm, so how am I supposed to think that you could see anything beyond that? I've traveled far more extensively than you did and seen the world in ways you can't even imagine, so my experience and understanding should be considered."

It was more than just that, she supposed. It was more than just understanding what had happened. It was about trying to make amends, though would her mother be able to make amends? This woman was proud, confident, and strong, and Serena had no idea whether or not she was willing to listen to anything she had to say.

"I know what you've been doing," her mother said. "Do you think that I can't feel it? The boy gave me that gift, at least."

Serena smiled at the idea of Rob being considered a boy. Maybe when he had first been Dragon forged, when she first met him, she could see him like that, but he was so much different than that now. She couldn't fathom him as that person any longer. It was hard even to remember what he was like, but there were times when she got lost in those thoughts, thinking back to when she first encountered him, and how naïve he'd been. How innocent. So much of him had changed, but so much of the world had also changed.

"Are you disappointed by what he's given you?"

Her mother paused, unsure, before staring back at the fire. "I don't like seeing beyond my realm," she said softly.

"Because you're afraid?"

"Because I know what it means."

"You don't know what it means. You haven't been willing to listen, nor have you been willing to even look beyond what we have here. And if you were, you might understand that there is much more than we've ever known. There is power here, but there is something more that our people deserve. Why can't you see that?"

Her mother frowned again, and she turned her attention back to Serena.

Essence swirled around her. Serena saw aspects of it, though not, in the same way, Rob often describes seeing essence.

"My father feared losing control of our realm," her mother finally said.

Serena frowned.

"You don't talk about him very often."

She knew so little about her grandfather. He was the dragon king before her mother was the dragon queen. He lived an impossibly long time, and had helped fortify the realm, helping to extend some of the borders, and to ensure the safety of essence. Serena knew very little about him, though. Her mother never liked to talk about him, and Serena wasn't born when she was alive. She had always believed that her mother didn't want to talk about the dragon king because it suggested that there was a time when she would no longer be the dragon queen. It was something that Serena had long believed, until she learned that one didn't have to perish for another dragon soul to rise.

Then it became more about her mother's stubbornness, and little else. That was probably enough, especially given everything that her mother did.

And Serena hadn't bothered to try to test for them. In the time that she had been connected to the palace, and subsequently to the tower, she had not even thought about what it might be for her to know more about her family, and those who had come before. There might be answers to help her explain the essence, the palace itself, and the kind of power that existed.

But then there was another thought that began to come to her, and it was one that Serena had not considered, but she should have long before now.

Arowend.

Some were here before, who existed in the realm, and those who had known about the connections between the realms. Serena didn't know if her grandfather was one of them, but if he had been, was he the one who was responsible for what happened to Arowend?

Serena focused on the connection to the palace, and there was a part of her that wanted to know, but that would involve reaching out to some power, something more than what she already had. She focused on what she already felt, and began to reach for the librarian, but hesitated.

She had someone here who might be able to help.

"What about him?"

"He warned me," she said, looking over to Serena. "He warned all of us that there was something dangerous to other realms."

"Really?" Serena asked, and once again, she wished she had somebody else here who could help her understand what was going on, and whether there was something more. Arowend could have been helpful, but if Arowend was here, there was a possibility that if he remembered those memories, it might turn him once again into the Netheral.

What of Tessatha?

Serena was tempted to connect to her friend, tempted to see if there was anything that she might recall from that time that would help her know whether her grandfather had been a part of what happened to Arowend, and what happened at that time, but Serena didn't want to risk harming her friend, and certainly didn't want to risk her friend getting hurt again.

"He knew something. He knew that there was some sort of power beyond our realm then, and though I have long known the Sultan and Nelah, I also knew there was a danger in us trying to connect. It's part of the reason that we remain separate."

"Because he feared," Serena said.

Her mother clasped her hands together, and she scowled at Serena. "Do you really think me so scared?"

"I saw how you were willing to hide when you feared the Netheral," Serena said.

Her mother fell silent for a moment.

"We did not want to lose what we had. We did not want to lose the safety and protection that we were able to offer our people."

"By not even attempting to provide it to them?" Serena asked.

"We provided them," her mother said.

Serena snorted. "You hid in essence well. You stayed away when the danger was there. There is nothing that you offered your people."

Her mother was quiet. "The others understood, as well," she finally said. "The Sultan. The Nelah. Even those beyond," she said, waving her hand as if to dismiss Gregor and the storm cloud. Did her mother know about the brambles? Perhaps not. She probably didn't know about Oro, either, as there were very few who understood that power, and it wasn't until Rob had been willing to test for something out in the water that she learned about that. "They understood the danger, and they understood that if we were to try to pursue something more between each other, we would find ourselves lost. That has been the way of the world."

"Even though your records likely would've told you that there had once been a connection between these realms," Serena said.

"A connection that had been separated, and for a good reason. Do not think that I know so little," she said.

For a moment, there was a bit of that confidence back in her voice, the same sound Serena had known her entire life, but then it faded. It was almost as if their dragon queen was retreating.

"Why are you so afraid?"

"Do you think you are the only one to have connected to the palace?"

And there it was.

Serena suspected her mother had known about her connection to the palace, but didn't think her mother had one. It wasn't until Serena had managed to link to that power, that she began to feel something more, some greater power, that had helped her understand that there was an energy that they might be able to draw upon. It wasn't until she had called upon the palace that she learned what it was going to take for her to find a way to become a dragon soul.

"You did not," Serena said.

"I did not, but he never taught me."

"So, my grandfather knew how to connect to the palace," Serena said.

Her mother nodded. "He did. It was one of his great secrets, something he didn't want to reveal, as… Well, I think that he understood there was a danger in it. The palace was power, and he thought that only certain people, those with potential, should be able to access that kind of power."

Serena started to laugh. When her mother looked at her, she shook her head.

"The palace is power, but the palace was also connected to other places, and if what you're saying is right, my grandfather knew that."

How would Arowend react to the idea that Serena's grandfather had been the one who had betrayed him?

And maybe Serena should be thankful that he had not remembered before now. How would he have reacted? Would he have grown even angrier? He would have every right to be so, though. She had seen what he'd experienced and heard about the awfulness he'd gone through, and Tessatha had shared what that time had been like.

"What?"

"I'm just amused by what you're telling me," Serena said.

"Because you have connected to the palace?" Her mother waved her hand again. "Do not think that your sudden understanding is some great gift. It might've helped you, but how long do you think that palace will continue to help you? At what point do you think it will withdraw that gift?"

"I don't get the sense that the palace is going to withdraw any sort of gift," Serena said. "And I suspect that the palace wanted someone to progress. It probably would've been content having you but seeing as how you were too afraid even to consider that possibility, perhaps the palace had no choice but to give it to the next best."

"I'm not so sure you're the next best," Serena's mother said.

She glared at her mother. Did it matter that she didn't believe in Serena?

For whatever reason, it did. She had wanted her mother's approval her entire life and hated that she struggled to get it. It had been so much different with her father. At least with him, she'd always known where she stood and that he was there for her, willing to help her, but with her mother…

With her mother, so much had been difficult for her, to the point where Serena never knew what she belonged to or if she could even be trusted.

"Can you feel the unity?" Serena asked.

"I can feel how things have changed, if that's your question. And your boy has continued to change things. Even now, it is changing. But then, I suspect you know that, don't you? You probably encouraged it. And you don't even understand the danger you are welcoming through it."

"I understand the danger," Serena said." We've been facing that danger but doing so with our eyes open, not our heads in the fire, trying to ignore what is coming. We recognize that there is something else out there, but we also know that if we allow that something else, that fear, to keep us from what we might be able to be, then we can never truly be free."

"What makes you think that you can ever be free?"

"How much have you seen changing?" Serena asked. "How much of what you felt is different than it had been before? Can't you believe that the world is better off? Can't you believe that your realm is better? You have your people who gained power, and understanding and have progressed beyond what they had ever been before. We have dragon blood," she said, her voice raising as she got more and more irritated with her mother. "We have those who reached for something beyond that, who now can grasp this unity. Don't you think that should be significant? Don't you think that is what we're deserving of?"

"I think that is what will destroy us," her mother said. "My father warned me. He said that there was something that would come. Something would take it from us if we tried to push too far. It would take *everything* from us."

Serena just stared at her mother. But not with the same irritation as she had before.

Her grandfather had known, which meant that Arowend must have known. But then, Arowend had warned her that he had remembered something, but his memories were scant and difficult.

"What did he fear?"

"He never said," she said, turning her attention back to the fire. "Only that there was something else out there, and that if we pushed beyond what we were and pushed beyond who we could be, something would come for us, and it would take everything that we have gained. It would take our people, our realm, and our essence."

That was too close to the truth to be a mistake, which meant that somehow, some way, her grandfather had known. He might have been a part of taking that artifact and turning it into a weapon. But there had to be something else, something more, that would help.

Arowend had thought that the weapon had been for him, to separate the realm.

And it made sense. As far as they had learned, the conjoining of the realms had certainly caused them to gain the notice of this other entity from everything Serena had seen. But what if there was something else the weapon could do?

What if it had been more than what they remembered?

What if the weapon had been designed not to destroy the realms, but to destroy this other entity? And what if the destruction of the realm, the separating of them, had been a side effect, rather than the ultimate goal?

If that were the case, then there was so much more that they needed to understand, and they needed to go to the one place that had answers, but it was also the one place that seemed as if it didn't want to give those answers up.

She had to go back into the tower.

Chapter Seventeen

ROB

Rob felt the Dragon pulling him.

The power exuded from this entity was beyond anything that he'd ever experienced before. It left him feeling raw. Fighting against a power like that was beyond his ability.

Which meant he had to find a way to become the unity.

But the unity here was powerful.

"I need you to pull on our unity," Rob said.

Arowend was getting dispersed, as parts of him started to separate. Rob was worried that if he waited much longer, some part of Arowend would be ripped apart completely.

He needed Arowend for this.

Arowend might be the only one capable of doing it, after all. Given his connection to the essence, how he was linked to it, and how he was little more than essence, it was possible that the only way they would survive would be by Arowend stepping up and helping.

"Why?" Arowend asked, his voice tensed and strained.

"This other unity is potent, and I need potency. I need my unity," he said.

"Is it yours?"

"It is the first unity—the primary, at least for me. And until I have some way of linking to that, I don't know if I could combat what's coming at me. And I need a way to hold onto it, to find some balance."

"Are you sure this is what we need to be doing?"

"No," Rob admitted. "But I feel like this is what we should do. We need to trust the essence."

Arowend was quiet for a long moment, and then Rob felt something coming from him. It was part of the dragon mind connection, but it was more than that. It was almost as if Arowend was sending emotion, feelings, images, and memories to Rob. And in them, Rob saw what Arowend had been through, how he had suffered when he had wanted to push, try to make sense of the essence around him, and how he had suffered when he wanted to bridge essence. His own people had betrayed him. Arowend had trusted essence at that time, feeling as if he had done what he needed to do. And that was what Rob understood. He wasn't sure this was right, but he trusted essence. And everything within him, everything that he had done so far, suggested to him that linking essence was the key.

But would it save them?

"I'll try," Arowend finally said.

And then there was a surge of power.

It came slowly, a dragging of energy that began to stir, a familiarity to Rob.

Arowend controlled that flow, and essence began solidifying within him again. Other essences still pressed against him, and he knew not to destroy. It was about balance, which meant he would have to work with this other essence before it destroyed him. He started to pull that essence.

Because of what Arowend was doing, the way he was sending the essence toward Rob, some part of Rob's own essence filled him, giving him greater power. That essence became a part of him. And he pulled on it.

There was a balance. It was unsteady, but perhaps that was all he could ask for. Still, there was a balance. Rob let that balance stay within him, lingering, as if he were teetering somehow, and the more that he held onto that essence and felt the balance, the more control Rob had over it. The longer he held the essence, the more the others stabilized, linking together and forming something more than what he'd already grabbed.

"Rob?" Arowend asked.

"You can stop," Rob said.

Arowend stopped pulling upon the distant sense of unity from their realm, and Rob felt the drawing coming to him, without any effect of Arowend pulling on it. More than that, Rob thought he could pull on it himself, much more easily than he had before.

And there was this other essence.

A painful explosion thundered within Rob, ripping through him in a way that felt as if it were trying to tear him apart. Rob tried resisting, but it wasn't even him that had to resist. The other essences inside of him knew what needed to happen.

Another explosion thundered, which was just as potent, attempting to tear Rob apart. He had to expand briefly, allowing the manifestation to fold away, until he pulled back together. Arowend swirled around him, helping Rob maintain his form, and coalescing downward.

"This is dangerous for you," Arowend said. "I'm not sure what's happening, but I can feel it."

"I think this other entity doesn't like what I did," Rob said. "I think we should retreat."

"I don't know if we can."

"Each time this power explodes, some part of me is torn, and I don't know if I can hold onto it. It's starting to strip aspects of me away."

There was another explosion. He had to disperse briefly enough for the other essence to swirl around him, trap that energy explosion, and then pull it back. He still had a link to this fifth essence, but the link was changing, so Rob had to counter it, but he didn't know if he was going to be strong enough.

Rob struggled to hang onto himself, having a hard time finding a way to maintain his normal form. Each time there was another explosion, he found that his essence burst, making it so that he could not maintain his form as well.

"We can't stay here," he shouted to Arowend, unsure if they could still communicate. It felt like there was some part of Arowend that was unable to link to him the way it normally did. Rob was accustomed to having Arowend's connection within his mind, but then again, he was also accustomed to having Serena's within his mind. Now there was an absence, likely tied to the fact that he was different, the fact that all the linked essence had changed him, making it so that he was somehow a different entity than he had been before.

But was he an entity? Or was he still Rob, only bound to a different type of essence?

"We need to keep you safe," Arowend said.

"The only way to be safe is if we retreat," Rob said.

It was a mistake for him to link to this other essence. "Can you hold onto your form as we go?"

"I can try," Arowend said.

"I think that I can propel us upward."

He slowly pushed, letting essence propel them upward.

It wasn't easy to maintain his form. Essence continually tried to shatter him, attempting to strip him apart, turning him into nothing more than an essence memory.

It was also trying to take away everything that Rob was. He had to find a way past it, if only he could hold himself together. His other essences helped, linking him. Every time Rob felt that essence, he began to detect some other aspect of it that was trying to fight him, bursting through him, the power that attempted to shatter everything that Rob was.

"Arowend," he said, trying to hold onto that connection to Arowend, knowing that it would be the key to whatever it was that he was going to be able to do, to the point where Rob had to hold onto it, had to feel that essence, and had to pull Arowend into himself.

But that was a mistake. He needed Arowend to maintain his own control, his own connection, and to be able to link to Rob in a way that only Arowend could do. Finally, he felt something beginning to swirl around him, the power that pressed, and then began to drag.

At first, Rob thought it was Arowend, and that he was holding onto him, dragging him back, but that didn't seem to be the case. Increasingly, he was aware of some other energy that seemed to be pulling on him. For a moment, Rob worried about that source of power and if it was going to be too much for him.

Rob didn't think he could withstand this for much longer. He didn't know if he dared risk linking more unity, especially if it attempted to harm him, while trying to hold onto this form.

But he didn't have a chance. He was pulled.

"You aren't taking my essence," Rob said.

He knew there was probably no point in doing so and doubted that there was any way that he was going to be able to overpower this entity — the Dragon, as the Eternal had called him. "You aren't going to — "

Pain surge through Rob. It was an enormous amount of pain, and it felt like some part of him was being stripped away.

"You can't have this essence."

Rob, tried to fight, and distantly, faintly, he could've sworn that he heard something. It sounded almost like it came from the thunder itself, like a storm was calling out to him, or as if the earth was groaning. "Mine."

Chapter Eighteen

SERENA

Serena couldn't help but question the power of the unity.

She paced the palace hallway, watching the soldiers as she did. The soldiers were oblivious to the fact that she was testing them. She was trying to make sense of the essence within them, hoping for answers, but she couldn't feel it every time she got too close to them, almost as if the soldiers were withholding something from her.

And if they were withholding from her, it meant that the palace and the unity connection were also trying to withhold something from her. Why would that be? It was strange, and more than that, it seemed almost impossible that the palace would decide to try to keep something from her, but perhaps it recognized that she was irritated by what was happening, and the way that she had been severed from an aspect of power that she might need.

The meeting with her mother was difficult because even though her mother was a difficult person, she told

Serena things that made her question how much of her own ancestors were responsible for what happened here. She needed those answers, but how was she supposed to find them?

Other than recently, her mother was the only dragon soul she'd ever known. But before that, it seemed to Serena that there should be some way for her to find answers by linking to the palace and understanding the people in the past and everything that existed within the palace prior to her mother. Was the palace essence, wasn't it? The palace carried with it memories. The palace was...

"I thought they would find you here," a familiar voice said, striding down the hall toward her.

Serena looked up, and she smiled at her uncle. He was dressed in a dark blue cloak, and the sword sheathed at his side, and an essence that circled around him. He had power, to the point where Serena could feel how her uncle was calling upon that power, how it swirled out from him, and the energy he was holding onto. She smiled at that, thinking about how Griffin would have once viewed her belief in his power and how he would've looked at her before she departed.

"I was just talking with my mother," Serena said.

He glanced past her, before turning his attention back to her. "I felt your arrival, but I wasn't sure what the purpose of it was. I didn't realize that you were here to speak with her."

"I wanted answers," Serena said.

"I suppose that's reasonable," he said, walking alongside her.

They made their way through the palace halls, past a series of soldiers that stood guard on either side of the walls, and past servants that were little more than manifestations of the essence. Serena still hadn't learned what the servants did, only that they were there, and seemed as if they were trying to offer some measure of assistance within the palace, something that made little sense to her. None of the servants should be serving the palace, not as little more than a construct of the essence.

"I've been trying to understand what she had done, and whether there is anything I need to do differently because of it."

"You can't tell me that you want to listen to what your mother has to say," Griffin said, arching a brow at her.

"It's not about what she has to say. It's more about who she is, and what she was. Not only that," Serena began, and she looked around, before focusing on the essence she could feel around her. She found herself linking to the unity, but even when she did, she wondered if there was a way for her to strip out some aspect of fire, some way for her to pull upon the power that had once been her birthright, but realized that while it was there, it didn't seem to respond to her in the way that it had before. And there was some part of the unity that had begun to change, something that her mother had alluded to, though Serena had known that it was changing. Maggie had suggested that, and she had seen it, given what Rob was doing and the way he was pulling on other essences, trying to link to power that was here. "I feel like I need to make amends for what I did."

"You need to make amends?" Griffin asked, with a

frown. "Given everything that your mother has done, the way that she nearly betrayed us and her own people, I'm not so sure you need to be responsible for anything like that."

"It's not that I'm going to apologize for what we did," she explained. "I want her to realize that I care about her."

"You do?"

Serena shrugged.

"Well, she is my mother, and I'm hoping to find some understanding so I can at least know what she did, and why she did it. It's hard for me, Griffin."

Griffin sighed.

"You know, seeing what my brother went through, makes it harder for me, as well. I always supported them, at least when they first got together, but there were differences, even then. Given what he has described, and how much he suffered, I'm left with unanswered questions. But then again, we have you, so perhaps there is nothing to be saddened by." He flashed a smile. "Besides, there were other things we gained from that connection. We understand the palace now in a way that we didn't before, and we understand everything you might be able to do and everything your mother was trying to hide from you."

"It's more than we realize," Serena said quietly.

"Why?"

"Well," she began, and it was difficult for her to say, because it meant acknowledging her family's role in it, especially given what she had seen from Arowend and Tessatha, and how much they had suffered. But it was something that she was going to have to acknowledge. Her family history couldn't be erased. So, all that was left was making amends. "I think my grandfather was one of the people who targeted Arowend."

Griffin paused, and there was a pulsation of essence from him, something that left Serena thinking that he was connecting to an aspect of unity, though perhaps it wasn't. As far she knew, Griffin had not gone into the tower, but she could feel that power coming out of him, perhaps in a way that left him accessing it only a little bit, accessing some part of it that changed something for him, and accessing something that blended the essence, the same way that Rob had first blended essences together.

"Your grandfather?"

"I don't know much about him. My mother never really talked about him before, except that he was an incredibly powerful dragon soul, and when he passed on, he gifted power to her."

"Do we know how long your mother has ruled?" Griffin asked.

It seemed like a strange question, but it really wasn't. As far as they knew, dragon souls could live an incredibly long time, and Serena's mother might have lived and served for decades. Centuries, even. And if that were the case, then she understood what Griffin was getting at. What if her grandfather had passed on after whatever they'd done to Arowend and Tessatha?

Then she would have an even greater connection to what happened, which might be even more significant.

And it would mean that her mother might have understood things that had happened back then.

She turned, thinking she might need to return to her mother, before changing her mind. "She didn't say anything about that," she said, and she tried not to be too irritated, but she couldn't shake that feeling, especially given that her mother continued to hide things from her.

"I can go talk to her," Griffin offered.

"I'm not sure it's going to make a difference," Serena said. "I can feel... Well, I can feel something. I begin to question if there is supposedly something else here that we need to understand about the purpose of unity. Isn't that what Rob is trying to get us to do?"

Griffin reached out and took her hand, squeezing it for a moment. He never touched her, at least not like this. This was something familiar, something comforting, like how her father reassured her. As he looked at her, he held her gaze, and it seemed as if he reached across with essence as well, trying to form a link to her, a way of connecting and comforting her.

"We need to decide what *we* want to do; not just what Rob wants to do. We can work with him, as I do think that young man is the right choice, but we must also make sure that we aren't following him blindly."

"I know," Serena said.

"But..."

"But I don't know," Serena went on, "I still feel like there are answers here that I don't have and answers that I really need to find, but unfortunately, I haven't been able to uncover them. I keep digging and digging, and I keep failing to uncover anything more. The only thing I get is more questions. Everything seems to be linked to what had happened before."

"And if we can uncover what that was, maybe we can uncover whether there was anything more that we might be able to use from that past," Griffin said.

That was Serena's hope, and part of the reason that she'd been working so diligently was Tessatha and Arowend, for that matter. The only thing that she had been able to uncover was that there was that emptiness that came after the destruction of the realms. It was that emptiness and power that Serena thought they needed to understand better. Until they did, she wasn't sure what they were going to do. She wasn't sure what they were going to uncover about the unity, and whether there was anything within it that would help them.

"Where do you think you're going to get your answers?" Griffin asked.

"I tried getting them for my mother, and I've tried waiting for Tessatha to provide something for me, but still, I keep digging and digging, and nothing really seems to be changing," she said.

"Are you digging in the right place? Are you digging in the right way?"

"I…" She didn't know. She smiled at her uncle. "Thank you for this conversation, Uncle," she said.

"That's it?"

"Well, I think there must be something within the palace that will help me understand my grandfather, and maybe help me understand the past, as that's what I'm connected to. Given what we've uncovered so far and everything we're dealing with, I think understanding the past, will help us understand the future."

The libraries weren't providing anything. Essence memories hadn't provided answers, either. The more she searched, the more she was convinced that the answers might be out there, but they were not in places she had looked.

Where could they be?

Tessatha and Arowend had been searching. And Rob had been going about things in his own way. And Serena even had the librarians looking into things in their way, checking for information, and searching for answers, but so far, she hadn't uncovered anything that she thought she might be able to use, so she had to keep digging.

As she stood talking to her uncle, she felt a strange link in her mind. It was like a tapping, some part of her that surged with a bit of unity, and she frowned. Was this some sort of attack? She waited for a moment, but as that power began to build, she felt pressure within her mind, and then…

"You're needed," her father said.

"What?"

"You're needed."

There was a surge of power, and once again, Serena was aware of it, but this time, she had a message that came with it. She was needed, but the tower needed her.

That was odd. She was never needed by the tower before.

She looked at her uncle, shared what she had learned, and ran to the main entrance. What she wouldn't give for Arowend's ability to separate into little more than essence, and if she could, then maybe she wouldn't have to run outside. She didn't think manifesting was the way to go, not if she was truly needed. She would need her physical form. Once outside, the gray sky looked down upon her, and the flare of essence from all over the city burst into her mind. Serena called upon that sense, and then she used a burst of her own essence, a burst of power, that sent her shooting upward.

She was distantly aware of a sense of essence that trailed after her, and she looked back to see Griffin following. Perhaps that was for the best. She might need help especially if she was needed.

She called Tessatha, and warned her that she might be needed as well, and tried to reach for Rob through the conduit, but there was no sense of him.

Could that be why she was needed? As Serena continued to let the essence carry her, she focused on what she could of Arowend, but there was nothing there, either.

The tower needed her.

That was worrisome, especially as she didn't know what it meant. She didn't know whether the tower was somehow sentient, but if it was, and it was calling upon her with that kind of power, then she could be walking into danger; she had to be ready for it.

When she saw the tower looming in the distance, she was aware of something that she'd not been aware of before. It seemed as if there was a power drifting from it. That was unity, but why was it directed outward more so than before?

There had always been a pulsation of unity, some

sense where it was going down, before going back outward. Now it seemed to be draining off more than it was going down into the realm.

Maybe that was why the tower needed her.

She landed, stopping in front of the tower entrance, and waited only a moment before Griffin was there. He straightened up and looked at her.

"Something's wrong," Griffin said. "And the tower called you?"

"Apparently," she said.

The idea that the tower had asked for her and sent Raolin was surprising and worrisome. Not because she wasn't willing to help the tower, but because she worried about what the tower might need from her, and how it might demand her service. She was connected to it, there was no doubt about that, but how would the tower want her to use her connection, and what would it ask of her?

She started forward, and the door appeared. When she reached it, she held her hand out, and focused on the essence within herself, holding that power as she stepped forward into the darkness. There was a sense of pulsation, the unity drawing her along the hallway, until she reached a door.

It was at the end of the hall. She knew this door and where it led but didn't know why the tower was calling her here. Her father appeared, stepping out of a doorway that Serena hadn't known was there.

"What's going on?" she asked, frowning at him.

Her father glanced at her, then at Griffin, and he focused on the essence. A sense of unity pulsed within him, something Serena hadn't seen from him before, but wasn't totally surprised that he had access to. He seemed to be better connected to the tower than Serena had expected him to be. Then again, he was always a scholar, more so than even Serena, so he would've spent considerable time testing the tower, testing the connection, and trying to make sense of that power.

"You're needed," he said.

Serena looked at the door.

"I get that, but the last time I was here, the tower didn't want to tell me what I needed to do, or what I was needed for. So do you want to tell me, or are you going to let me go in there blind?"

He took her hand.

"I'm going to warn you," he said, and the moment that he did, a surge of panic worked through her, "what you will find in there is going to be terrifying. But you must find a way past it."

With that, he waved his hand at the door and pulled it open.

And then she saw a Rob.

And it looked as if he were getting torn apart.

Chapter Nineteen

SERENA

Essence was ripping Rob apart. Serena could see it, even though she wasn't sure why it would work that way, as he had been a part of unity from the beginning. He was the very first one bound by that unity, and the first one to truly understand it. That essence was stripping free something of him, tearing away his entire being.

But there was something different from what she had seen from him before. Not just that the unity was trying to peel him away, but some part of that unity felt different.

She could get close, but she didn't dare get too close, fearing what might happen if that unity also began to work on her. She needed to work quickly to make sense of what was happening here. Even as she got close to Rob, she was unsure how to help him.

"What happened to him?"

"He came here for answers," he said.

She arched a brow at her father, surprised that he knew, then again, he had been inside the tower.

"What kind of answers?"

"They went searching for others."

Others.

Unity.

And Serena could feel what Rob had done and how he was separated. She recognized that there was another link to him, something more within him that had not been there before, the way the essence was blending and blurring and changing him.

But it was doing more than just changing him. It was changing his connection to this tower, and the power supposedly trying to hold him in place. Serena wondered if there was anything that she could do to help hold him in place.

But she realized the tower was already doing that.

The markings on the wall took on a different meaning for her.

She had known that there was power here and that it was old, and the connection it provided was considerable, but she never really understood them, as she didn't have the opportunity to stand and master them.

Now she could feel something more.

That power was stretching away, changing, and shifting. And Rob was changing and shifting. That essence was blurring through him.

For a moment, as she stood there, watching him, she had a different question: Was he progressing?

Rob would be the first one of them to find a way to progress. He had been chasing knowledge and power because of that understanding for as long as she had known him, and she fully expected Rob to find a way to move past the limitations they had already uncovered and find a new path for himself. And if he did, what would that mean?

Would it mean that he would be changed into something of essence itself?

They had long believed the final form of progression would be dragon form, and in that case, it would mean that they would have the essence and be able to blur and blend into it, the same way that Arowend had.

But as far as they knew, Arowend hadn't actually progressed; he had simply taken on essence memories and was able to manifest them. This felt different.

And as she watched, she couldn't help but feel like she was losing Rob.

She didn't want to lose him. She wanted to do anything that she could to pull him back, to help him, but maybe that wasn't what Rob wanted. She knew that if she were to push here and try something he didn't want from her, he would probably be angry with her. He would believe that whatever he was doing was necessary for whatever they thought they would have to face, and he might be right about that. She didn't know what they were dealing with nor the extent of the threat, but she did believe that there was something more, and until they fully understood it and were able to overpower it, she would have to find a way to move past that and help Rob in whatever way he wanted.

"What do you think?" she asked, glancing over to her father, who was standing over her shoulder.

"The tower warned me that you're needed," he said.

"I might've been needed, but I'm not exactly sure whether this is something that Rob doesn't want. Given everything I've seen from Rob, this could be a progression," she said, filling him in on what she thought about and how she felt about this power. "I don't know, to be honest. I can feel the essence working through him, and... Well, I worry that if I were to try to do anything here, it would disrupt whatever Rob has already accomplished."

"Look at him," Griffin said, getting close and holding one hand above the hilt of his sword. "Do you think this is what he wants? I can see the way the essence is pulling on him."

"You can see it?" Serena asked. That suggested that Griffin was better connected to the unity she had realized, but maybe it shouldn't be all that surprising to her, as her uncle had always been willing to progress. He may not have stepped inside the tower, and he may not have learned what he needed to find a different form, but she had little doubt that her uncle would be able to figure out something, if given enough time.

"I think *all* of us can see it," he said. "It's not unclear. It feels like he's getting torn apart, as if the essence were being ripped free from him. Is that what we want for him?"

"I don't want any of this for him," Serena said. "But I want to help him and allow him to do whatever he thinks he needs to do. I'm willing to help and do whatever I need, so that Rob can be what he needs to be."

And that's what it came down to, didn't it? She had to

step back and not be so afraid of what Rob wanted. She needed to give him a chance to be what he was supposed to be.

She could not intervene.

"This is dangerous," Tessatha said, near the doorway. "I can feel it. I can see traces of it. There are other essences here," she said, stepping forward and using a long, metallic rod to trace a symbol on the ground, before stepping around Rob and making a few other symbols on the ground near him. When she finished the circuit around Rob, she looked up, then pressed a bit of her essence through those markings. Serena had never seen Tessatha using power like that. It reminded her of some of the ancient power.

Had Tessatha been withholding something from her?

Serena doubted that was the case and thought Tessatha was simply using some aspect of her power that was different than what she'd done before, to the point where Tessatha was not trying to hide something so much as she was trying to use aspect that she had not necessarily needed to use before. Or maybe some aspect of power had been discovered. Serena certainly had enough of the librarians working around the realm, trying to find something in the ancient memories that might help them. Tessatha was a scholar, so she didn't necessarily need the librarians as Serena did. She might have had her own way of finding information, her own way of uncovering everything that existed, and her own way of restoring lost memories.

"Look at this," she said, and she jabbed the pole, pointing to Rob. "You can see at least three other tracings of unity within him. Each of them is distinct, which suggests that he has bonded to others."

"Three others?" Serena asked.

She had known that he had connected to Alyssa's unity, so at least one other wasn't nearly surprising to her, but knowing that he had managed to connect to more?

Was that the problem? Had he bonded to this power too soon? Maybe Rob had pushed too hard. That wouldn't be terribly surprising to learn, as this was Rob, after all.

"There are three others," she said, before she paused for a moment. "And perhaps a fifth, but it seems to fluctuate," she said." Can you see it?"

Serena shook her head. "I don't see anything."

"It's this room," Tessatha said; she swept her gaze up the walls before turning her attention to Rob again. He looked pained, his face filled with anguish, but there was something else about him.

He was a manifestation, at least wherever he had gone.

And the fact that he had lingered in this form, and it didn't have any awareness of what they were doing around him, suggested that wherever he'd gone, possessed great power.

He had extended so much of himself that he had pushed beyond the boundaries of what they were able to do. Serena had never manifested quite so potently before.

And maybe Rob hadn't chosen to. After all, he had come into this room and had been drawn, she suspected. There was the power of the unity here, enough so that Serena could feel it flowing around her, and she suspected that Rob had been drawn by it. If she were to manifest, she had a distinct sense that the unity here would draw her upward, probably like it had drawn Rob upward.

Maybe that's why she felt the unity outside the tower, the way that she did. There had been something pushing on her, something that was pushing on him.

"You think the tower betrayed us?" she asked, looking at Tessatha.

"I think the tower is helping," she said slowly, turning to the walls. She used the rod and pushed some of her essences into the walls. A series of markings on the wall began to glow. They started slowly, then one after another, each marking continued to intensify, growing with more vibrancy than they had before. She frowned at that, but then her father stepped over the wall, joining Tessatha, and he traced other markings, letting them glow just as well. "If you feel this, you can tell where the tower is offering its influence. I can't say anything more than that, but it seems to me that the tower is trying to help us somehow. Perhaps… Well, perhaps the tower is trying to help Rob in some way. I can't tell."

Was the tower holding him here? Or maybe the tower had allowed him to manifest, but now there was another power working against him.

She had been called here.

"Help me," she said, calling out to the tower.

She waited, she knew the tower had some way of connecting to her, but the tower hadn't spoken to her directly in a while.

It had spoken to her father instead.

"Help me," she said again.

There was no answer.

Her father stepped over to the wall; he traced his fingers along it, running them slowly and steadily along the surface until he paused, glancing over her shoulder at Serena. "I can feel pressure here. Whatever the tower is doing, it is helping but failing. I think that is why you were called here."

"*You* called me here," Serena said.

"I called because I could feel the tower's urgency. I think I was the closest one."

"Where is Arowend?" Tessatha asked.

Serena frowned.

If Rob were here, in this manifestation, she would've expected that Arowend would also be here. Hadn't they been traveling together lately, especially as they'd been searching for answers, trying to understand the heralds, and the power this other entity wanted from them?

"He was here," Serena's father said. "He went with Rob. Actually, I think he went before Rob."

Tessatha covered her mouth, and she gasped.

"No."

They all turned to her.

"What is it?"

"If he went," she started, looking up toward the ceiling. Serena followed the direction of her gaze while also feeling the power of the unity flowing, so she understood the implication.

Arowend had gone before Rob?

Arowend was the essence.

If the unity propelled him out, then it was entirely

possible that Arowend had been scattered. And if that were the case, then what might've happened to him? Where would he have gone?

The only answer was an obvious one.

Rob had gone after Arowend.

And now Rob couldn't return.

Serena paced around the inside of the tower, focusing on the energy that she felt there. The tower had called her, which meant that the tower wanted her help because the tower believed that Rob needed something from her.

She had a unity connection but also a connection to Rob, didn't she?

And this close, she thought she might be able to use that connection, borrow from the conduit, and perhaps even offer him something he did not have otherwise.

Maybe she could help Rob and drag him back. The more she thought about it, the more certain Serena was that this was the key.

She stepped through the ring of markings Tessatha had made and neared Rob. Some aspect of it was familiar, and it obviously was the unity from this realm, but some aspect of it was unfamiliar. Though it was, Serena tried not to let that bother her, and tried not to let that keep her from getting closer to Rob, where she needed to be. She focused on what he needed, on the power that she knew he required of her, and she held her hand out, feeling for that power and something that she thought she might offer to Rob. The more she moved closer to him, the more she began to feel power, but it wasn't the power that she needed.

Instead, she needed to focus on the conduit, that

connection, and the energy that she knew Rob had. She needed to focus on what they shared together. And so, she opened herself to that, borrowing from the energy that was around her, the power of the unity that flowed through the tower, and through the realm, to the point where she could feel all of it bursting into her, and she sent it bubbling through that conduit.

His essence started to fortify.

Some of the strangeness that was pulling apart began to ease, to the point where though that power was swirling around him, and though there was no familiarity of power that was working its way around him, she could see that he was withdrawing, that some part of the strange connection that was attempting to rip him apart had begun to fade and change, and that some part of her Rob began to return.

It was a strange thing for her to be aware of, a stranger still that she could feel, but it came through the conduit. But the conduit wasn't a one-way conduit.

She could feel what Rob was experiencing.

And she could feel some part of him that was threatened, the way that power was trying to strain and pull and...

And bulge.

There were parts of it that seemed as if they were exploding.

Every so often, that explosion would strain against Rob, and these other essences would push, and seem to pull him back together. As she added more of the unity around her into that conduit, she began to feel some part of Rob beginning to recover. The more she did, the more she recognized that whatever she was doing was helping.

Then she felt another surge.

This was stronger than the others.

It was unity, but it was a strange form of unity, coming from some part of Rob she had not known before. It bulged against her, foreign and painful, as it attempted to shred him in a way Serena could barely hold onto.

Some other external entity helped hold him together. She was adding what she could through the conduit, but she began to wonder if it was going to be enough. But as that other entity began to add its own form to it, and helped Rob, Serena recognized it.

It was Arowend.

That power was coming through, and Arowend was offering something more than he had before, to the point where Serena could feel everything he was doing and getting, and…

It was going to be too much.

Tessatha seemed to recognize it. Serena didn't know why, or how, but she must have felt something from Serena, the fear that she had through her own connection to Serena, and she stepped forward, winking to Serena through the dragon mind connection, and she poured her own unity outward.

Serena could feel some part of Tessatha going through that conduit.

"You're giving too much," Serena said.

"Not too much," Tessatha said through gritted teeth.

"Tessatha," a voice said, coming through that conduit, though it seemed unfamiliar.

It was Arowend, but he was using Rob, using his connection, to try to reach her.

"I'm here," Tessatha said.

"Tessatha," he said, again.

"I'm here," she said.

And then, Tessatha did something that Serena had never experienced. She pushed essence through Serena, manifesting how Rob had often manifested through the conduit, but in this case, it felt as if the tower propelled Tessatha, pushing her, and carrying her beyond.

At the same time, she felt a pulsating of power.

And then something gave way.

Serena had been yanking on that power, trying to pull it toward her, and until it gave way, she wasn't sure what she was doing, and she didn't know if she would even be able to drag Rob back to safety, but as she pulled, she recognized that it was working, and that he came back to her.

And then she collapsed.

Chapter Twenty

SERENA

Serena came around slowly.

Strange energy flowed around her. She worried that she'd lost some part of the unity. She opened her eyes and sat up. She was still inside the tower, and the symbols around the walls were just as she had remembered, even though there was now an energy that hadn't been before. It was almost as if the tower itself were trying to protect them.

She focused on unity, and was thankful she still had that connection. There was still something that was drifting from them, some aspect of that unity that was fading, but increasingly, Serena could feel it easing until it was no longer pressing outward with as much force as it had before.

"Easy," Griffin said, kneeling next to her. She could feel his hands running along her arms, checking her for injuries, but that wasn't where she would've been injured. She had been thrown back. She remembered what she was doing and the power that she was holding onto, as it flowed into her. She didn't know if it was a burst of the essence, this other entity that had slammed into her, but she knew that it was more potent than anything she'd ever felt before.

"Rob?"

"He's here," Griffin said. "Unconscious, but here."

Serena tried to sit up, but her uncle was holding her back, trying to keep her from moving. She shook him off. She was drawing upon the unity, and so it was easier for her to do that, knowing that she had the power within her to push Griffin away, though she was also careful not to push too hard. This was her uncle, after all, and she didn't want to harm him.

"What happened?" she asked.

Griffin propped her up, and for a moment, he looked over at her, before turning his attention to where Rob lay in the middle of the room.

He looked fine.

That was all that Serena could say about it because she wasn't entirely sure if he was healthy or injured in a way, but at the same time, he didn't look as if he were suffering in any sort of way. He looked…

Fine.

She focused on her essence and on the connection that she had with Rob, and as she did, she began to realize that he had unity, at least the kind of unity that she had, but there was something else within it that she had felt when she was within the conduit. She was tempted to focus on the conduit and try to go through it, thinking that maybe she would find some answers in it, but even as she attempted to do so, she realized that there was a danger in it. She might harm Rob, and given that he had already been attacked in some way, her main focus was keeping him safe.

So, she struggled to her feet and looked around the room.

Tessatha lay crumpled along the opposite wall.

"What happened to her?" she asked, nodding to Tessatha.

"I don't know," her father said. "She came over to you, and then I felt something potent. I've been trying to make sense of it, but the tower isn't helping in this case."

"She manifested," Serena said." I felt it. I don't know what's happening, but I felt… Well, I felt something. I think that it's tied to whatever it was that Tessatha did to help Arowend."

At the time, Serena had recognized how she was pushing the power out and had recognized just what Tessatha was attempting to do because she didn't want to lose Arowend. She had manifested, sending so much of herself through the conduit that it was a danger. Serena knew it was a danger and felt Tessatha's uncertainty, but she also recognized something more.

She recognized that there was a part of Tessatha that was willing to do it, almost eager to flow through the conduit and help Arowend.

"Is he back?" she asked, looking over to Griffin.

"I don't know," Griffin said. "I was waiting on you to check him."

"You didn't go and check yourself?"

"I figured that there was only so much that I'd be able

to do. And besides, the tower didn't want me to get that close," Griffin said, glancing up at the ceiling. "Each time we tried to get closer to him, I felt the tower pushing against me, as if the tower were irritated that I'd even try." He grunted, and then shook his head, laughing softly. "Maybe it's more my imagination than anything else, but I can't help but feel like the tower is a bit of a bully," he said, raising his voice a little bit as he did. "Not wanting others to get close to their favorites."

Serena rolled her eyes at her uncle.

"I'm not so sure that Rob is their favorite," Serena said, as she strode forward.

She focused on the unity around her and slid through Tessatha's markings on the ground, crouching next to Rob. Griffin stayed behind her, and she could feel the essence coming from her uncle, as if he were waiting, willing to give her something.

She traced her hands along Rob's face, pushing his dark hair back from his brow, while turning his head from side to side, trying to detect anything that might happen to him. She could feel the power and something odd, but she wasn't sure what it was.

He had been drawing upon essence, a unity different from what she possessed here. And it was holding him intact, but for how much longer? Serena couldn't help but wonder if the unity he'd been drawing upon might've changed something for him, and perhaps it would've made it so that he wasn't strong enough for what they would have to face. Or perhaps now that he had linked the unity, binding this realm to other realms, he may have changed the essence around them so that none of them could use it.

She tried not to think about the consequences of it, but it was difficult for her to look past it and think of anything other than the challenges that Rob might have given them.

All because he thought he knew better.

She let out a heavy sigh and then focused on the conduit.

"Rob," she said, pushing through the conduit, trying to connect to him. "I need you to wake up."

She felt an awareness in his mind, but that was about it. There was some sense of him there, but whatever she felt was faint enough that though she was trying to reach for it, and trying to make sense of it, she didn't know what more there was that she could do.

She wasn't a healer. Essence could heal, she suspected, but she didn't know what to do with the essence to help Rob. In the past, when she did that, she used her connection to others to help her. Sometimes it had been her mother; other times, it had been Maggie or even Tessatha. And at this point, Serena wasn't even sure if any of them could help her with Rob, as the injury he sustained was considerable.

There was another person she thought could help, but where was he?

She looked around. "Arowend?" Serena asked.

"He's not here," Griffin said.

"But he was there. I felt him. Whatever was happening, Arowend was holding Rob together in a way that had bound him, and I think Arowend was the reason Rob survived."

It was a strange thing to acknowledge, but then again, this was Arowend, and increasingly, Serena began to question if she had read Arowend wrong.

"He didn't return," Griffin said. "Maybe he's still out there, and trying to return? To be honest, I don't know if Rob has really returned, but I can feel that some part of this unity essence is not pulling upon him in the same way as it had been before, so I do think that whatever you did for Rob, and in this place, seemed to be enough." He looked around, before settling his gaze on Tessatha for a long moment. "But I don't know."

Serena wished she had an answer. She wished she understood, but she didn't have any answers even as she tried to make sense of what happened here and the power there was. Tessatha had helped, Arowend had helped, and...

What had she done?

She helped pull Rob back, but even as she did, she felt as if some part of him had left her, remaining distant. She could feel the essence within him. There was that connection to the unity, and that part of him that was still bonded to who he was, and to the tower, and to this realm, but there were other parts of it that were different, parts that she could feel, parts that she knew, and parts that left her thinking that whatever answers she might be able to uncover, were beyond her comprehension. Serena needed to understand it better and know what more she could do, but even as she focused on it, she came up with no answers.

But they were there.

She sat next to Rob, holding onto his hand.

Griffin settled beside her.

"What if he's gone?" she asked, looking over at her uncle. "What if we can't pull him back?"

"Then we have to go on," Griffin said. "That's what Rob would want, isn't it?"

"I don't know," Serena said, as her bottom lip trembled. "I know that... Well, I know that Rob would've told us to keep fighting, and to try to find a way to progress, and we would do whatever we could to gain the knowledge and the power that we need for us to do those things, but how can I go on without him leading?"

"He's not gone," Griffin said. "At least, he's not gone yet. Do what you can to help him."

"I don't know if I can do anything to help him. I feel something, but his essence is different now. There's some part of him that's changed, some that has shifted beyond my comprehension. I can feel that he's bonded to this other unity, and I don't know what to make of it, nor do I know what that means for us."

"For *us*, or the two of you?"

Serena smiled to herself. "To us, as a realm. And to us, as a couple."

"Are you a couple now?" her father interrupted, from the far side of the room. He was still crouching next to Tessatha, pressing a series of markings along the wall. Serena wasn't sure what he was doing, only that it seemed like he was trying to activate unity essence in a way that might be helpful to Tessatha.

Maybe it would help draw her back. If she had gone

through the conduit and manifested in a way that Rob had, it was possible that she was with Arowend, and he was holding her together the way he did for Rob. And if so, perhaps it was for the best that they had not returned. And maybe the tower could help her and Arowend, the way it had helped Rob.

"I don't know what we are," Serena said. "We've not had an opportunity to try to figure that out. We've always been too busy."

"You can never be too busy for love."

He looked at Tessatha, and Serena smiled slightly.

Maybe that was a lesson that she should have taken from Tessatha.

Tessatha and Arowend had an impossible romance. Arowend had died. Tessatha had been frozen in time by the brambles. And somehow, they had survived. It might look different than before, but they had pulled through it, and now the two of them were…

Well, Serena wasn't even sure what the two of them were anymore, as she didn't know what happened to Tessatha, and whether there was any way for her to pull her back. What she did know, however, was that Tessatha had been willing to fight, and she was willing to do whatever it took to help Arowend. Wasn't that love?

What would Serena do on behalf of Rob?

She didn't know. Would she sacrifice herself the way Tessatha did? There were limits to her capabilities. Everything had limits.

But the essence was so different, especially the essence that had worked for Tessatha and Arowend and everything they experienced throughout their lives.

Maybe Tessatha had known that there was no way she was going to suffer. Maybe she had already understood what she had done, what she was willing to do, and how she was willing to press herself outward.

Maybe there wasn't an answer.

Perhaps that was the key, as Serena simply didn't know. The only thing that she knew was that she needed to help Rob.

She squeezed his hands.

She focused on the conduit. It was her only option to help Rob. She continued to probe through that conduit, letting the connection flow to her, and began to feel the unity she recognized within him. She had to follow *that* unity. The unity from the tower between Rob and her seemed to have one certain frequency. She focused on that.

That was one component of Rob.

But even as she focused, she knew there were other aspects here. There were other trembling powers within Rob. So, she needed to probe through those, to try to make sense of it, so that she could feel the kind of essence that worked within him. All she needed was an edge to uncover one additional aspect.

She'd been to Alyssa's realm. She recognized that essence, didn't she?

And there was that part within him. Serena knew that it was there, and she knew that all she had to do was find it, follow it, and flow with it, and then she would understand more about who and what Rob had become.

Then she felt it.

It was as if she were stepping off to one side, and she

could feel some part of herself different and distant, but that other part of her gave her understanding, and she was able to feel that bit of Rob. It was different, but it was also unique and familiar.

She stepped to the other side, and once again, she felt another sort of essence.

Now that she understood what she needed to do, she continued to move, following that sense, and shifting from one place to another, as she attempted to draw upon more of it. Each time she moved, she felt some other bit of power within her.

And she thought she needed to draw upon that other bit of power.

Then she felt something else. It was deeper, settled inside the core of Rob. This was unfamiliar — and familiar.

Serena only recognized it because she had felt it was trying to push against him and rip him apart. It was there now, settled deep inside of Rob, and it seemed as if it were pushing, bulging, and trying to disrupt.

She wanted to scoop it out, but that wasn't what she needed to do.

This other essence. That was the key.

She had to blend it.

How, though? Serena didn't feel as if she were strong enough to do that.

But she didn't have to be. The tower was.

And so, she focused on the unity around her, the unity inside her, and the essence within Rob, and she pushed.

Chapter Twenty-One

AROWEND

AROWEND FELT DISCONNECTED.

He'd been fighting for so long, trying to hold onto Rob's form, that he lost track of his own form. The battle had raged for far longer than he'd ever experienced before, to the point where Arowend was no longer sure he could save himself. And maybe that was the point of all of this. He came out here, attempting to try to make amends for what he'd done, knowing that it was going to be difficult for him to do. He came knowing he was the only person capable of making this journey. And when he left, he knew there was a possibility that he might not return. It had been terrifying, but he had done so with a firm resolution, something that had settled inside of him, as if his own essence had come to terms with what he was willing to offer himself and the sacrifice he would make.

Then he felt Tessatha.

That shook him.

Tessatha had always shaken him. Memories of her filled him. The very first time, he had seen her, a young scholar at the university, working with her unique form of essence and pouring over a stack of books. Arowend was almost afraid to approach her, but he had done so because he wanted to understand her essence and know what she was studying. He had been so isolated at that time. He didn't know his essence very well, but well enough to have been accepted into the university, where he could continue learning how to master and manipulate ice. There were others from all the realms who had different forms of the essence and could use them in ways that allowed them to control great power.

He approached her tentatively, holding onto his essence that was balled up tightly within him, afraid.

She looked up and smiled at him.

There was something disarming about her smile that melted the cold within him. He sank down into a chair across from her before he even knew what he was doing. They started talking, and from that day on, they never stopped talking.

He hadn't thought of Tessatha in that way in a long time. Why now? Some part of him blended and blurred, some part of him strained and stretched, and some part of him… was coming apart.

Arowend had felt that before.

Back when he has ripped apart while fighting on behalf of his people, trying to help them, and essentially having been told that he was not wanted.

Why wasn't he wanted?

Arowend had fought, wanting to help his people and

his land, and attempted to do everything possible to achieve this.

But they didn't want him.

He pushed those thoughts aside.

He was Arowend.

Wasn't he?

But in this form, with this pain, and there was pain, he felt like the Netheral.

Rage built within him. Arowend was aware of that rage, which had helped hold him together for centuries. And it had been centuries.

He felt that rage, and it bubbled up within him.

He attempted to hold onto his power, holding onto himself, but every time that he tried to do so, he could feel some part of him getting torn free, ripped apart, to the point where he could no longer hold onto who and what he was. Arowend struggled and strained, trying to be that person, trying to be something more, but every time he strained for that power, he could feel something working against him, and he felt as if he were getting separated into smaller and smaller pieces. Why wasn't Rob helping?

That thought lingered.

Hadn't Arowend been willing to sacrifice on behalf of Rob? He had stretched and pushed everything in himself to offer Rob the benefit, to hold him together when his manifestation was failing, but Rob wasn't doing the same thing for him.

Some faint and distant part of himself told him that Rob could not, that he had connected too much power, that he had been the reason that they had an opportunity to escape in the first place, but all he knew was the pain of separation, and the memory of what he had lost. Arowend — the Netheral — could feel it; he could feel the way he was getting stripped apart.

And it hurt.

Pain raged within him.

Power rage within him.

And power meant that he could pull himself together.

Wasn't that what he wanted to do? Wasn't that what he needed to be?

If he could call upon that power and find a way to draw it through himself, Arowend could find a way to overcome the pain, and be the one responsible for it. With enough rage and power, Arowend — the Netheral — knew that he could overwhelm those who wanted to destroy him.

And he *would* destroy them.

He would rip through them the same way that he was ripped through.

That power pulsed within him, the power he had known for centuries, which had left him living in a way that was not living.

He roared, but there was no one there to hear him roaring.

He tried to explode power, but he felt something pressing against him.

What was it?

Why was there power trying to work against him?

Arowend—the Netheral — would fight through that, destroying it the same way that he would destroy Rob, helping him. Then he would return and rip through everything and everyone else, doing whatever it took to get his vengeance. He had been stripped free of his power, life, and love. He had been stripped free of everything that he was supposed to be.

And he would have vengeance.

Then he began to feel another essence.

The Netheral pressed against it.

But that essence touched him. There was a warmth. And within that word came a familiarity.

The Netheral raged.

He knew what was happening. It was another type of essence trying to harm him, the same type of essence that had always tried to harm him. If he let it get too close, it would find its way to weasel through him, and it would eventually succeed, tearing the last vestiges of essence free from him until he was nothing.

He had survived by holding together, holding onto himself, and he would do so now. So, he battled.

That touch came again. It was faint, but it was there.

Once again, Arowend battled, trying to rage against that sense of essence and ignore the power that was touching upon him, knowing that he wanted nothing to do with what was out there, trying to reach for him. Arowend knew that essence was struggling against him, and he struggled with it. That touch seemed soothing, but it was a false soothing, he knew. He had already felt it, and he knew what would happen to him if he let them soothe him into nothingness. They would tear him apart, tear everything apart, and separate him from all he had been.

They would separate him from Tessatha.

That touch came again. Now it was stronger. It seemed closer, as well.

There was a warmth within it… and something familiar.

For a moment, Arowend tried to lash out, but now the essence that came at him was even more potent than before, to the point where Arowend wasn't even sure he could counter it as he had. He tried, but he felt some part of it working against him, some part of it trying to struggle with him, and straining against everything he had done. That essence was potent.

The essence strained against him in a way that Arowend couldn't counter.

He bulged, but that touch soothed him again.

And then he heard his name.

Not the Netheral.

No. That had become his name, but it was not his name.

He was Arowend.

He strained, struggling with that power, and tried to bulge against it once again, but even as he did, he felt some part of him countered and resisted.

More than that, some part of him knew that he should not fight.

He was the Netheral, but he was Arowend.

He was both.

He was the Netheral when he was separated, the Netheral when he had been filled with rage, but that rage was still a part of him. He was Arowend through it all.

He heard his name again.

There was that touch of essence again, and it slithered toward him, sliding into him, and blended with him.

And it was familiar. It was comforting. It was home.

"Tessatha?"

That essence continued to swirl, flowing through him, and though Arowend could feel it working, he wasn't sure that there was anything that he could do to counter it, and he wasn't even sure if there was any way that he wanted to try to counter it. He wanted to let his connection with Tessatha fill him, as that power built within him, coming to him in a way that left him feeling like he might be able to draw upon something more. Arowend could feel that, and he let it fill him.

"This is dangerous," he said, awareness surging into him.

Gradually, that warmth continued to build, pulling some part of him back. He wasn't sure what it was doing, nor how it was working, only that he could feel that essence constricting.

But it wasn't just her essence that was constricting. She was holding onto his essence, pulling some part of him back, and tying him together.

Tessatha was helping.

She was doing what Rob should have been doing.

As he thought of that, Arowend became aware of another type of essence.

There was that foreign essence that had been bulging within Rob, and Arowend had been looping around Rob, trying to hold him together, but with a startled connection to Rob, Arowend realized that Rob had been doing more than he had known. Rob had been sending out his own form of unity, trying to link to Arowend and add some of that connection, gifting it in a way that was meant to hold Arowend together just as well as Arowend had been trying to help Rob. They had been swirling around each other, essence around essence, power around power, as they blended and blurred their power, until…

Until Tessatha.

"There you are," she said.

He could feel her. It was a manifestation, no different than how Rob had manifested, but she was here so strongly that he worried for her. He could still feel that foreign entity pressing upon him, but he recognized that whatever was happening, whatever that foreign entity had done, and whatever Rob had done by linking to it, had lost some of its efficacy.

"What did you do?"

"I came to you," she said.

And he *could* feel her. It was so different from what he had felt from her before. Arowend had been an essence memory, and Tessatha had been real. That had created barriers between them that neither of them had wanted, but they had known they would deal with. They had to if they wanted to be together. Arowend had learned to solidify his essence and try to manifest more fully, but there were still limits to what he was able to do.

But Tessatha…

Tessatha could manifest at any time, and she had, but it was not the same.

This felt different.

It felt more real in a way that he had not felt with her in so long.

He wanted to cry, but he wasn't sure that such a thing was possible in this form.

"You're sacrificing yourself," he said, realizing the consequences of what she had done. He could feel her essence and the way it was pulling. He could feel how she'd sacrificed for this manifestation. It wasn't dissimilar to how Rob had done it, though he had the distinct awareness that Tessatha had done so intentionally, knowing how much she had given and its consequences.

"You needed me," she said. "I could feel what was happening. I knew you wouldn't be able to return unless I came."

"Tessatha," he said, and their essence blurred and blended.

For a moment, that was all they were. A mixture of the essence, but then they came apart. He could feel her, and she could feel him.

"We have to get you back."

"Not yet," she said. He felt what she was doing, but he wasn't sure what it was.

It was almost as if she were calling upon some aspect of the essence, trying to draw it deeper. As he focused on what she was doing, he realized the reason. She was summoning more of his essence.

When she said he was almost lost, he hadn't realized how close he had come. He was slowly being torn apart. And maybe it was happening far longer than he had realized, perhaps even longer than Rob had realized, as Arowend had been disconnected from the tower for longer than Rob had been. And Arowend didn't have the same advantage of linking to the tower, blending his own essence, in the way that Rob had.

What could he do differently now?

Nothing but wait for Tessatha.

And she was helping. He could feel what she was doing and how she was calling his essence back together, pulling him back together, and allowing him to be Arowend, not the Netheral.

Distantly, Arowend began to wonder what that meant for Tessatha, and what would happen to her as she continued to push some sense of power out from herself, gifting it to him. Would she be altered in some way that would leave her incapacitated, or would she be able to recover from this?

Arowend simply didn't know, as he couldn't tell from what he could feel, only that there was this emptiness he had been feeling before he began to detect the way Tessatha was trying to call him back together.

He felt himself, and over time, he began to feel some part of himself coming back together, stretching and straining, drawing back into a sense of something more, something that suggested to him that he could be more, but how was that possible for him? Arowend wasn't sure how to make sense of it.

"Tessatha," he said, calling out to her. He knew that he needed to reach her, in some way, but as he attempted to do so, he couldn't feel anything other than the strange sort of emptiness that he knew. "Tessatha."

Each time he called out her name, he thought he could connect something more to her, and he might be able to bridge a bit more of that bonded connection to her, and...

And he had hoped that he would find something there that he could use, but unfortunately, as Arowend continued to reach out to Tessatha, he felt an emptiness and an absence of her.

There had to be something there for her, but as Arowend attempted to find it, he couldn't feel what he knew to be there.

Then warmth flooded into him again.

At first, he wasn't sure what it was. Essence, possibly. There was certainly some bit of essence that was there, but he didn't know what it was, nor did he know why he could feel it so profoundly. But then he began to feel some part of a familiar form of essence that he had always known or seemingly had always known.

Tessatha.

He spoke her name again, using essence this time, but it was not just his own essence that he was using to reach out to her. He was using the kind of essence that he could feel between the two of them, which seemed as if it were bridging who and what they had been, a connection that had formed between them.

And it was a connection. Arowend could feel the bond that was there, but more than that, he could feel that they were meant to be together.

Tessatha.

He breathed out her name, even though he had no breath. He spoke it with essence, with every bit of his being. And slowly, far too slowly for Arowend's preference, he began to feel some part of her coming back to him. He began to recognize that she was there, and, more than that, he began to feel her emotion drawing toward him.

Then he called on her once more. He needed to find something that would help him understand what happened to her, but he also needed to try to find a way to link the essence that she had filled him with, something that would grant him an understanding, and perhaps the ability to do something more with that power. Arowend had to connect; pulling on that essence was the only way to do that.

As he did, he began to feel Tessatha. This time, it was he who held her together.

He realized that she had pushed so much of herself outward that she had exposed her manifestation to danger, and more than that, she had nearly lost a part of herself. Because Arowend was there, and because he was pushing out with that power, he gave her the opportunity to come back together.

And that was what she needed. He pulled, feeling the sense of Tessatha and everything that she was, everything she could be, and everything he wanted for her, flowing back into her. And as he did, he felt the connection between their form and recognized something more about it.

Though the connection between them formed, something that seemed to be the essence, he also recognized that a connection failed her. She had lost one, and Arowend feared what it meant for her.

How much had she just sacrificed?

Chapter Twenty-Two

ROB

Rob opened his eyes slowly.

He felt strange but wasn't sure why. A power pressed on him, but it was unfamiliar. He felt unity, the same kind that he felt when he first went to the nexus, but now there were other powers linked to him.

As his memories returned, he gasped, and understanding and awareness of what he'd done and why he'd done it came to him. He had bonded essence to try to create enough power that they might overwhelm the danger they had encountered and push back the Dragon. Rob had succeeded, or so he thought, but at what cost?

He had used that essence, linking some part of it to himself, in such a way that he wasn't even sure if there would be any way for him to expel that essence from himself. And at this point, he wasn't even sure he *wanted* to expel it.

As he tried to connect to his essence and the other essence around him, he realized there were at least five distinct types of linked unity inside himself. It reminded him somewhat of how he had linked to the different realms in his land, and yet, unlike then, when he didn't have any control over those essences, now he felt as if he had some measure of control, even if he wasn't sure how he could use that power.

And as they blurred together, he felt the changing. It was the same thing that had happened before and had been happening in his realm. And Arowend had been there, helping Rob...

Arowend.

He looked up, but he wasn't sure where he was. Everything was dim, though he felt the unity around him.

Arowend had been there with me.

What had happened to him?

"Easy," a voice said.

Was it a voice, or was it a dragon mind connection?

Considering the last place he'd been was the other realm, surrounded by the Dragon and that power, he was concerned about what it might do and how it might attack him.

"Rob," a voice said.

He blinked to clear his vision. There was essence, but not all of it was familiar to him. Some felt strange and foreign, leaving Rob wondering if he could control it—or if it would overwhelm him.

"Easy, Rob," the voice said, and now he recognized it.

"Serena," he said.

Hands touched him again, but Rob couldn't see, though he could feel her. Now that she was close to him, he was much more aware of her essence. The conduit should help him understand what more had happened. Rob used that conduit, but the lack of familiarity with the essence made it difficult when he attempted it.

"Something's wrong," he said.

"I know," Serena said.

He sensed that she was moving around him, though he wasn't sure how he had that sense. Eventually, he realized it seemed to come from the essence she was radiating.

"I had to work with the essence inside of you. I wasn't sure what I was doing, but there are several other forms of unity, I believe, inside of you."

"I had to link to them," Rob said, and he explained what he did, sharing with her how they had traveled using the towers and the unity to explore beyond.

"That was dangerous," she said.

"I know," he answered, and he did. He could feel something about it, but he could feel that there had been little choice in the matter, as increasingly, he felt as if he had needed to try to make sense of it. He had to know.

"When you returned, you were having a hard time," she said. "And there was a different kind of essence within you, seemingly rebelling against everything you were doing. I had a hard time trying to combat that."

"I think it's this *other*," Rob said.

"That's what my father suggested, as well," Serena said, and she took both his hands. When she did, there was a surge of power that came from her.

Rob recognized an aspect of unity but also that whatever she was pushing through him was different. It was unique enough to hold onto it, and he felt that familiarity, anchoring himself to his realm. It helped him find something familiar about himself, and his power. Gradually, he managed to find that energy, and used it to help guide him back. Doing so cleared something for him. He could see again, and he saw Serena watching him.

Was that worry in her eyes?

Her golden hair was pulled back, and her face looked bruised. What had she been doing in his absence?

"What happened to you?"

"Oh, nothing," she said. "But I'm glad to see you, as well. What happened?"

"I called on the local essence," Rob said. "Maybe I wouldn't have known about the local essence, and how that flows, had I not detected these other unity essences."

"Perhaps," she agreed. "And I'm not going to tell you that you made a mistake, but I think it was. You and Arowend…"

She trailed off as she mentioned Arowend, and Rob heard the hiccup of a note in her voice, and he realized that something was wrong, and that Serena wasn't going to tell him unless he pushed.

"What is it?"

"I don't know what happened to him," she said.

"He's not back?"

Rob would've expected that Arowend would have returned just as quickly as he had, as the two of them had been linked together. More than that, Arowend had been holding Rob together. Then again, Rob remembered how Arowend had started to separate, and how he might have lost some part of himself, to the point where

Rob would've needed to do something more to help with Arowend.

"He didn't return. And Tessatha..."

"What happened to Tessatha?" He started to sit up.

Serena took a deep breath and fixed Rob with a hard stare. "Tessatha went after him. She manifested, but now it seems her connection to her body is tenuous. I don't know what to make of it. And my father thinks she might not survive it."

Rob was quiet. They had known that manifesting carried certain dangers, but the idea that they might manifest and risk sending too much of themselves beyond, had always been more of a theoretical possibility, not something that Rob actually expected would happen.

And Tessatha...

Tessatha had so much more experience than them and knew how to control her essence in ways Rob was still working with. It came from her long and vast experience with essence, but more than that, it came from her connection to Arowend, and how much he had shared with her.

"We have to help them," Rob said.

"I agree," she said, "but there's something else you need to know. When you returned, there was another essence here. I had to push on it. It changed something, but I don't know what it was."

"My unity," Rob said. He sat up and looked around.

He didn't recognize the room they were in, though it seemed to have a certain amount of power to it. Maybe they were still in the tower? He wondered how long he was unconscious, but something through his connection to Serena told him the answer anyway.

Days.

Days that he'd been out. Days that Tessatha and Arowend had been missing. Days that the Dragon had an opportunity to continue to push, knowing that Rob had begun to link to essences.

He slowly got to his feet, stretching. His muscles were sore, and part of it seemed to come from the fact that his own connection essence was different than it had once been. Some part of him was different, as well.

He had to come to terms with this newfound unity.

He had connected to those powers, linking to them. It should strengthen him, but maybe first he had to bring them together, blending them the same way as he had once blended the different powers of his realm.

He didn't know what that might be like, or how he could even do it.

Rob turned his attention inward, finding his own connection to unity the way that he had once connected to ice when he was trying to find the other powers of his realm. And he realized that he didn't need to blend them, as this was blending on its own, which he already knew.

Having connected to Alyssa's realm, Rob had started feeling that change in his own unity here. Could he separate them out again if it were necessary?

"Rob?" Serena asked.

"I can just feel what's happening," he said, and he explained to her what he had observed. "I suspect it's the same thing you've detected all around the realm. Unfortunately, I'm not sure what to make of it."

He looked up. The room was smallish, with a low ceiling, a single door along one wall, and no windows. There was just a bed and a basin of water. Nothing else. It was almost as if this was as sparse and stark as possible. He could still feel the unity around him, though.

"I've been trying to make sense of what we're dealing with," Serena said. "Because everything seems to be tied to this essence, right?"

"As far as we can tell," Rob said.

"And were it not for the tower, we wouldn't necessarily feel the unity similarly. At least, I wouldn't necessarily feel the unity similarly. You, on the other hand, have a different means of doing so."

"Mine is tied to the nexus," Rob said.

"Exactly," Serena said, as if she'd been waiting for him to say that. "And I haven't been able to reach it. At least, not recently. I think there are answers there, but I don't know how we could find them without going together."

"You can only reach it by manifesting," Rob said.

"Then let's manifest. I know it may be dangerous for you, and that you've just recovered, but I don't know how much time we have, Rob."

Rob felt for the conduit. As he did, he recognized something. Serena had been holding something from him.

Something that she had detected. The presence. It was powerful.

And it was moving.

He manifested.

Rob wasn't even sure how that would feel, but when he was manifested, it seemed almost easier for him to gather these other essences together, and he separated from himself, hovering. Through the conduit, a connection that seemed to be more potent now that he was manifested, he called to Serena, who joined him in the manifestation. He carried her downward and toward the nexus.

It was a different sensation going in this manner than it had been when he had first found it. But reaching it, finding that chamber, and stepping free, Rob felt the reassurance that he had Serena with him. She immediately began to look at the walls, as if testing for something.

"What is it?"

"It's this place," Serena said, looking over at him. "Can you see it?"

"I don't really see much here," Rob said.

There was still very little of that energy, just enough that Rob was aware of it there, but even as he focused on what he could detect, he didn't know if there was some part of it that he was supposed to be able to identify. Perhaps that came from the fact that he was manifesting with a different type of unity essence than he had before.

"Maybe it's just me, then."

"What is it, then?"

"There are markings here, Rob. Markings like the tower. Markings like inside that room in the tower. All of this is connected." Serena looked around. "And I don't have any idea why."

Chapter Twenty-Three

SERENA

Serena could feel something around her, something, unlike anything she'd ever experienced before. Ever since the tower gifted her knowledge, she had known about the types of patterns, but she couldn't read them. There was something about this place and this essence, even though it was only residual, and not there in full, that Serena thought she needed to make sense of. She had been struggling with it ever since she stayed at Rob's side, waiting for him to regain consciousness. She tested the type of essence that flowed inside him, without clearly understanding what she had done when she forced that other type of unity into him.

But now she was left with different questions. Some ancient entities had marked this place. They had stored the unity.

Rob looked at her, as she walked up and ran her fingers along the etchings on the wall.

"The symbols here, I suspect, were designed to pull

essence down here and store it. I don't know if that's something dangerous, or perhaps intentional, but...." She frowned, and she looked around again. Without having an opportunity or time to study, she wasn't sure that she was going to be able to know. "I just can't tell you, Rob. I don't know what to make of these markings, nor do I know how to read them well enough to be able to tell you anything about them."

Rob was standing at the edge of what looked like a pit, and given what he had described of the unity, and the nexus himself, she suspected that the pit once contained the power that he somehow pushed out into the realm.

"I've been aware of the drawing of unity from the very beginning," Rob said softly. "It's always felt like it was coming from this place, but when I was in the other realms, I felt as if that unity was drawn upward. I could still feel it, though it seemed to have slowed a little bit. There is a pulsation to it."

Serena frowned. She felt something similar, though she hadn't thought about why or how she felt that power. The only thing she knew was the power was there, and there was some part of it that she thought she could follow. But then again, it was that part that Rob actually followed.

"So, we have some ancient that called power downward until you arrived?"

"And until I reached the nexus, we didn't have any trouble with this other entity. That must be significant, as well."

"Oh, Rob. You can't blame yourself for this."

Rob was quiet for a moment, and she felt for the conduit, trying to make sense of what he was dealing with, and whether there was anything she could say or do that would help Rob find his way, but unfortunately, she couldn't tell. There was an emptiness.

"I'm not so sure that I can't," he finally said. "Think about it. We know what Arowend and Tessatha were involved in, and we know what these others were doing, and how they must have known that there was some other danger. It's because of them that the land is shattered again. But if it hadn't been shattered, Arowend and Tessatha likely would've found the nexus, and likely would've called power here, and... Well, they may have started this long before us. So, it waited until I got here. And then..."

"And then you chased this power," she said.

"I wasn't chasing power for the sake of power," Rob said.

She smiled.

"I know you weren't, but you still chased it."

She was right. He *had* been chasing power, trying to understand progression, and perhaps not fully understanding everything they were potentially involved in. And without that, there was the real possibility that he had advanced too quickly, the very same thing that so many others had warned him about, pushing himself and his people into a danger that they were not fully equipped for.

And maybe they never could be equipped for it. The others that had come before them had a different kind of power and understanding, than Rob. He was fully aware of that power and everything they were capable of doing, and he recognized that he could feel some part of that draw on him.

Could he have been used?

She knew Rob wouldn't like the idea that he might've been used, but what if something had pushed him in this way? Maybe this other entity knew there was a nexus and could not reach it without additional help. And knowing that Rob would take the action he did, this entity might have drawn him into something that Rob couldn't handle otherwise.

"We can study the symbols," Serena said to him. "And if we give it time, we can uncover what happened here. I'm confident that with enough time —"

"I don't think that we have time," Rob interrupted.

He turned to her, and stood on the precipice of the pit, leaving Serena a little nervous that Rob might simply fall into it. "I can feel it. I don't know how, and maybe it's just that I'm somehow now connected to this other entity because I've linked to this other essence, but I don't know that we can wait. There is more power here. It's pushing and building and coming for us. It's inevitable."

There was a weariness to Rob that she hadn't felt before. It came through the conduit and the tone of his words.

He was tired.

And he should be. Rob had been fighting from the moment she met him. From that first time, he had been going after power, trying to become something more, trying to make sense of something more. Everything he did was about fighting, straining, and struggling, and he scarcely rested.

How could he not be tired?

She had to support him. Because if she didn't, Rob might be unable to do this.

Maybe he wouldn't be able to do it, anyway. She didn't know what they were dealing with, much like Rob, but they could either shatter their gains and return their realms to what they once were or plunge ahead and hope they find something greater.

Her mother would've shattered the realms. Maybe even her grandfather.

The mistakes of the past could not be the mistakes of the present, because they would make mistakes for the future. How much had they lost as they tried not to progress and learn? How much had her people suffered unnecessarily?

Bonds had never been formed that could have been. People had never interacted, or known each other, the way that they should have. Essence had been neglected, and people thought they had to struggle to access it in ways they would not have.

No. Serena could not sit idly by and wait. She had to do something, only she wasn't entirely sure what that something was going to be, only that she had to help Rob do it.

"We can do this," she said.

"I don't know if I can," Rob said. "I feel the linked essence, but because of it, I can feel something else out there. It's bigger than me. Stronger than me. And it knows its essence better than me."

"Haven't you felt that before?"

"This is different," Rob said softly.

"Then we can find answers."

"How?"

The answer was obvious.

"Think of everything that you've done in the time that you were here, Rob. What key features set you apart from this other entity, and others who came before you? What do you think makes you unique?"

"I don't know. My drive to progress?"

She chuckled.

"If it was only about that, then I suspect there would have been others who would have been able to find essence and find a way to progress, before you did. It can't be only about progression. It must be about more."

"Then what is it?"

"Your desire for connections."

She felt like that was the obvious answer, as it was the one thing that had separated Rob from so many others. It separated Rob from her mother. It was what had made Serena care so much about Rob, because she knew Rob was willing to fight for others and help lift others up when he was trying to make that journey. He wasn't holding others down so that he could progress. He wanted everybody to progress along with him.

"And we can use those connections now. In fact, I think that we have to."

"I don't know if those connections are strong enough."

"Not if we use them the way that you've been. It's not about strength, is it? That's perhaps our gap, but —"

"Perhaps?"

"I don't know if it is or not," Serena said. "As I don't know because we're missing knowledge that I think will make a difference for us. If we have an opportunity to push, we might uncover something more to help us. Even if it's just understanding."

She closed her eyes for a moment, and she connected to the librarians.

There wasn't just one anymore. Now there were many, and she could feel them. It was almost as if some part of the unity had bonded her to them even better, bridging her to that power, and so when she summoned them, she felt the librarians respond. Power burst into existence as all of them manifested.

Serena looked over to Rob for a moment, who was frowning at the librarians there. "You called us, Mistress?"

One of the librarians stepped forward and smiled at her, which Serena found amusing, as she still didn't know what to make of them. They were manifestations, but she didn't have a sense that they were the same sort of manifestation that Arowend was, nor were they even the same sort of manifestation that Eleanor was. They were power and reflections, essence memories. But they seemed to be interrelated and interconnected. More than that, she was left wondering if perhaps these were left intentionally. Maybe the ancients had known that the people who followed after them would need some means of accessing power, and had left the librarians, for them to have a way of connecting to the power that existed out in their world.

"I need to know what you've learned," Serena said. "Because we've now found another place of markings."

She motioned to the nexus, and the librarians turned as one, before she felt a stirring of essence flowing between them. It was unusual for her to detect, as she was completely aware of the way that the essence was working, but she couldn't tell what they were doing, nor was she aware of how they were using it, only that it flowed between them, jumping from one librarian to the next. They were speaking to each other, she thought. And the way they were doing, it left her with a vague feeling of confusion, partly because she couldn't help but feel that power was far more potent than she thought they were capable of. "We know that these are similar to the markings found within the tower, and we know that the power in the tower is connected to the nexus."

"I have found something about that," one of the librarians said, looking at Serena. "There have been ancient markings found all throughout your realm."

"Which part of the realm?" Serena said.

"All of them," he said. "Many of them are on lost structures. The essence memories are hard to parse, but finding places of learning and essence memories there has allowed us to draw upon some of those memories. We have begun to find more and more of those memories and more of those markings. I suspect that we can unearth even more if we have time."

"We don't have time," Rob said.

One of the librarians turned to him and bowed his head.

"Understandable, master, but I'm afraid this is slow

work. We've recognized that there is an ancient entity that was here before all." He stepped forward and looked down into the nexus. "At least, an ancient power. Then something began to change. I'm not entirely sure what it was, only that we have begun to piece together snippets of information. Thanks to the mistress, we've been able to uncover any of it at all, because she was gifted by so much of it from the tower itself. Without that, I don't know if we could find anything more."

"What we need is time," Serena said.

"And it's the one thing we don't have," Rob said. "Because of me. If I had waited to push through the tower and follow the unity, maybe we would've had more time."

She wasn't accustomed to Rob sounding or acting like this. She wasn't accustomed to this sort of malaise from him, but then again, she couldn't imagine everything that he'd been through, and how he was injured in the process.

And adding to that was the possibility that he recognized that Arowend was still missing, and Tessatha was missing, and that they might never return. How many more would be lost?

When they had fought against the Netheral, Serena had agonized over how many people they had lost. With each challenge they dealt with, the risk to people increased. That was what her ancestors had feared, she suspected. And it left her wondering if maybe they were right. Could that be what her mother and even her grandfather thought?

Dangerous thoughts.

Those were the kind of thoughts that meant that they would stay ignorant and powerless, and they were the kind of thoughts that meant that her people would continue to suffer, and struggle, and would never be able to find a way to progress, advance, and find the power that they needed. If they waited and did nothing, this other entity would come. She had seen the effect of the heralds and the subheralds, what they were willing to do to the essence, and how they would siphon it off. All because they were there to fuel this other entity?

But it had to be about more than just fueling this other entity.

It had to be about something more.

Progression?

If it was about progression, at a certain point, progression did not involve essence.

At least, that had been her experience, there was always some aspect of essence that had been important, some blurring and blending of it that had been necessary for her to gain a measure of understanding and control and to find her way to more power, but power wasn't the only thing that progression required.

Knowledge.

Maybe the other entity was after a way of stealing the knowledge of different realms and using it for their own purposes. If there were something in this realm that would help provide them with information about it, then they would know what they needed to do. The heralds hadn't helped Rob other than to reveal their fear of this other entity.

And why wouldn't there be something here?

If she believed that the nexus was formed artificially, and she did. She believed that the tower was connected to it, a storehouse for that power, which she did, and if the librarians were right that these ancients had provided them with other markings that would help them understand the power that was scattered throughout the realm, then why shouldn't she go to the source?

"We need to return to the tower," Serena said.

Rob looked over to her, a deep frown furrowing his brow. "There's nothing in the tower for us. It's just a point of power."

"It is, but it's connected in a way that other things are not. Think about that, Rob. Connected. The same thing that you have always done. I know that you're blaming yourself. But it wasn't until you came and linked the powers that we succeeded at progression. You awoke essence that had long been lost."

"And it wasn't until then that I began to attract the attention of this other."

"Perhaps we would've always drawn that attention. If the ancients knew about this, and knew what was out there, and if these ancients were as powerful as we believe them to be," Serena went on, sweeping her gaze around the inside of this chamber, and feeling as if there was obviously something here that would help them, if only they had an opportunity to draw upon it, "then don't you think the ancients left more for us? I think that the tower itself is the key."

"We were just in the tower," Rob said.

"We were in one part of it. I think it's time for us to return to the chamber you were summoned to."

Chapter Twenty-Four

ROB

Rob stood inside the room in the tower, feeling the strange energy all around him. He had felt this the last time he was here with Arowend, but with him gone, Rob was now left with an emptiness. Maybe he should share this with Serena, so that she understood why he was struggling, because Rob was definitely struggling. It was not just that he missed Arowend, but he felt responsible for what happened to him. Arowend had gone because Rob had suggested it. And now, if Arowend was lost, it was because of Rob.

How many times would Arowend have to suffer because of others?

Rob looked over to Serena, who was staring up at the walls. The librarians were also surveying the walls, though Rob wasn't sure what to make of them. She had summoned six librarians, though he knew from experience that she could summon even more. He didn't know what she thought she might accomplish as she summoned them, only that there seemed to be something to the librarians and how they were analyzing everything here.

Maybe Serena had a point, though.

Could it be that everything was tied to a connection? Rob certainly knew that he had formed connections, and those connections had been pivotal for everything that they had accomplished, but at the same time, Rob was left wondering whether there was going to be any other way for him to master those connections.

"I don't feel anything here," he said.

Serena glanced in his direction. "Why do you think that you should?"

"Well, last time I was here, I felt something from the tower. Essence, at least. And in this case, I don't feel it quite as potently as I did before. It was pulling on me."

"Maybe because you've linked something," Serena said.

"I linked it but didn't link it to this land," he said.

"It's possible," one of the librarians interrupted, without turning, "that you've become some sort of nexus for this land yourself, Master. You were the one to free that power, and you're the one who has connected to things in ways that we do not fully understand." Only then did he turn to Rob. "You're the only one who has progressed how you have. Your levels are different from other levels. Perhaps that's the key."

Could it be?

There was certainly no doubt in Rob's mind that he had done something to the essence, and he had somehow changed it, but even in doing so, Rob wasn't sure what that meant, nor was he sure how he had managed to bridge it, only that he must've done something.

The essence here was changing.

And…

And as he focused on his own essence, he felt some part of the tower begin to shift. The tower was little more than a manifestation. They had known that from the very beginning, and now he could feel some part of that construct changing.

The tower had not yet started changing, but if it did, maybe he could link to it the same way that Serena had. That would help him understand it. He had a conduit and a connection to her, and she had one to the tower.

Rob may not have the natural essence that had formed the tower the same way that Serena, Tessatha, and Arowend had. So far, Rob knew that they were the only ones who had progressed by going through the tower though Rob believed that there were others who could do that, if only they were willing to take the risk. And it was a risk. But he could connect to the tower itself if he used the connection he made.

Once again, he was reminded of how Serena was sometimes smarter than him.

Sometimes?

He would have laughed to himself if it wasn't so obvious. Serena was usually smarter than him. Connections might be the key.

And if they were going to be able to defeat the Dragon — or even just hold it back — then he may need to use those connections in ways that he had never even fathomed before. He was going to have to use connections to search, so he connected to Serena, before feeling for her link to the tower.

It was bright and potent, but also seemed to tether her in place.

"Help us," Rob said.

He spoke through essence and through his unity, though his unity had changed. Every passing moment made it feel like that unity was blurring even more, blending in a way Rob couldn't quite control as he felt that essence within him; he pushed it outward.

And the tower responded.

The tower had never truly responded to him before, because he had never truly needed to.

But then, Rob was the one who added the nexus to the realm, and because of that, he had to think that he had offered this realm something more, a possibility that had not existed before. And now Rob thought that he might be able to find it, and to make sense of it.

The tower loomed inside his awareness.

Rob focused on it, and as before, he could feel some part of that essence surging, something that was building in a way that linked with him and gave him another sense of understanding.

"Help us," Rob said again.

There was still no answer.

Serena watched him. She didn't say anything, but then again, Serena didn't need to say anything for him to understand what she was thinking. Serena had given him the technique. Connections.

He pressed outward, pushing down and focusing on what he could feel of the tower and the connection the tower possessed. This tower was linked to the realm, and into the strange and unique places that had once been testing zones, places that had helped him and the others find a way to progress and understand their power. The more he connected to those places, the stronger his link to the tower became.

Rob had visited those places. He had felt their power. He had used that essence.

He could blend them and force this unity.

But Rob wanted connections, and he didn't want power.

There was a stirring.

There was no other way to describe it other than that. Rob could feel that stirring from the tower and realized that it might provide him with answers.

"Help us," he said again.

Much like the last time, he felt an emptiness.

He pushed and began to feel something changing, essence building and bridging to him, the power now lurching inside of him.

He focused on the tower again.

"Help us," he said again.

Rob pushed again, drawing upon the unity he had forged and the connections he had made, as he continued to strain outward. Some of them were tenuous, as there were two forms of that unity that were not nearly as strong as the others, and then he reached that fifth form, one that threatened to overwhelm him at times, but Rob could feel it there, nonetheless.

Only then did something bloom inside of him. It was a blurring, but then again, the essence had been blurring inside of him for quite some time. Rob tried to make sense of that blurring. He continued to push, struggling with it, and hoping that he might find something more, but even as he did, that energy and essence didn't link to him the way that he wanted to.

"Help us," Rob said.

This time, he felt the tower.

There was no other way to describe it. The tower had changed. Rob had already started to suspect that, as he could feel some part of the tower differently, but he wasn't entirely sure what it was.

Now, as the tower opened to him, it seemed as if it were trying to share with him that there was something more Rob might be able to uncover.

"Help us," he said again.

"You do not need help," the tower said.

Rob froze.

It was a strange, booming voice, filled with power. It was more than just unity; maybe it was a blurring.

"Help me understand," Rob said. "You're a construct?"

He wanted answers, but he also wanted to ensure he wasn't offending the tower, as if it were more than just a construct. Rob knew that he was going to have to be careful with what he said, and how he implied the changes that were there.

"I am a creation."

"A creation of the nexus?"

There was a pause, and in that pause, Rob became aware of Serena's reaching through him, connecting to him through the conduit. She wanted to be there and understand the same way that Rob wanted to understand.

"I am a creation," the tower said again.

"What about the nexus?" Serena asked; an image appeared, which came from her mind, one that carried the patterns within the nexus and patterns within the tower. The fact that she could form those in her mind was a marvel, partly because Rob had a hard time focusing on those patterns on his own, let alone trying to force an image through to the Dragon.

"The nexus was created to protect this realm," the tower said.

"What about this other entity?" Rob asked.

There was a moment of pause, much like there had been each time. And he realized the reason behind it. He hadn't pushed any sort of image through the same way that Serena had. Rob didn't have the ability even to form one, as he never saw the Dragon. But maybe he didn't have to see the Dragon for him to push through something that would help this tower construct explain to them what they were dealing with, and what they faced before. So, he began to focus on feelings. It was power, but then he thought about the heralds and the subheralds, and he used the ones trapped in his realm, along with those he had faced, and everything he had experienced. He sent them as a surge of emotion mixed with essence, but it was more than just that.

He could feel something. He thought of the essence of the Dragon. Rob thought that was going to be the key to all of this, if only he could make sense of it.

"It is ancient," the tower said.

"We know it was ancient," Serena said, her voice more soothing, though it carried power.

She projected another image of symbols scattered on the wall. Was she using them in a specific pattern?

Rob couldn't tell. Maybe that was all that she was doing, but maybe there was something more to it. Maybe she was drawing on the tower itself.

But the tower's essence was changing, and Rob didn't think they could use any part of that changed essence for her to focus on the power that she needed.

"What we need to understand is what purpose it has. Why is it trying to come for us?"

"It consumes," the tower said.

Rob could feel Serena. And then again, he also knew that the Dragon consumed. He had seen it himself. He showed Serena and the tower a series of images. It started with Alyssa's realm, and then he moved on to what he had seen in the other places, how that power had been stripped away. There was only a hint of unity, but nothing more than that. It had consumed.

That was what the heralds and the subheralds were after. They wanted to help the Dragon find that power so that it could consume.

"Why does it do this?" Serena asked.

"To progress."

Rob held Serena's gaze for a moment. "We knew that," he mouthed to her.

"We know it, but there has to be something more to it than just progression, Rob. Progression can't just be about power."

"Maybe it is," Rob said.

"But why?"

Rob realized that the question was not just for him, but it was for the tower, as well. And it was one that he shared. What reason would the Dragon have for continuing to gain power? Maybe it wanted to progress, but maybe it was about more than just progression. The real question that Rob didn't have an answer to was about what would happen if he were to progress next.

He had long thought that it was dragon form. But what was that? The ability to take on any shape? That was simply essence. And he had seen those with that power. He had helped them find their power and purpose. Arowend and Eleanor and several others had.

So, it couldn't just be a dragon form.

"There has to be more," Rob said, agreeing with Serena. "It must be about finding a different kind of power. What is it? What are we dealing with, and how are we going to be able to stop it?"

"There is no stopping," the tower said.

"There has to be something," Serena said. "What does it want?"

That was the real question, Rob knew. And maybe if they found what it wanted, maybe they could finally come to terms with a way of slowing it. But it wanted essence, didn't it?

Rob had seen it, and had felt it, and had known that. When he had been connected to it, however briefly he was, he had felt the way that essence had bulged, and it was powerful. He had no idea how many different unity essences it connected, nor did he know what it would do if it targeted him again, only that he had felt that power, and insufficient near it.

"It wants to move beyond."

The tower fell silent.

Rob frowned, and he turned to Serena. "Move beyond?"

Serena was quiet, and her expression was solemn.

Rob couldn't tell what was bothering her, but he could tell something was bothering her. "Serena?"

Serena let out a heavy sigh, and though he could feel she attempted to reach for the tower again, he also detected that she did not manage to do so. The tower seemed to have given all that it could. And given that the tower was connected not only to Rob's essence, along with the others, but also seemed to have been connected to the Dragon, maybe it was prevented from sharing anything more. The fact that it had shared this much, at least, was helpful.

"What is it? What do you think it wants? It has to be about more than just essence."

"The tower said it wanted to move beyond," Serena said. She looked up, before turning her attention back to Rob. "We've been trying to make sense of these writings, and something Tessatha said to me makes sense now. There have always been markings here that alluded to something powerful. We thought they were the ancients, but what if it was beyond the ancients?"

"What's beyond the ancients?" Rob asked.

"What else could it be? The tower means it wants the power of the gods."

Chapter Twenty-Five

ROB

THERE WAS A FAMILIAR PULL OF ESSENCE ON ROB. Something bulged against him, and Rob strained to hold onto that essence, trying to exclude himself from it. There was a limit, though. He feared that he had reached it.

Serena watched him.

"What do we do?"

"I don't know," he said. "I can feel... well, I can feel the unity, and I can feel this power bulging against us, but I guess I don't know."

"You know what we're talking about," she said. "We're talking about this other entity trying to become something greater."

Rob shrugged.

"Isn't that what we've been talking about all along, though? What have we been doing but trying to progress and become something more?"

"This is more than just trying to progress," Serena said. "This is about trying to become a god."

The idea sounded impossible, but so too did so many of the other things he'd been dealing with. How could it not? But at the same time, Rob also wondered if perhaps this was what they needed to do, try to understand whether there was going to be any way that they could control and overpower it. This other essence seemed so significant and vast that Rob had to believe it was close to succeeding.

And if it were close to succeeding, what would happen if they were to permit it to gain even more power? What would it do then?

Serena watched him. "I've seen that look in your eye before," she said.

"There's no look," Rob said.

She snorted.

"There's definitely a look. And I see it in your eyes. You're starting to think about what would happen if *you* were to have that power."

"Actually, I wasn't, but now I am. Can you imagine what it would be like if we were to progress that much and have that kind of power?"

He had never considered the possibility of becoming some sort of deity, but if he were to continue to progress, wouldn't he eventually reach a point where others viewed him as something along those lines?

When he was younger, his people had long believed that the dragons were some sort of sacred entity, something impossible even to comprehend, because, in Rob's mind, they had been. Now that he knew about the dragons, or at least knew about what they believed of them, Rob couldn't help but feel as if what he had seen and experienced, and everything he knew of them, was wrong.

But his people had dragon skulls. As he thought about it, he had to believe that those were forgeries. Some way that somebody had created something for his people to celebrate and worship.

What of the essence?

When he was younger, he believed that essence was tied to dragon tears, or perhaps blood, that had spilled into the ground, allowing others to connect to it. And maybe it was. It seemed hard to believe that much, but there were so many strange things that he had encountered, that it was possible.

"You're right," he said, looking over to Serena. "None of this makes any sense. But I do wonder what would happen if the Dragon were to gain that power."

Serena looked up at the tower. The walls around them glowed, and it wasn't until Rob realized that she was putting some essence into it that he understood why. She was gifting some part of herself to the tower, or perhaps the tower itself was trying to connect to her in some way; either way, it was building some connection, bridging it in a way that was seemingly designed to call upon the energy that was all around them.

"I have a feeling that the tower, and those who came before us, did not want that."

"Well?" Rob asked. When Serena arched a brow at him, he shrugged. "Why don't you ask the tower? You have a different connection to it than I do. You are far better bonded to the tower."

"It won't matter," Serena said. "But we can't let this other win."

"What would happen?" Rob asked.

"All would fall," a voice said from all around him.

It was the tower, but it spoke aloud, rather than through the dragon-mind connection. This caught Rob by surprise.

"What do you mean all would fall?" Rob asked.

"All would fall," the tower said again, though he noticed that there was some sort of resistance coming from the tower, as if the tower were struggling in some manner.

It's the Dragon.

It was trying to push and keep the tower from sharing something.

And if it succeeded…

Rob didn't know what would happen, but he did feel like he had to try something.

"Let me help," he said, pushing his essence upward, trying to connect to what he felt around him. He wasn't sure what was there, nor was he sure about what he could do, only that he thought that he needed to add more of himself to it, so that he could stabilize the essence.

A strange, rumbling energy flowed through him.

"What will be lost?" Rob asked.

"Everything," the tower said.

And a series of images formed.

Rob saw lands — realms — scattered. There were dozens of them. Dozens upon dozens. Some of them were mountainous, some looked as if they had once been vast and open plains, and some looked as if they were deserts. All of them reminded him of various aspects of his realms. And all of them having been drained of power.

He felt others, some that were familiar, including those that had linked to him, and there were still others beyond that. Rob did not know how many of those of the realms there were, and he did not know whether there was anything that he would be able to do to save them, but what he saw — and what he felt — was an extensive connection of power, something that was beyond anything that he had even considered.

Those images flashed in his mind so quickly, leaving him seared, as if some power ripped through him until they were no more. Even then, Rob struggled with it.

"Did you see that?" Serena asked.

Rob nodded.

"That's what's going to happen here."

Rob shook his head.

"No. That's what's going to happen everywhere."

Every land would be ripped apart. That power would be stripped free. It would be given to the Dragon.

And then what?

The idea that the Dragon wanted that kind of power, that it was willing to strip it away, leaving them with nothing, left Rob wondering whether there was anything he could even do.

"How can we stop this?" Serena asked.

Rob allowed himself to focus on the power, wondering if there was any way that he might be able to do anything. And he turned his attention to the tower, posing that question to the construct of the essence, wondering if the tower would know anything.

"You must oppose it," the tower said.

Rob started to laugh.

Serena shot him an annoyed look, but she also frowned. "How are we supposed to stop this entity that has grown so powerful?"

"You must do what you do," the tower said. Now the voice was going fainter, and as it did, Rob tried to push some of his own essences into it, wanting to stabilize it again, but it wasn't working as he had hoped.

"You want us to link to this power," Rob said.

"You must find a way."

The tower flickered, and Rob realized what was happening.

Unity was getting drawn, pulled on the tower, and making it so the tower didn't have nearly the same connection that it normally did. It was draining, and it was fading.

The pressure continued to build.

Given his previous experience, Rob feared the source of it. And he worried about how it was drawing on the unity now.

"What do you suggest?" Serena asked.

"Well," he began, "I think we need to find a way to make additional connections; there are too many places out there. And to be honest, I have no idea how to do it without having somebody there to hold me together. With Arowend missing...."

"You've linked to these other places, though. Shouldn't that be enough?"

He looked up. The answers weren't here. The answers were beyond.

And the only way to understand that was to use the tower. As he let essence flow from him into the tower, the symbols began to illuminate, bursting with light. That didn't come from him, though.

Rob turned, and he realized that it wasn't Serena. It was the librarians. They were activating different symbols around them.

"This seems to summon some of that power," one of the librarians said.

Rob felt it when the tower lurched.

A shape took hold. Then Arowend stood in front of him. And so did Tessatha.

But they were different. At least, Tessatha was different, though Rob wasn't exactly sure what it was at first. It took a moment for him to realize that she was somehow disconnected from her physical form.

A wave of essence flooded through him.

It came from Arowend and Tessatha at the same time. It was a blended sort of essence, as if they were working together, and he understood what had happened.

"Are you sure?" Rob asked.

"We are. This needed to happen. We don't have much time," they both said, connecting to him uniquely. "We must act quickly."

Rob turned to Serena. "Did you feel it?"

"Only through you, and only vaguely, and I don't

know what it is that's happening, but I have a sense that whatever it is might be dangerous. Do we have to be concerned about it?"

Rob breathed out. He could feel what was happening, and even though he wasn't sure whether they were going to be able to succeed, he understood.

Arowend and Tessatha were nearly ripped apart, and they saved each other. They had blended their essence in a certain way. It was a connection.

And in some ways, it was similar to how Rob had formed connections; only what happened to them was unique in the way that it had linked them, binding them in a way that had built some power together. Rob wondered if he and Serena could do that, but then again, it would take separation from their bodies.

What he had seen and felt from them suggested that a significant power was coming, the Dragon, and it was building. Rob had managed to catch a glimpse of that power, but he sensed that there was *more*.

He hurriedly shared with Arowend what he had found in the tower.

"How can we stop it?" Serena asked.

"There's only one way," Arowend said.

"We have to link," Serena said.

"I think so," Arowend agreed. "But doing so is going to be difficult." He looked at Rob. "Do you think that you are connected enough that you'll be able to withstand this attack and whatever it is that it tries to bring to you?"

Rob had to believe that he could, and he had to think that there was going to be some way for him to be able to handle it, but increasingly, he wasn't sure if such a thing would even be possible. He could feel that power, and he was left wondering if maybe it was going to be more than what he had.

"I have to try."

He looked at the others. "I would like to have more time to prepare, but I don't know that we have it."

"You won't be alone," Arowend said.

"You can't do this," Rob said. "The last time you did—"

"Last time I did, I was alone. This time I will have Tessatha with me."

"You should return to your body," Serena said.

"There is no return," Tessatha said. "And this is what I'm supposed to do. This is the way that I'm supposed to be. I was not a part of it before. I can be, now."

"How?" Rob asked.

"I think the only way is what you've done in the past," Arowend said. "And I start to wonder if perhaps you had it right all along. You have wanted to form connections, as it holds you in place, and it binds you together, binding the realm, and everything that you've ever done. That is what you need to do now, I suspect."

How could Rob use that, though?

Rob had a unity connection, but would it be enough?

He looked at the others. "We can try. All of us. But I need you to stay here," he said, looking at Serena. "I need you to provide me with a focus. A way back."

"Rob…"

Rob shook his head. If he were to do this, and if he were to fail, he had no desire to have Serena drawn away.

But if she were to come with him, maybe he would have a way of anchoring to her in some way that would help him. Rob certainly didn't know if that was going to be enough, if anything that he tried would be enough for what was happening, nor if there was going to be the kind of power that he needed to draw upon for him to bring that energy back. But he thought that he was right. If he were to do this, and if he were to lose Serena, he would never forgive himself.

But then, it may not even matter if he were to fail. The Dragon and that other power would escape, and there would be too much beyond that Rob couldn't work with, and too much that would be lost. As much as he wanted to combat what was there, and that power, he may not be able to.

He nodded to Arowend, and then he manifested.

He felt as if he had just recently returned, and felt as if doing so now, separating this way, and feeling this power escaping from him, was far too dangerous, but at the same time, what choice did he have but to keep trying? Rob felt as if he needed to push beyond and let some part of himself escape to find a way to counter. If he could link more and find a way to master more, he could defeat the Dragon.

Or at least he could delay it until they had a chance to understand.

He turned to Serena, having manifested in this chamber where it felt as if some part of himself was completely separated. If he failed, he would be the essence. If he failed, he suspected that he would be drained, and that some part of him would drift off into the nothingness, leaving him separated.

"Hold onto me," Rob said. "Use everybody. We need everyone here."

"And if it doesn't work?"

"If it doesn't work, then there is no stopping this."

There was an inevitability to it. If they were dealing with some creature that wanted power to the point that it was going to devastate everything, to try to ascend to some sort of godlike power, then there may not be anything more that they would be able to do anyway.

Rob had no idea what he would do if this worked. He had no idea how he would use this essence if he succeeded, but he had to try.

Arowend swirled around him.

And then it seemed as if Arowend swirled into him.

It was odd, but it was also familiar. He had known Arowend from all the linking they had done, so Rob understood his essence and how he was connected to him. Rob thought that he might even be able to draw upon that in a way that would help him, but it was the power that Arowend was drawing, the way that essence was connecting, that Rob didn't fully understand.

As it flowed, he felt Tessatha's presence, as well. Three of them formed something else.

They bonded to Rob in a certain way. Rob was connected to these other essences, and Serena was there. He felt the tower, he felt the different types of unity, and he felt the Dragon. A certainty of essence is coming his way.

Rob pushed.

The tower pulled him, taking him up, but this time

there was no strain of power like there had been, nothing but the essence of slowing. He didn't feel ripped apart. At first, he thought it was because the tower was somehow helping, but he realized that it was tied to what Arowend was doing, how he held Rob together, bridging him in some way that kept him from getting shredded.

It happened rapidly.

And Rob went with it at first, but he remembered something. The tower had shown him something.

Follow the flow, but let the flow move him, guide him, and find a way to help the others.

"There are other places," he began, and he sent that knowledge through to Arowend, but realized that he didn't need to. In this manifested form, and connected as he was to Arowend, Rob could feel everything, and had his knowledge, and it seemed as if he had Arowend and Tessatha's knowledge.

They were essence.

He had never felt Arowend quite like this before. There were times when Rob worried that Arowend was little more than a memory, but that wasn't it at all.

Arowend was the essence.

And though he was, he still could be more.

"How do we find it?" Arowend asked.

"The tower," Tessatha said.

Her voice whispered softly in Rob's essence connection, but he heard it. He knew. He could see her in his mind, as if she were formed there, connecting to him in a way she would bridge to him.

They started toward one of the other realms. They passed beyond the boundary of what he had connected to, and Rob began to feel pressure. It was foreign, but there was definitely a unity sense out there. Rob immediately latched onto it, pulling it to him. In the past, when he had pulled up on the unity, he struggled to pull it down and hold onto it in a way that would hold him together, but in this case, Rob didn't struggle with it nearly as much as he had before. Arowend and Tessatha working with him, helped Rob to hold onto it.

They kept moving.

And he felt propelled. It was almost as if the memory that the tower had given him, the essence surges that he had seen, and shown him something more.

He was pushed again.

They found another place. Once again, Rob felt that drawing and used the unity, linking it to him.

Arowend and Tessatha helped solidify it. Each time Rob did it, he felt some part of his essence changing. Some part of himself was changing. The unity was sliding through him but was also blurring and blending, becoming something very different from what it had been before. Rob strained to hold onto it, struggling to make sense of what he felt, but he could not tell what it was.

And then he felt a shuddering of power.

Arowend and Tessatha surged, holding onto Rob, keeping him together in this manifested form. They sacrifice parts of themselves, but they hold him.

"There are more," Rob said.

And he could feel them, distantly—many more. The memory of what he'd seen from the tower showed in his mind, and all he needed was to reach for those other places, that other unity, those other realms.

But he couldn't.

This other power was coming.

And it was powerful. Rob had felt some part of that power before, but he'd never experienced it to its fullest extent. Even now, as he did, he wasn't sure that he had ever felt anything quite like it before. There was a vast and enormous sense of energy. It seemed impossibly large.

An image formed, and Rob recognized the source of it, realizing that it came from the Dragon as it gave Rob a vision of what it was and the power it possessed. A dragon mind connection, but one so powerful and vast that Rob could not refuse it. It showed him power. So, much power, more than Rob could even fathom.

A godlike power.

And it was terrifying.

Arowend and Tessatha held onto Rob, swirling around him, trying to hold him in place, but Rob wasn't even sure if that was going to be enough. He could feel that essence, the way that was building, and the effect as it continued to squeeze down on him, attempting to rip him apart.

It was the same thing Arowend had done to the heralds.

Even though Arowend and Tessatha were there with him, he feared it would work. He had come, but he was unprepared.

Rob was not enough. How could he stop a god?

Chapter Twenty-Six

ROB

Rob struggled with the power that was bearing down upon him.

Connected to him, he could feel Arowend and Tessatha having the same difficulty, but their difficulty was different. They had a hard time holding together, even though they were trying to maintain this connection. They were bridging Rob to these other essences, helping to hold him together as he struggled to find a way to build some part of the power that existed within himself, but even as he attempted to do so, he could not find a way.

The Dragon pushed.

Rob had felt the Dragon several times now, and each time that he had felt it, he had recognized the way that power was building, and he recognized just how much it was pushing down on him, getting to the point where he could do nothing but strain against it. The Dragon was there, and then…

Then Rob felt it.

It was buried in his mind, some aspect of power, and he felt the strangeness of that building against him, struggling to try to overpower him. This pressure bore down on Rob's mind, attempting to strip essence from him like Arowend did while dealing with the heralds.

Had they given the Dragon the idea?

If it were connected to the heralds the same way Rob was connected to others, such a thing would be possible. That terrified him.

"You have the last connection," the voice said.

Rob didn't even know if it was spoken aloud, or if it came through some link that he shared with it. And maybe he did. He certainly forged a connection through that essence, so regardless of whether he wanted it or not, that connection was there, pressing down upon Rob and bearing onto his mind.

"You will give it to me."

Rob struggled, as he knew that he needed to try to find some way to give it back, but he couldn't do anything other than a struggle, fighting against that power, struggling against the energy that was there, attempting to constrict down into his mind.

"You have what I need."

Somehow, Rob managed to find some way to speak. It was difficult, as he could feel everything within him quaking, struggling with it, but he knew he needed to find a way to move past it.

"Why do you want it?"

All around him was a bleak emptiness.

Rob couldn't tell what it was, only that he felt nothing. The emptiness, that absence of essence, struck him the most. And that's what worried him, as well. That emptiness filled him with worry about what else he might encounter and whether there would be any way for him to battle through this.

"Release it."

"If I release it, you destroy everything I know."

The essence squeezed him.

It had been a long time since Rob felt essence bearing down upon him like that. So long that he had forgotten just how painful it could be. It reminded him of when he had been little more than a dragon forged dealing with the dragon mind and feeling that power as it attempted to constrict around him, working through him as it squeezed.

And this time and in this place, Rob could feel that energy. He felt it squeezed. He felt Tessatha and Arowend being squeezed. He felt everything they felt, the pain they experienced, the terrifying worry that they would be stripped of all they knew.

The essence constricted, drawing down on Rob.

He had to fight, but he didn't know if he would be able to generate enough strength to resist. The Dragon had shown him just how little he was compared to it.

Rob tried to concentrate his essence the way he once had when he fought against dragon minds, pulling that power down inside, but that wasn't going to be enough. He pulled it down into little more than a tight ball but constricting it like wasn't enough and did not change him. Essence continued to build, pressing through him.

It was overwhelming.

And he would be overwhelmed. He would have his essence ripped free.

And once his essence was gone, that of the realms would follow.

The Dragon would succeed.

He felt Arowend and Tessatha pressing through him, giving him a bit of strength, but it wasn't enough. They were no different than him. Powerful, but how could they be powerful enough to stop God?

Rob had known the Dragon was powerful, given that the heralds and the subheralds were willing to fight on its behalf, but he never considered the possibility that it would be this powerful and that what he felt would be this overwhelming. As it began to work through him, Rob struggled. He had to push, didn't he? But how could he, when he felt so much pain, an overwhelming desire to simply let go, abandon everything he was, and give up?

"Save yourself," Rob said, speaking through their connection with Arowend and Tessatha. "I don't know if I can do this."

"You can," Arowend said.

"I can't. I'm not strong enough. I don't have enough power. I don't...."

"Don't let it rip you apart," Arowend said. "Don't let it turn you into what I became. Be stronger. Be *more*."

Rob didn't know how.

It was a simple thing to say that he should be more, that he needed to find some way to do that, but it was much more difficult for him to understand what that was going to entail.

"I can't," Rob said.

Everything within him cried out; everything within him rebelled at what he was feeling, the energy that was there, and the way it was threatening him. Everything within him told him that he couldn't do this. That he was not enough.

Arowend surged, sending some part of himself through that connection, and as he did, Rob became aware of not only Arowend, but also Tessatha.

He felt something from Tessatha.

It was a choice. She had made a connection. She had opened herself to Arowend, and had allowed herself to be connected, to share that connection, to get *lost* in that connection.

And there was a prodding, a hint of a reminder, a bit of something that suggested to Rob that he could do something similar. That he needed to do something similar.

And hadn't he already?

Rob had always been about connections. He had been trying to forge those connections, make those links, understand them, and know what more he might be able to be. He had not lost himself. That was the key here.

That's what Tessatha was trying to tell him. He was still himself, even though he had blended with them and formed some sort of connection.

Rob pulled on that awareness, pulling on his connection to Serena. And he pulled on that connection that he had to his realm. That was going to be the key.

Through it all, he felt the Dragon, this deity, trying to press through him, trying to overwhelm and destroy him.

Rob continued to push. Then he pulled.

It was the same way that essence had flowed for him while working with the unity, both in his realm, and elsewhere. Pushing and pulling. Some of it was given to his land, and some was taken from it.

Rob wasn't fast enough. Power exploded from the Dragon, coming toward him like a darkened storm cloud and surrounding him. He was little more than a small fragment of essence. He, Arowend, and Tessatha.

He had never found the Dragon directly or faced it before, but now Rob felt it. He felt that power, the way it was coming to him, and the energy that he possessed.

The cloud pressed toward him, and Rob resisted, attempting to push against it.

He had essence. That was one thing he possessed, but not nearly in the volume he needed.

He pushed, nonetheless.

If he did not fight, he would fall.

And so, he tried.

Maybe he could find some way to shatter that cloud, disrupting it long enough for him to find a way to overpower it, and claim it for himself. Rob had done something like that before, so why not now? He focused, using the unity essence inside of him, creating a beam of energy and sending it away from him.

It hit the cloud and simply vanished.

He had to try again.

Once again, Rob tried, pushing outward with several different attacks. Near him, he felt Arowend and Tessatha adding to what he was doing, and a burst of incredible power, far greater than anything he had ever sent at one time, went streaking away from him. Rob had drawn it from himself, the essence of the realms, and other places he had linked to.

And the Dragon absorbed.

Again and again, he tried.

Strangely, though, it seemed as if this essence didn't care. It simply waited.

And Rob hesitated. If he continued this course, he was going to give the Dragon exactly what it wanted. Essence. His essence. No. He couldn't do that.

But fighting wasn't going to work.

And Rob knew that he was not enough. Even pulling on the connections he'd formed to the unity essence in the other realms, he still wasn't enough.

Distantly, he felt something tugging at him.

He thought maybe it was Arowend or perhaps Tessatha.

The cloud started to build. It was constricting around him, swallowing him.

It was inevitable.

Rob could do nothing against it.

Distantly, he was aware of that tugging. Was it some part of the unity tower trying to draw upon him? He latched onto it.

Then he felt something through the conduit.

"No," Rob said.

The conduit had connected him to Serena.

Worse, though she was there, she was reaching through, allowing herself exposure to this other essence, and this power; Rob knew that she was going to be in danger. He had to protect her, somehow, but even as he attempted to do so, he could feel the power working against him, pressing on him, and, unfortunately, overwhelming him.

"No," he said again.

But Serena came, and worse, others came. It was as if Serena had linked to everyone that Rob knew.

But shouldn't she have?

She had said the connections were the key.

There was Gregor, storm cloud, Maggie, Serena, and Raolin. There was Griffin, Ashmond, Yoral, and countless others that Rob had worked with over time that he had been training. Boris shone brightly in his mind, as if he were linked to life in a way he had not been before. It had been too long since Rob visited Boris, but their shared connection remained. And there was Eleanor, little more than an essence memory, but in essence, a memory that had solidified and became something greater, no differently than Arowend and Tessatha.

It was throughout the realms. All the realms.

Each of them surged in Rob's mind. Each of them came through, and each of them would get swallowed. But something was different.

The Dragon pressed down. It squeezed, corrupting, building, but somehow Rob and his people pushed back.

The power building on him was inevitable.

They were fighting and had an essence, but they did not have the strength.

Rob tried to fight, trying to ensure his people did not suffer, but he didn't know if it was going to be enough. How could they handle something like this?

He had felt the staggering power of the Dragon.

Even its singular power was more than what Rob and his people possessed.

But did it have to be?

Something was changing.

They were linking together.

Rob had done that to defeat the Netheral in the first place. He had linked with others. He had turned the dragon souls into something more.

Now there were dragon blood, dragon souls, and countless others that were filled with the essence Rob had helped them gain. Everybody around him, everybody that he had connected to, shared in power Rob could summon. Somehow, the cumulative effect of these different types of essence was more than what he could have summoned on his own.

And as he felt that essence pushing and pushing and joining him, Rob reached out. It seemed so simple, but it was surprisingly complicated. As he reached for that power, he sent it sweeping away.

Then he pushed. The cloud was there.

"You don't need to do this," Rob said. "There is a way to be more powerful if you bond to others."

"I will take it all," the Dragon said.

"Why?"

Rob didn't know who spoke through him, but the question came. Was it Maggie? No. It was somebody he hadn't expected.

The dragon queen.

Was she here?

"I will take it all. Then I will remake everything."

"You would destroy to rebuild?" The dragon queen

asked the next question, and this time, Rob felt her through that connection; he began to wonder if she was helping or not.

They had struggled with her so much, but he had also understood.

"It's the only way."

"It's not the only way," Rob said, and he felt as if he were talking to the dragon queen as much as he was talking to the Dragon. And maybe he was.

Power didn't determine everything that they did, but her power was certainly significant. And everything that Rob felt from the dragon queen, every way that he felt that power pressing, suggested to him that there had to be something more that he might be able to borrow, some other aspect of power that he might be able to draw upon, if only he were able to find it.

Was it just the connections?

But he had seen others attempting to destroy to remake.

And sometimes, it worked. Arowend was different because he had been destroyed and then remade. As were Tessatha and Eleanor. But was different better?

He brought Arowend toward him. "Would you change anything?"

"I would not have been destroyed," he said softly. A series of images flashed. Rob nearly turned away from them, but they came through his mind, and went through the connection that he had to everybody else. This was Arowend getting ripped apart, and the pain and anguish that he'd experienced. Rob had felt some part of it before, but it was far more acute this time. "This is what destruction is like. I might've been remade, but I am different. I might even be less."

"You're still here," Rob said. "Because we formed connections because we chose not to destroy. If I wanted to destroy, I would've ripped apart the Netheral. I would have ripped through the brambles, and lost Tessatha. I would have destroyed the heralds," Rob said, and with a surge of essence, he linked to them, using what he felt of Serena, and her vast exposure to the essence in their realm. "Destruction is not the answer. We must progress."

The Dragon laughed, and the cloud swallowed Rob.

Everything went dark.

Rob strained, and he knew that he did not have enough power. He knew that the Dragon had more and could never be defeated, not like that. Rob did not have the strength.

Not alone.

But he had long ago learned that he didn't have to do all of this alone. He had others with him. Others that he had brought. Others who were still linked to him. Power bloomed in his mind.

He felt Alyssa join. There were others there, others that Rob didn't know.

He had linked to them, somehow.

Was it because he had added these other realms?

One by one, those other entities began to bloom, joining him, as if they wanted to be a part of this. Rob knew none of them, but perhaps he didn't need to know them.

They lent him power.

He felt as if he were linking to all the realms in a way he hadn't before.

That energy had always been there, blending and blurring, the different types of unity swirling together, but now it felt different. Now it felt solid. Now it felt like he could truly use it. Rob expanded that essence, and as he did, it exploded outward in a cloud of brightness.

The dark energy continued to fight him, swirling around him. Rob struggled with it, knowing that there was no other way that he would be able to fight, but knowing that he had to try to do something here. He pushed.

And everybody that was connected to him pushed with him. Everybody conjoined with him, adding aspects of power, building on to that, given Rob more than what he had before.

And it came through him. It continued to expand. It swept through, mingling with this darkness. Rob started to burn through it, using what he had felt of Arowend, before realizing that was a mistake.

He could not destroy. He had no idea what would happen with this essence if he destroyed it, but he feared it would be lost.

"This is going to hurt," he said. "But if I'm right, it will change everything."

He told Serena what he was going to do, and then he pulled, drawing the Dragon down and into the unity essence towers.

Chapter Twenty-Seven

ROB

Rob stood outside of the unity tower. He could feel the pulsation of the essence, and it now felt stronger. It was unity, true unity, or at least as much as Rob thought it could be. He felt essence all around him. It came from nearby, and it came from others that were far from him. Others that Rob had yet to find and meet. All that power continued to blend, telling Rob that there was more he needed to find here, if only he were willing to do it.

Serena took his hand. She squeezed.

He felt her in ways he was thankful for, as he appreciated his connection to her and how much she had done for him, willing to give him something more.

"Are you sure it's going to hold?" Serena asked.

Rob could feel the drawing of the unity tower here…

And he felt it in other places. It was a strange awareness for him but an awareness that flowed through him.

"I think this was what we had to do. We couldn't destroy."

"What happens if it escapes?"

"It's not a matter of escaping," Rob said.

He had felt it when he had been there, feeling the Dragon and drawing upon that power. He knew what he needed to do, even if he wasn't sure that was going to work at that time.

Don't destroy.

That had been the key for him.

And yet, Rob had made that mistake a time or two, but he was not doing the same thing the Dragon had done. He had learned.

"The essence towers are the construct designed to restore essence," Rob said. "I wasn't sure at the time, but I could feel the pulling and pushing. Even now, you can feel it. It's there. Those towers blend the essence, draw that down, push it out through the realms, and link them together. The towers were the key all along."

"But what happens if it uses our power?"

"I think we did something different," Rob said, and he was sure of it now. "We were drawing upon unity, but that is the key. *We* are the unity. Our essence. People. The realms. All of that is the key."

He turned away from the tower, though he saw a Raolin approaching, satchel in one arm, his notebook under another. He radiated power. Rob couldn't tell how far he had progressed, only that he certainly had.

"How is he?" Rob asked Serena.

"Better," she said. "At least, better than he has been.

He progressed, but I think he might've skipped a step or two. He's at least as powerful as me. Maybe more. He seems to have a different connection to the tower."

Rob smiled. "It's good. He was lost for so long, that I think he deserves to have that."

"I know, and it's even stranger that he has started to visit with my mother again."

"You do know that your mother was there with us," Rob said.

"I know," Serena said. "And I was surprised by it, if I'm honest with you. I can't believe that she was willing to be a part of it."

"I'm not even sure how much of that she contributed, but she did help me see that it wasn't about destruction. I don't know what would've happened had I tried to destroy."

Maybe Rob would've been consumed by that essence. He might've felt an overwhelming desire to do the same thing the Dragon had done. Maybe nothing would've changed. Maybe this other power would have been prudent for Rob to be able to counter. Regardless, he was thankful for what he had done.

"It's strange to see them together again," Serena said softly. "They aren't together, but they are talking. So, there's that."

There was a swirl in the sky overhead, and Rob glanced up. He felt it and saw little more than a cloud, barely more than that, but it was enough. He smiled.

Arowend and Tessatha had stayed.

They were a unique form of essence, now blended.

They were two that had become one. Rob thought that surprisingly romantic, and he wondered whether he might be able to do something in time with Serena, if he were to choose that.

It would mean giving up who he was. It might mean giving up *what* he was.

But can I stay in this form indefinitely?

"What's next?" Serena asked.

"I don't know. I felt like I had to progress for so long, I no longer knew the answer. I feel like I should, though."

"You don't want to progress?"

Rob flicked his gaze overhead. "I thought the next step was dragon form. And maybe it is. And maybe Arowend and Tessatha have reached it. But even if it's not, even if there is something beyond like the Dragon wanted, is it worth it?"

Serena squeezed his hand. "I don't know. I think only you can answer that."

Rob smiled tightly. "I don't know if it is. And I don't know if it ever could be."

He breathed out. What was he going to do? It felt like an eternity since he'd been chasing progression, wanting to know how to advance to fight, grow, and be ready for what he had to face.

Now he didn't have that same urgency.

How long, he didn't know. Maybe some new threat would come. Maybe he would have to find a way to progress again, regardless of what that might look like.

But for now, maybe this was enough.

Serena focused on the conduit between them. She

connected to him. Essence flowed. It was unity, a power blending much greater than Rob had ever felt.

They would explore. They would see these other realms. They would see how much they could restore, and they would make sure that those the Dragon conquered were freed.

But for now, he could rest.

For now, he could be with Serena. And perhaps they already had their blending of the essence. She smiled at him, squeezing his hands, seeming to know his thoughts. He leaned over, kissed her, and then sighed heavily.

"Why don't we visit the valley, then visit your realm, and then...."

"Then we can do whatever you want," Serena said.

"I like the sound of that," Rob said.

As he let his focus wander and felt everything in the realm. It felt peaceful.

It felt connected.

And that was all Rob ever wanted.

The Blood of the Ancients series may continue, but don't miss a brand new series set in the same world: The Serpent Stairs.

Dan Michaelson / D.K. Holmberg — The Serpent Stairs — Essence Wielder Book 1

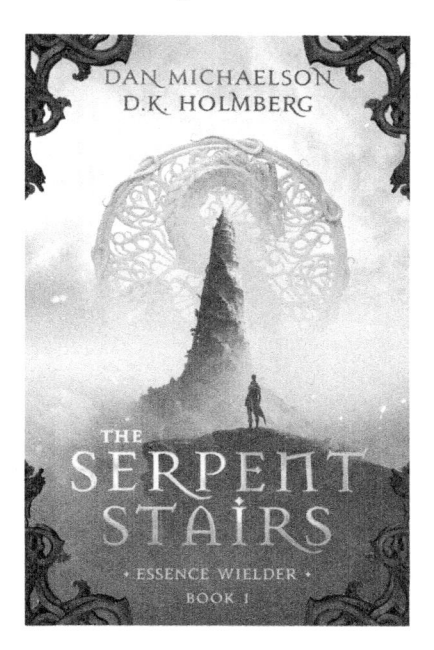

Dax Nelson was destined to protect the empire. When he's gifted the power of an unusual essence, everything changes.

The Great Serpent grants a gift of powerful essence to those who come before him. The experience, and the gift, is unpredictable but all have a vision of the Great Serpent so they can understand the purpose of their essence.

Not Dax.

With his new essence, rather than learning from his father, he now must go to the Academy to learn to control his essence. It's not fire as all in his family possess, but even the most powerful in the Academy don't know what it is—or what it means for Dax.

And the only thing he remembers from his visit to the

Serpent Stairs may be key to stop an attack on the empire, if he can understand his essence in time.

Series by Dan Michaelson

Cycle of Dragons

The Alchemist

Blood of the Ancients

Similar Series by D.K. Holmberg

The Dragonwalkers Series

The Dragonwalker

The Dragon Misfits

The Dragon Thief

Cycle of Dragons

Elemental Warrior Series:

Elemental Academy

The Elemental Warrior

The Cloud Warrior Saga

The Endless War

The Dark Ability Series

The Shadow Accords

The Collector Chronicles

The Dark Ability

The Sighted Assassin

The Elder Stones Saga

Printed in Great Britain
by Amazon